THE SEASIDE HOUSE

A MARINA COVE NOVEL, BOOK ONE

SOPHIE KENNA

The Seaside House

A Marina Cove Novel, Book One

By Sophie Kenna

© Copyright 2023

Cover design by Craig Thomas (coversbycraigthomas@gmail.com)

GET A FREE BOOK!

Sign up for my newsletter, and you'll also receive a free exclusive copy of *Summer Starlight*. This book isn't available anywhere else!

You can join at sophiekenna.com/seaside.

1

In the space of a single breath, Charlotte Keller's life had toppled like a fragile house of cards.

She tightened her grip on the white porcelain sink of the shared dormitory bathroom as beads of sweat trickled down her forehead, stinging her eyes like fire. The icy tendrils of the dark and secret words she'd overheard snaked through her body, coiling themselves around her heart and leaving her gasping for air.

As she looked into the mirror, a painful prickling sensation crept across her body, settling in the center of her chest. For a moment she didn't recognize the woman staring back at her. Blinding fluorescent light and the pungent undertone of disinfectant clawed into her skin.

Charlotte clenched the sink until her hands trembled and burned. She took a deep, shaking breath and held it hard against her throat, trying to force down the primal scream churning inside her lungs. Just moments ago, her greatest concern had been the empty void of her plans for the future staring back at her as she and Sebastian dropped their youngest daughter off for her first year at Columbia University.

How quickly everything could change.

An hour earlier, Charlotte was following behind Allie as she skipped up the steps two at a time to Furnard Hall, Sebastian in tow carrying the last of her boxes up to her dorm room. Allie had been fluttering around the condo like a hummingbird all spring, counting down the days until her semester began in May immediately after her high school graduation; she'd enrolled in an early summer program before her official start in the fall in order to get a jump start on her economics program. A vague queasiness had taken root within Charlotte as the day loomed in front of her, but she had carefully pushed it down as she did her best to share her daughter's eagerness to begin the next chapter of her life.

"So what's on the docket tonight, kiddo?" asked Sebastian as he deposited the final box on the floor of Allie's small double room that she'd eventually share with her childhood best friend. The room was austere and cramped, but plenty of sunlight flooded in through the windows, making the space appear larger than it really was.

Allie hopped onto her bed and let out a deep sigh, legs sprawled out in front of her and a grin on her face. "There's an orientation where they put the summer people in groups to get to know one another during lunch, and some sort of live music thing later. It'll be cool to meet some other students."

"That sounds really fun, honey," said Charlotte, tears unexpectedly springing to her eyes. A memory of Allie as a preschooler ripped at her, the little girl twirling around in their living room in her favorite turquoise skirt, showing off her plié as Sebastian clapped along, her huge green eyes crinkled with laughter as she ran into Charlotte's open arms for a hug.

Allie held out her hand to Charlotte and pulled her closer. "I'm going to miss you too, Mom," she said, her eyes glistening. "I'm not that far away. I'll get to see you all the time. You won't even notice I'm gone!"

"It's going to be so quiet without you kids running around. I'm going to have to leave the TV on all the time just for company," said Charlotte, brushing Allie's hair back behind her ear.

"Well, you still have Dad! You guys can travel the world now, have some adventures, get into trouble!" Allie said. "Give the old folks in all those pharmaceutical commercials a run for their money."

Charlotte laughed as Sebastian's phone rang. "I've got to take this real quick, it's work," he said as he frowned at the screen. "Duty calls. Why don't you girls unpack a few things, make this room feel a little more homey?"

Ten minutes later, Charlotte and Allie had unpacked her bedspread, placed some framed pictures on the dresser and end table, and hung a few posters of Allie's favorite indie rock bands on the wall. Charlotte unearthed a vase from one of the boxes and placed a single sunflower she'd brought, Allie's favorite. She and Allie had grown sunflowers in the terrace garden every year since she was two years old, running outside each passing week to check how tall they were getting until they towered over them.

"Where's Dad? It's almost noon, I'm gonna have to get going soon," said Allie.

Charlotte frowned. Sebastian absolutely had to take a work call during the precious few minutes they had left with their daughter? She had made peace with the importance Sebastian placed on his work long ago, but he should be there to see his last child off to school.

"I'll go check on him, sweetheart, just give me a minute," said Charlotte as she headed into the dorm hallway. Sebastian was nowhere to be seen. After walking the length of the hallway, she spotted the stairwell around the corner from the elevator, pushed down on the bar, and opened the heavy gray door.

Sebastian's hushed voice echoed down through the large stairwell from several floors up, then stopped abruptly. "Hang on," she heard him whisper. Something in his voice gave Charlotte pause; something flitting across the back of her mind, raising her hackles. She released the door and it clanged shut as she hastily crossed the landing and descended the first three steps, pressing herself tightly against the wall.

Sebastian's head appeared in the gap above her through the flights of stairs as he surveyed the landing. He couldn't see her. His head disappeared as he continued his phone call. "Never mind. Anyway, I had fun last night too, Steph. I miss you. But we talked about this. I can't just drop everything and meet up whenever you want."

Charlotte felt the blood drain from her face. Steph? Who was Steph? A hundred faces ran across her mind. Sebastian's high profile had him rubbing elbows with so many people, Charlotte was never able to remember them all. All the fundraisers, the fancy dinners, the meet-and-greets; tapas at Castello, mimosas at Il Cane Blu, box seats at the opera.

Sebastian's voice dripped with furtiveness as he lowered it to almost a whisper. Charlotte strained against the deafening silence blanketing the stairwell. Standing on her tiptoes, she stretched upward toward Sebastian, fingers gripping the railing.

"Me too, Steph. Okay. Just give me a few hours, I'm in the middle of some stuff. Let's go to your place again, Charlotte's gonna be home tonight. Uh-huh. Why don't you have some cocktails ready for us around seven. Uh-huh. Can't wait, babe."

The words drilled down through the stairwell and sliced through her skin with reckless abandon. It was as though all the air in the room had been suddenly siphoned out.

An involuntary moan escaped her lips as she pressed her palms against her mouth. Leaping up the steps and across the landing in two bounds, she slammed open the door and escaped into the hallway toward the bathroom as nausea sloshed through her like a tidal wave.

THE SOUND of giggling in the hallway broke her trance, and the door to the shared dormitory bathroom swung open as two girls entered. Charlotte hastily ran her hands over her face and through her hair as she straightened her back and tried to appear nonchalant. The girls quickly quieted and exchanged glances as they walked past her. With trembling hands, she turned on the faucet, splashed cold water over her face, and forced a steady breath.

Maybe it wasn't as bad as it sounded? She tried envisioning Sebastian actually going behind her back with another woman but came up empty-handed. He had never so much as glanced at another woman in front of her in the twenty-six years they had been together. As she watched the marriages of her friends crumble around her, she had always felt lucky to have someone so solid. *He's one of the good ones*, everyone had said.

Sure, he was tall, dark, and handsome. If that was your thing. And wealthy. Scratch that. *Ridiculously* wealthy.

Or so everyone thought.

Women's heads had always turned, but they really took notice when they learned his name. *The* Sebastian Carter, yes, yes. The sole heir to the great Carter Enterprises and its vast fortunes, left to him by his father, the esteemed Rubeus Carter.

But the money hadn't been important to Charlotte. She knew nothing about his wealth when he first brought her into the fold, after she ran away from her home on Marina Cove when she was eighteen years old, craving safety, stability. It was his easy manner, the devil-may-care grin in his eyes, the thick tenor of his voice wrapping itself around her like a warm blanket. He had always made her feel she was on steady ground.

Except that in the long years that followed, his staggering fortune had slowly dwindled to nothing. An extensive series of bad investments, a recession or two, and a stubborn refusal to adjust his upper-

upper-class Manhattan lifestyle to the ever-mounting evidence that he was going bankrupt. Billions of dollars, evaporated into nothing, like a lake in a terrible drought. He'd kept promising Charlotte that the next investment would be the one to restore the empire to its former glory. Each one had pushed them deeper and deeper underwater, her sense of safety going along for the ride.

And now, this had happened.

Whatever he and *Steph* were doing behind her back, it was bad. No sense in denying that. Her mind reeled as she tried to reconfigure the words she had overheard into new patterns, a different context. *Let's go to your place again, Charlotte's gonna be home tonight.* Maybe they had been meeting for work?... Another sickening lurch swelled in her stomach, almost bringing her to her knees. They had been together in her home. He was going to see her tonight.

Can't wait, babe.

Well, you don't usually call coworkers *babe*. It was impossible to tell exactly how far things had progressed, but she wasn't stupid. Everything she had taken for granted was being stripped away from her in the blink of an eye.

A horrible sob squeezed against her throat like a

dam about to burst as she imagined the worst. Charlotte straightened her skirt, raised a shaky arm, and wiped her brow with the sleeve of her blouse. Whatever this was would have to wait. This was Allie's day. No way was Charlotte going to ruin it with some big confrontation, some falling apart in front of everyone. She was going to hold her head high, and appreciate the precious seconds she had left with her daughter as they wisped out of her grasp like vapor.

CHARLOTTE RETURNED to the dorm room to find Sebastian and Allie sitting on the end of her bed, laughing together. Allie stood up, bubbling with anticipation, and took her mother's hand. "Well, I should start getting ready."

Charlotte pulled Allie close and wrapped her arms around her, etching the warmth of her body and the smell of her coconut shampoo into her memory. "I love you so much, Allie," she whispered into her hair. "I hope you have the time of your life. Promise me you'll savor every moment, all of it...You never know when it'll all change."

Allie pulled away slightly and looked up at her

mother, eyes rimmed with tears. "Are you all right, Mom?"

Charlotte forced a small laugh, brushing the tears from her own eyes. "Of course, sweetheart, this is all just a little…I'm just going to miss you, that's all. I'll be fine. We'll be fine," she said as she glanced up at Sebastian. "You're such a wonderful girl, Allie. I'm so proud. I know you're going to do great things."

"With her brains and Carter charm, she sure is," said Sebastian, pulling the two of them in for a hug. Charlotte noticed a conspicuous absence of the warmth and security she usually felt in his arms. He suddenly felt like a stranger.

Allie squeezed them one final time and let go. "Thanks for everything, guys. It's gonna be strange being away from home…I think the longest I've ever been away was a week for summer camp." She grinned, looking back and forth between them. "I'll call you tomorrow to let you know how everything went, okay?"

"Sounds good, Allie girl. We love you." Sebastian reached for his coat. "Try not to get into too much trouble, okay?"

Allie laughed as she walked her parents to the elevator at the end of the hallway. Sebastian put his arm around Charlotte's waist as they stepped in.

Charlotte looked once more into Allie's eyes, those big, beautiful green eyes she had first peered into as the doctor lifted her up and placed her against Charlotte's chest. Allie smiled and winked at Charlotte as the doors slowly closed between them.

2

Charlotte inserted her key and pressed the elevator button that would take her to the very top of The Windsor, their Upper East Side penthouse condo on Park Avenue. As the light for the 30th floor illuminated, she shook the rain from her umbrella, and sighed deeply as the doors opened directly into their expansive living space.

Something jumped up on her out of nowhere and a wet, sandpapery tongue slapped itself all over Charlotte's face. Laughing, she kneeled down to Ollie, her wild and uncontrollable chocolate lab always filled to the brim with unlimited glee and love, and pulled him into her chest, placing a smooch on the top of his head. "I missed you, boy," she whispered into his fur as he panted happily and grinned his gigantic dog grin.

Tossing her keys on the kitchen island, she poured herself a glass of water and stared through the floor-to-ceiling windows at the Manhattan sprawl below. Although the condo was undoubtedly enormous and spanned two stories, the ceilings were inexplicably low, and combined with Sebastian's sea of bric-a-brac and busy earth tones and uncomfortable but trendy postmodern furniture, the place had always given Charlotte the feel of a crowded underground bunker, always pressing in on her. The deep rumble of thunder drifted in, punctuating the steady dripping of rain and the round-the-clock din of Manhattan traffic.

All of this, her home, possibly gone at any moment. For some reason, Sebastian didn't seem to be worried quite enough about their current financial state. Confidence, perhaps. Arrogance, more likely.

Sebastian had a meeting with investors after they'd left Columbia. So he'd said. Charlotte knew he was going to meet his other woman. Young, beautiful, perfect *Steph*. Total silence had drowned the car as their personal driver crawled through traffic on the way home, although Sebastian apparently hadn't noticed until he dropped her off at the front of their high-rise and asked if she was okay. Charlotte hadn't said anything; a part of her dimly registered that she was in shock and needed to gather her thoughts, alone. She watched helplessly as Sebastian left her to be with someone who wasn't his wife, his love.

I had fun last night too, Steph. I miss you.

Everything since she'd overheard the words had taken on a surreal quality, like watching the world from behind frosted glass. Charlotte's mind skittered. She clutched the glass of lukewarm water in her hands so tightly she barely realized her knuckles were aching.

Before she knew what she was doing, Charlotte set her glass down so fast it tipped over and shattered, spilling water all over the ground. She hurtled up the spiral staircase that led to the second floor of their condo, Ollie loyally bounding up behind her. Scampering down the large carpeted landing like an animal in pursuit, she thrust open their bedroom door.

Charlotte scanned the room, the blinding wall-to-wall snow-white carpet and furniture boring into her eyes. She approached their broad king-size bed and ripped off the duvet as the collection of decorative pillows spilled onto the floor.

The sheets went next, along with the pillowcases and mattress cover. The bare mattress stared back at her. Ollie stood guard at the bedroom door, a grim expression on his face.

Panting slightly, she lifted all the edges of the mattress, scanning the platform it rested on. She went to the headboard, inched her fingers behind the heavy wood, and pried the bed away from the wall. Shoving aside the end table, she got on her knees, reached behind the bed, and swept over the floor with her hands.

After scattering the contents of Sebastian's end table all over the floor and rifling through it in a manner that made her feel like a woman unhinged, she stood up, took off her heavy gray blazer, and wiped away the sweat forming on her brow. With an increasingly detached resolve, she watched herself head into the large walk-in closet, flick on the light, and proceed through the rows of his dress shirts, suits, and pants, emptying pockets, examining collars.

Nothing.

Feeling a fresh swell of nausea, she rushed into the en suite and steadied herself on the bathroom countertop. A familiar prickling numbness was crawling across her arms and legs as the room seemed to sway. *No no nononono. Not now.* It had been so long since she'd had an episode.

Charlotte glanced over to the full-length mirror and examined the 44-year-old woman before her, barely recognizing her.

She should be angry, of course. Livid. The horrible thing was, it wasn't anger flaring inside her. Reaching deep, she slowly found the dark mass roiling in the pit of her stomach. To her profound chagrin, she realized that it was shame.

The rational part of her knew it was crazy to feel ashamed, but regardless, a part of her felt that this had somehow been her fault, something she had caused.

Charlotte had sensed a bit of distance growing over the years, but had always chalked it up to the normal ebbs and flows of a marriage. Sebastian always seemed to be working, and Charlotte put everything she had into being there for her children in all the crucial ways they needed her. It was hard for them to make time together. It was simple inertia; life was a balance, and she had done the best she could. Maybe she should have tried harder to make more time for him, to keep things interesting. Keep the spark alive.

Maybe it was an emotional affair? That didn't sit any better; the thought of Sebastian falling in love with another woman drove hot stripes of agony through her abdomen. She really had no way of knowing the exact nature of his infidelity until she confronted him.

Which wasn't that simple. Her whole life was wrapped up in his...the children, their home, everything. With a sickening lurch, Charlotte realized for the first time just how dependent on him she was. She had nothing of her own. No home, no income, nothing in her name. And with Sebastian on the brink of bankruptcy, she had no safety net.

A significant part of her wanted to pretend she hadn't heard him in the stairwell; just bury her head in the sand, continue on her merry way. Or just hope for the best... that he'd made a mistake, and was still committed to her. After all, Sebastian hadn't left her yet. Maybe there was still a chance for them. People came back from this sort of thing all the time, didn't they?

The wretchedness of the past few hours was taking its toll; Charlotte felt the strands of her thoughts tying themselves around one another, melding into a writhing, snapping mess pounding against her skull. She was a woman alone, and had no idea what to do next.

AFTER SHOWERING and pulling on her favorite fluffy pajamas, she padded downstairs toward the kitchen. Five full minutes of staring into her fridge had done nothing to spur her appetite, so she plunked down on the white leather sofa in the living room, scratching Ollie's ears and flicking through the infinite channels of their satellite television. Unable to find anything good, she turned it off, and just listened to the gentle pattering of the rain against the windows as Ollie nuzzled up against her leg and silent sobs racked her body.

After a few minutes, Charlotte wiped her eyes on her pajama sleeves and lifted a framed picture of her and Sebastian they kept on the end table. Their oldest daughter, Mariah, had taken the picture with a camera she was learning to use after they'd gotten it for her as a birthday present. She knew her middle child Liam had been somewhere behind Mariah, hands in his pockets and brooding about something, and Allie was bouncing around nearby, cloud-gazing and carefree. Charlotte and Sebastian were framed against the backdrop of 3rd Avenue, wind whipping at their hair. She was gazing up at him as he laughed at some forgotten joke, captured for all eternity.

Mere weeks after he'd asked her on a date while she waited on him in a small cafe in Brooklyn, he'd whisked her away to Paris to stay for the summer. She'd only been living in the city for a month and was sleeping on the couch in a tiny apartment with one of her sister Diane's friends, stashing away her tips to create a new life for herself away from the mess she'd just run from. They'd spent three perfect months in his beautiful Le Marais apartment in the 4th arrondissement; evenings under the stars on the rooftop terrace sipping drinks and taking in the views of the Seine and Île Saint-Louis, sneaking around the narrow cobblestone streets and hidden alleys like children, lying in the grass in Place des Vosges while she read him her favorite Neruda and Keats, sunlight drenching their skin. After living on a tiny island off the coast of Massachusetts that no one had ever heard of for all eighteen years of her life, she felt she was at last experiencing some of the beauty and adventure out in the great wide world.

It had all been a beautiful dream, a much-needed escape from the harsh reality of what had happened at Marina Cove.

Sensing a desire and an opportunity to reconnect a bit with Sebastian, Charlotte had reached out a few weeks ago to the owner of his old apartment and learned that it was now available for short-term rentals. She'd planned a whole trip for them to revisit their old haunts and spend some quality time together now that their three children were gone. She'd wanted to surprise him with the trip after they dropped Allie off at school. Obviously they couldn't go now. Not when she had no idea what was going to happen next.

It was going to be crucial to be rational about it, whatever she decided. Her plans for the future hadn't included any of this. She had already been agonizing for months about what she was going to do after Allie left...it had made more sense to research things slowly, plan her future out carefully, so that she wasn't just wasting time or doing the wrong thing. The first flickers of desperation had been making their anxious whispers heard deep within her over the last few years, warning her that she might actually need to start earning an income of her own if things didn't turn around. Sebastian's reassurances had always quieted the whispers for another few weeks, only for them to eventually return in an ever-growing chorus.

So each time the thoughts bubbled to the surface of her mind, she'd carefully pushed them down into the shadowy corners she rarely frequented, where they belonged, until she had more time to think once Allie was on her way. After all, Sebastian was smart and well-connected. Surely, she'd reasoned, he'd figure something out.

A sudden sensation of the floor dropping out beneath her broke her reverie, and she returned the framed photograph to the table. Everything in her life seemed to be coalescing, converging on something. What she needed was time to think. She needed some girl time with her friends. They'd know what to do.

3

"And so Grayson's all, 'Baby, it's not what it looks like!' and the au pair's, like, right there behind him, pulling her dress back on!"

Kylie and Riley laughed hysterically as Brielle glanced at Charlotte and rolled her eyes. "Come on, Kylie. How's that funny again?" she said. "Tiffany must be devastated."

"Lighten up, Brie." Kylie narrowed her eyes. "If you ask me, Tiff had it coming. All that looking down her nose at everyone, *Isn't Grayson just the bestest? Isn't Grayson just the perfectest? Isn't Grayson just the hottest?* I couldn't take it anymore."

The four women were seated on the outdoor patio of La Cuillère D'Argent, although Charlotte had suggested a different restaurant when she'd texted her friends the night before. It was too loud here on the terrace, the sounds of car horns and drivers cursing always closing in and drowning out the conversation. The waiter slithered up, conspicuously taking in the pearls, the solid gold bracelets, the cashmere, giant dollar signs bulging from his eye sockets.

"*Bonjour, belles dames*. What may I bring to you on this fine morning?"

"I'll have the nick-oise salad, and lots of Chardonnay," said Riley.

Kylie sighed loudly. "It's pronounced *nee-swahz*, dear." Riley's face flushed as she stuck her tongue out at Kylie.

"At once, *Madamoiselle*." The rest ordered, and the waiter slinked away, humming to himself.

Riley removed the ridiculous white fur and leather gloves she called her "driving gloves" (absurd, as she'd never even gotten her driver's license) and ostentatiously splayed her hand on the table, revealing what must've been a ten-carat diamond ring. Brielle brought both hands to her mouth and gasped. "So Hudson finally proposed?"

Riley grinned, rolling the ring around to catch the sunlight. "Well, not exactly. But he's going to, soon. We picked this out over the weekend. Well, I picked it out. He doesn't know anything. Isn't it just perfect?"

A distant part of Charlotte registered that a ring that size would've paid for her entire childhood home many times over, but she pushed the thought aside. Maybe she could snatch it away when Riley wasn't looking and sell it. It would keep her afloat for a while. "It's beautiful, Riley. I'm happy for you."

They continued to admire the ring as the waiter returned and lowered the tiny silver plates that would barely hold a cup of coffee. They'd all ordered a salad and wine except Charlotte, who'd chosen two large croissants and a side of bright pink macarons. Charlotte reached for the butter as the other women watched her out of the corners of their eyes, and defiantly began to slather it on a croissant, taking a huge, crunchy bite.

Truth be told, Charlotte hated this restaurant; it was all pretension, the kind of place that refused to print prices on the menu. She'd always found the food bland, uninspired. A place that catered to the wealthy who were far more concerned with posting pictures of their food to social media than the taste. Supposedly one of the most "authentic" French restaurants in all of Manhattan, she found it nothing at all like her time living in Paris.

That glorious summer, Charlotte had befriended a woman living a few floors down from her, Amélie, a pastry chef at a charming little place on Rue Saint-Paul called L'étoile Pâtisserie. Charlotte spent afternoons with Amélie learning to make all sorts of things she'd never even heard of, let alone tasted. Mille-feuille, choux à la crème, tarte tatin; they'd play old Frankie Valli records way too loud, covered in flour and sugar, carefree laughter and great conversation coursing through the kitchen. A whirlwind of tastes and smells, her appetite for creation blossoming. She'd never felt so light, so free.

Charlotte looked around the table at her friends, all connected one way or another to Sebastian's large circle of influence. She'd never quite found herself fitting in with the social elite; she always felt like she was watching from the outside, but over the years she'd eventually learned the rhythms of gossip, the brands to wear, which schools to send her kids to. It was sort of a bizarre guilty pleasure, just grabbing the firehose of cash and spraying away with everyone else. Money had eventually ceased to really mean anything to her; Sebastian's inherited wealth had been unimaginably vast, and it was decades since she'd had to consider the cost of anything.

That is, until recently. Suddenly, the cost of the food in front of her unearthed an old feeling from deep within, dusted off after years of disuse. A feeling of scarcity.

No one else knew of Sebastian's financial problems, certainly not her friends. After all these years, she still didn't really know Kylie or Riley all that well; apart from the surface, she knew very little about them on a truly personal level. But they were fun, mostly, and well-connected. They seemed to know everyone, which helped Charlotte, who had a hard time keeping track of who had inherited what and who was marrying or divorcing whom. At first, her heart was sore with longing for her childhood best friend Sylvie, whom she'd left behind when she fled Marina Cove, but over time, she became more comfortable letting go and following the well-worn grooves of the day-to-day as a newly minted spouse of the ultra-elite.

Fortunately, she had Brielle. The wife of one of Sebastian's old work partners, Brielle helped Charlotte navigate the confusing and often treacherous waters of the Manhattan social elite. She'd always felt that in some way, Brielle, like her, was a fish out of water.

As the women blithely continued their gossip, Charlotte broke in suddenly. "Sebastian is having an affair."

The words escaped into the air around them, casting a blanket of silence that smothered every corner of the patio. Charlotte's eyes welled up as Brielle took her hand.

After several moments, Kylie said, "Did you sign a prenup?"

"Honestly, Kylie, how rude," Riley gasped, her hands raised to her mouth with a look of feigned shock.

"Tell us what happened, honey," said Brielle, ignoring the others.

As Charlotte explained what she had overheard, the three women nodded in understanding. "I went through it with Sloane, as you know," said Kylie. "Honestly, it didn't end up being that big of a deal. It wasn't like I hadn't been a bit of a bad girl myself. Anyway, even with the prenup, I got a tidy little package out of it. We still keep in touch."

"I would never cheat on Sebastian," said Charlotte. "I've never done anything. And I thought he hadn't either."

"Well, boys will be boys," said Kylie. "It was bound to happen sooner or later. I say dump him."

"Shut it, Kylie," snapped Brielle. "Not helpful. Charlotte, did you talk to him yet?"

"No," she admitted. "I only overheard that bit before I bolted out of the stairwell, and with dropping Allie off and everything...I couldn't process it. I think I'm still in shock."

"Well, who knows what he was actually talking about?" Riley said with an empty expression that made her closely resemble a goldfish. "Like, that could've meant anything, right?"

"Right, Riley. Maybe they were talking about playing tennis together," said Kylie. "Get real. He's obviously a horrible jerk, dear, and I say kick him to the curb and collect your payout."

"I did sign a prenup." Not that it mattered anymore; there was nothing left for Sebastian to protect. Charlotte sighed, leaning back in her chair. "I was eighteen when he asked me out. When things got serious, he told me about his second ex-wife 'taking him to the cleaners' when they divorced, and he said he'd vowed to himself to always have a prenup." She ran a hand over her face. "He said he didn't want people using him just for his money. It actually made a lot of sense to me at the time. I didn't care about his money. I didn't think twice."

"I know, hon," said Kylie. "We've all signed them. Sloane tried to get away without parting with anything, but I've got a magical little word for you. *Alimony*. Make him pay."

Her friends had no idea about the looming bankruptcy, of course. They couldn't conceive of anything other than a limitless well from which to draw. All that work, all those years. The prominent Carter Enterprises, a Manhattan institution, reduced to ashes.

Come to think of it, she didn't really understand exactly what Sebastian did, which mostly seemed to involve fancy dinners, traveling, and fundraisers. It was something with investments, or lending. Hedge funds? He was never interested in talking about his work.

At any rate, there wasn't half of anything for Charlotte to get if she did decide to divorce him. She could quite literally become homeless. A horrible feeling of vertigo made her place both hands on the table to steady herself.

"Seriously, though, what if whatever he did wasn't that bad?" repeated Riley. They all looked at her. "I mean it. What if it's like, they were just hanging out and maybe he regrets it?" she said with a blank look as Kylie rolled her eyes into the sky.

Brielle, who had been mostly listening so far, leaned forward and looked Charlotte in her eyes. "As much as I hate to admit it, Riley has a point, somewhere in there. It's possible that this wasn't some huge, horrible thing...You know me and Slater went through something like this last year. It was a disgusting, terrible mistake, and yes, it crushed me, but he was so apologetic and desperate to make things work that we got over it. And now look at us," she said as she sat upright in her chair, smoothing her hair carefully. "We're better than ever. I'm not telling you what to do, but just don't do anything rash...you might regret it forever."

Charlotte picked at the sleeve of her blouse for a few moments. "I don't think I can stay in that house with him right now. If I'm being honest...I'm afraid to find out exactly what happened. I'm probably better off not knowing."

Brielle gave her a sympathetic nod. "You probably just need a little space to process things."

"I don't want to confront him until I have some sort of plan...I can't just up and go. I don't have a job, anywhere to stay..." Charlotte felt like a fraud, playing dress-up with the big kids in this ridiculous restaurant.

"You can stay with me and Jackson," said Kylie. "We just remodeled the guest house. I think that's just what you need. Our pool boy is single. For now." She smirked.

Charlotte rolled her eyes inwardly. Extra time with Kylie and her nonstop train of gossip sounded like more stress, not less. "That's okay. Maybe I'll just get a hotel, or something..."

"Maybe you should get out of the city for a bit," said Brielle. "You're all tied in with everything here. You should go someplace nice, with a beach. Why don't you go visit your family? Don't they have a place out on Marina Cove?"

"What's Marina Cove?" asked Riley, her nose wrinkled in confusion.

Marina Cove. A memory surfaced of basking in the sun on a hot July afternoon, cold glass of lemonade and a book in hand, while the seagulls flew overhead and the breeze carried over the crystal blue water. It was certainly a beautiful, relaxing place.

Until it wasn't. After everything that had happened, she'd left for New York City, and hadn't really kept in touch with her family since then. As far as she knew, her younger sister Ramona was the only Keller sibling who still lived on the island. Charlotte was pretty sure Ramona was still running the family inn, but they weren't on speaking terms. Charlotte had left Marina Cove a year and a half after that Christmas Eve she'd tried ever since to push into the corners of her mind, the one where her family came undone at the seams, and Ramona felt that Charlotte had abandoned them.

But she didn't know the real reason Charlotte had left the island all those years ago.

No one did.

It was something she'd carried with her since then. And she wasn't about to add to her life's complications right now.

"It's lovely there, but not really an option," said Charlotte. "I don't really speak with my family anymore. We just sort of all...fell apart." A memory flashed across her mind, Charlotte's father laughing and chasing Ramona and her across the shore one night, rain pouring down on them in buckets, Ramona clutching Charlotte's hand as they splashed through giant puddles and screamed with delight. Silence hung over the table for a few moments. "I'll figure something out."

Brielle gave her hand a squeeze as Kylie and

Riley exchanged glances and returned to picking at their tiny salads. "Well, at least we have the fundraiser tonight to take your mind off things. That'll be fun."

Oh no, the fundraiser. She'd completely forgotten. Sebastian was a guest of honor, and she was expected to be in attendance. Although squeezing herself into an uncomfortable dress and feigning interest about high society matters didn't exactly sound fun, there was a true comfort in just going on autopilot, losing herself in the familiar patterns, turning her mind off for a few precious hours.

Her friends meant well, but hadn't been much help. She needed space to think clearly. The worst had already happened. Because when it came down to it, you were really only talking a spectrum of horrible betrayal. Whatever Sebastian had been doing, Charlotte's life was going to change irrevocably.

What she needed to decide before she confronted him was whether to give him another chance. She didn't want to make any permanent decisions in the heat of battle that she couldn't easily take back. Charlotte had long ago learned the terrors of uncertainty, and she no longer let herself get caught off guard.

An idea sprang into her mind. Instead of canceling their trip to their old apartment in Paris, maybe they could still go as planned. Get back to their roots. Paris was really where it all began, after all. Sometime over the years, they had lost their way. She loved Sebastian, and she knew in her heart that he loved her too. Or at least he had...Perhaps it wasn't the swoon-worthy kind of love, all passion and fireworks, but it was safe and warm and steady, and that had always been enough for her.

Maybe if they could return to where it all started, she could see how she really felt about their future together with more clarity. Away from the fancy high-rise, the socialites, the big city that could swallow you whole in a flash. They could spend some real, quality time together, for the first time in what felt like years. Then, hopefully, she would know what she wanted. And then she could face the truth, whatever it was, armed with a plan.

4

"And so I said to him, 'That sounds lovely, Higgins, but you had better buy me dinner first.'"

Raucous laughter and back slapping ensued as Charlotte struggled valiantly not to roll her eyes. She, Sebastian, and ten or so of Manhattan's super-elite were gathered in a tight circle amongst the crowd in the enormous hall on the uppermost floor of the famous Château du Ciel high-rise. She struggled to take a full breath as the fabric of the black dress Sebastian had chosen for her cinched imperiously around her waist, forcing her to suck in her stomach to avoid the back zipper bursting away and exploding some idle flute of champagne.

The last twenty-four hours had a thick, dreamlike quality to them, like the moments after waking from a nightmare. The steady prickling of unease that scuttled about within her since she was a teenager had been amplified lately, her heart thrumming relentlessly against her chest. Sebastian happily flitted in and out of the condo on his various errands and meetings, blissfully unaware of her abject misery. How was that possible?

What was this fundraiser for again? She felt a tiny stab of guilt as she realized she'd never even asked Sebastian. It seemed to her there was always another fundraiser, another shockingly expensive dress selected for her, another giant plastered smile. It wasn't that she minded them, exactly; she was happy to be part of anything charitable, even if the cynical part of her knew that most of these people were donating primarily to see, be seen, and capitalize on the tax benefits. She wondered vaguely if anyone else here was putting on a facade, spending money they didn't actually have to maintain appearances.

Charlotte closed her eyes and took a breath, trying to interrupt her racing thoughts. At least Brielle would be here tonight.

"...and so we finally told her that if she kept hemming and hawing about it during our meetings, we'd just have to find someone else to take her place on the board," an imposing blonde woman was declaring with tremendous fanciness to the other fancy women in the circle, all with fancy positions on boards and committees and charities. Camila. Camille. Carmella? Charlotte found her mildly terrifying. They'd met several times, but Charlotte always seemed to black out momentarily as people were introduced to her.

"Wesley, you've got to try these things. Exquisite," said one of the men standing inside their circle through a mouthful of pastry as he snatched another from the large silver trays being circled around the floor by a sea of waiters dressed all in white. None of the other women had taken anything from the trays. After debating for a brief moment, Charlotte grabbed a few of the apple tarts for herself, trying her best not to draw attention.

The blonde woman was watching Charlotte. "Wesley, love, why don't you fetch me another glass," she said as she shook her champagne flute in his general direction. As Wesley scampered away, she asked, "So, Carlotta, what is it that you do, dear?"

"Charlotte, actually." She cleared her throat, unable to raise her voice to an appropriate volume for some reason. "Well, I'm a stay-at-home mom. Or

I was, anyway...Sebastian and I just dropped our youngest off at Columbia."

"Ah...well, good for you. I could never tolerate that sort of life, all those dirty diapers and the screaming," she said, crinkling her nose and looking over Charlotte's shoulder, clearly scanning around to see if there was anyone more interesting. "Thank goodness Wesley and I had someone for all that. So what are your plans for the future, now that you're all alone at home?"

Well, in the short run, getting out of this conversation. Maybe smashing her apple tart against Camellia's smug face and frolicking away in delight. "I'm still weighing my options."

The woman's lips formed into a tight smile as she eyed Charlotte up and down. She was being evaluated. "Charming. Well, I suppose we all must find ways to pass the time. Best of luck, dearie."

Charlotte didn't break eye contact as she took a particularly large bite of her tart. The woman gave her a final smirk as Sebastian and the other men began hotly debating about the months-long tumbling of the stock market and what it meant for everyone. Where was Brielle when she needed her? Charlotte knew she'd be floating around somewhere.

Excusing herself, she moved through the room in no particular direction, keeping an eye out for her friend. The room was getting muggier and the air more stifling as the crowd seemed to multiply. Dozens of massive crystal chandeliers hung precariously low throughout the enormous hall, flooding the room with hot artificial light. As she wound through the throngs of people milling around and approached the center of the room, she spotted a towering porcelain structure with five huge basins stacked at least fifteen feet high. Intrigued, she made her way toward the looming fixture and saw an avalanche of molten chocolate pouring from each basin into the next, forming a huge pool at the bottom large enough to swim in.

As she idly wondered what they would do with this much chocolate when the night was over, she grabbed a dipper and poured some over a large plate of strawberries. Someone might as well enjoy it.

"Yoo-hoo," a voice sang behind her. She turned to find Brielle holding a bowl of chocolate in one hand and a plate piled with cream puffs in the other.

"I'm glad you're here," said Charlotte, gesturing back to the group she had left. "Not sure how much more of that I could take tonight."

Brielle's face grew serious. "So...how've you been doing with...everything?"

Charlotte set down her plate and took a breath as the tears threatened to form. "Well, apart from sobbing and screaming to myself anytime Sebastian isn't around and not sleeping a wink last night, I'm great."

Brielle nodded sympathetically and took Charlotte's arm in hers. "I'm so sorry, hon. Have you given any thought about what you're going to do? You talk to him yet?"

Charlotte looked over her shoulder and scanned the room to find Sebastian. He was clearly telling some story, holding court, everyone laughing. "No, not yet." Large tears were beginning to stream down her face as she quickly swiped them away. "I'm really scared, Brielle. I feel like my whole life is ending. What am I supposed to do? I don't know what rabbit hole this is all going to go down. I can't just leave. I have nowhere to go."

Brielle's mouth opened and closed several times; she was clearly unsure of what to say. Clutching her arm tighter and facing Charlotte directly, she looked her in the eyes. "I honestly think that whatever it is, you shouldn't just assume it's going to be over forever.

I think...maybe you should consider giving him another chance. He doesn't deserve it, babe, I know, but your whole life is wrapped up in his. You have your kids together. Even if you leave him, you'll have to face him basically forever. Birthdays, holidays, everything." She grabbed a napkin from a nearby tray being walked past and offered it to Charlotte. "I know it's horrible...I'm just saying, maybe just try to hear him out, keep an open mind. Don't do anything rash."

Charlotte bristled. This was her marriage. He had made a vow to her all those years ago. A vow she had taken seriously. Should she really stay with him just because her life was wrapped up in his? Didn't she deserve better than that?

The sound of a fork against a champagne flute echoed through the room. "Hello, hello, check one-two. Is this thing on?"

The crowd opened some space around an immaculately tuxedoed man holding a microphone, a gigantic wolfish grin plastered on his face. "Welcome all, welcome all to tonight's charitable event. Thank you all for coming. First, let's give a big hand to my man, Sebastian Carter. Without his generosity, our worthy cause would never have been possible. Not that he had to dig around in the bottoms of his pockets, exactly. We regardless thank you for your largesse."

A polite tutting rippled through the room as the man flashed his enormous, blindingly-white teeth. Charlotte shifted on her feet, her heels already causing a dull throbbing in her lower back.

"Well, I was just about to settle in for a nice lengthy speech, but my wife is giving me *that look*, so I'll just say, thank you all for your generosity tonight. The Mason H. Billingsby Children's Squash League now officially has the funds to open ten additional courts, along with a sparkling new dining terrace, a therapeutic recovery bay, and a relaxation sauna. Now maybe our kids will finally be able to beat those riff-raff from Long Island in next year's tournament!"

Laughter and applause swelled through the room as Charlotte grimaced. So that was where tonight's flood of money was going. Where on earth was Sebastian getting it all? Was he seriously taking them deeper into debt, for this? She glanced at Brielle, who returned a blank expression. Guess she felt it was a good cause.

Now Sebastian was listening intently to someone, nodding and smiling broadly. A perfect lock of salt-and-pepper hair fell across his forehead; his eyes twinkled with amusement. Somehow he almost looked younger at fifty-eight than he did when she first met him. It didn't seem fair how his looks flourished as hers seemed to wane.

A beautiful brunette appeared next to him, maybe a couple of years younger than Charlotte, maybe not. Without looking at the woman, the smile dropped from Sebastian's face as he pointedly created a few inches of distance between them and turned slightly away from her. Charlotte's heart stopped beating for a moment, and she spluttered as the missed beats gathered and lodged themselves in her throat. The woman gestured animatedly with her hands as she spoke, apparently continuing some part of the story, and Sebastian laughed nervously as he eyed her out of the side of his vision. Something rippled up Charlotte's spine and settled between her shoulder blades, some warning from the ancient recesses of her brain.

Suddenly, the woman turned her head and stared directly at Charlotte. An unmistakable look of recognition passed over the woman's face, a knowing look, as one corner of her full lips turned slightly upward and her eyes narrowed almost imperceptibly. It was subtle enough to mistake for a polite smile.

Beads of sweat had broken out across Charlotte's forehead as her vision shrank to a tunnel. It was her, Charlotte was certain of it. Some remote part of Sebastian clearly felt a shift, and he turned his head and caught Charlotte's gaze. A split-second glance at the woman next to him. Then, back at Charlotte. His expression was blank as time crawled to a stop.

"Charlotte, you okay?"

"What?" Brielle's voice had broken the trance. The sounds of laughter and clinking glassware returned as the darkness slowly receded from the edges of her vision. "It's nothing. It's nothing. I'm fine," she forced out through a shaky exhale. "I've got to go. I'm sorry, Brielle. I have to get out of here."

Brielle was speechless as Charlotte turned on her heel and frantically scanned for the nearest exit. Bile formed in her throat and threatened to overtake her. The last thing she heard as she forced open the large double doors was Sebastian's anxious voice calling after her.

5

Darkness gathered outside as Charlotte paced around the condo aimlessly, waiting for Sebastian to return from the fundraiser. She'd spent the interminable cab ride back to The Windsor in wall-to-wall traffic, weeping silently and clenching her fists in the backseat as the driver kept glancing up to his rearview mirror at her, a sorrowful look in his eyes.

Charlotte checked her phone to see the time and noticed a missed call from Mariah. A weak smile formed at her lips. Talking with her children always made her feel better.

Mariah picked up on the first ring. "Hey, Mom!" She sounded groggy. "How did things go with Allie yesterday?"

Oh, it had been just terrific. "Hey, sweetheart. I was sorry to see her go, but you know how excited she is. I still can't believe she's gone."

"I know, me neither. Listen, I only have a minute, I have a date tonight with this guy Derek from the hospital." Mariah was a medical student at the Boston University School of Medicine, and almost never took a night off from her studies. Charlotte sometimes worried about Mariah's workaholic tendencies, but she always seemed to be keeping everything together okay. "I just wanted to say hey and see how you were holding up. Is Dad there? Did he cry dropping her off?" she asked through a smile.

A brief pause. "Your father's fine...we were at a fundraiser tonight, he's not home yet." *He's probably off philandering with his other woman, shattering your mother's heart into a thousand pieces.* "He's probably still schmoozing...you know how he is." Mariah gave a knowing laugh. "I'll tell him you called when he gets home. How are you doing? How are your classes going?"

"Oh, fine...busy. Well, that's sort of an understatement..." She heard Mariah stifle a yawn. "I miss you guys."

"Oh, honey..." Charlotte did her best to hide the tremble in her voice. "I miss you too."

There was a pause. "What's wrong?"

She always knew. "Just a long, long day is all. I'm okay. It's so good to hear from you." Her voice cracked on the last word.

A moment of silence passed. "It's good to hear from you too, Mom. I know it's been a while since I've been back...work and all. I'll be there for the 4th of July, though, right around the corner."

"I know, sweetheart." Charlotte forced a small laugh. "Everything just seems to be happening all at once. Don't you go worrying about your old mum, though; she's made of tougher stuff. Now, tell me all about this Derek."

She listened intently as Mariah's musical voice plinked out a soothing melody that began to melt away the horrors of the last day. As they said their goodbyes and Charlotte ended the call, she pulled out a heavy wooden chair and sat down at the end of the long, marble-topped table in the dining room. The sound of the wind whipping through the air carried into the condo as darkness settled in the sky. She tapped her fingers nervously on the table.

Something had shifted within her as she spoke to Mariah. She felt something clicking into place, a course correction. If Mariah had come to Charlotte with this same problem, what would she say to her? What would she want for her daughters?

Here Mariah was, working her tail off going after her dreams, head held high and conquering the world. Somewhere along the way, Mariah had grown into a woman before her very eyes. She deserved to have the life she dreamed of. Didn't Charlotte deserve it too?

An image of her own mother swam before her eyes, her mother as she was before her family had begun to unravel that Christmas Eve when she was sixteen. Always singing, floating from room to room in her graceful way. The tinkling of her laughter, the flush of her cheeks, the well-worn crinkles around her mouth from her enduring smile. That particular feeling of warmth and safety in her arms that only mothers could provide.

Less than two years later, Charlotte left Marina Cove and had never been back. While many years had passed since she'd seen her mother in person, Charlotte kept in touch sporadically. Not that it had seemed to matter much. Something had broken irrevocably within their family.

Charlotte suddenly found herself flush with a yearning to be with her family, her mother. She supposed it was an instinctive sort of urge, a vestige of infancy when the greatest need in the world was a mother's loving embrace. Underneath all the pain and loss, her mother was still in there. The woman who'd carefully taught her the ways of being a woman in the world, whose patience and love had helped make Charlotte into who she was today. Maybe there was some way to find that woman in her mother again, and Charlotte could feel safe once more.

Fear and uncertainty weren't going to stop her from standing up for herself any longer. Sebastian didn't deserve a trip to Paris with her. The details of what he had done didn't matter; he had broken their marriage vows. It didn't matter if they hadn't had the perfect marriage; besides, such things didn't exist. There was no excuse.

Somewhere along the way, Charlotte had lost herself to a desperate need for certainty and predictability. Her whole adult life, in one way or another, had been dictated by Sebastian, and she'd allowed it in the interest of maintaining the status quo, at any cost. And now the safety net of wealth she'd long taken for granted was no longer there. It gave her a sudden feeling of claustrophobia, a prison of her own making. She needed to get away from Sebastian for a while, to get away from the city, the people, all of it. Go back to where it all began. Somewhere safe to clear her mind and allow herself the time to work out what she really wanted. No one was making her decide between a divorce and a lifetime with Sebastian right this moment. Regardless of what would happen between them, it was time to find some way of making a future and a life of her own. A life that Sebastian didn't control.

Charlotte decided then and there that after 26 years, she'd return to Marina Cove. Ramona would be furious, of course. But sometimes, you just had to go home. And truth be told...Charlotte didn't really have anywhere else to go. Who else could she turn to as her life imploded, if not her family?

Her phone chimed in front of her. *There in five.* Charlotte sat up straight in her chair, squared her shoulders, and took a deep breath. Her entire life was about to change.

As the light from the elevator in the foyer illuminated, signaling Sebastian's arrival, Charlotte rose from the dining room table and waited for the doors to open. The jumbled mess of thoughts and feelings that had tumbled and ricocheted within her since yesterday had at last stilled. She held on to the clarity with gratitude, and smoothed her hair back as the doors pulled apart and Sebastian entered the room, tentatively looking at her standing before him. Ollie gave her a nuzzle and planted himself next to Charlotte, staring daggers at Sebastian on her behalf.

"Charlotte...I want to talk to you." He watched her as he slowly removed his tux jacket, set it on the kitchen table, and loosened his bowtie.

"I heard you talking to her yesterday, Sebastian."

He froze mid-movement and watched her carefully. "Talking to who?"

"*Talking to who*," she spat. "*Steph*. You left to talk to your other woman while I was down the hall with our daughter..." Her voice cracked as tears sprang to her eyes. "Sebastian...why...how could you. *How could you do this to me?*" A hot flare of anger rose in her throat as she strode across the room toward him and squared up against him. "*After twenty-six years! I gave you twenty-six years of my life!*" A single sob escaped her lips as she glared up at him. Up at those big, dark blue eyes that she'd gotten lost in all those years ago. Those same eyes that looked up at her as he got on one knee in the sand, salty wind whipping against them in the moonlight, as he asked the question that would create what should've been a bond that would last a lifetime.

Sebastian sighed and slumped his shoulders. "It isn't what you think. That's actually what I wanted to talk to you about."

Charlotte laughed humorlessly. "That was your precious *Steph* next to you tonight. Right? You're only trying to cover for yourself because you're afraid she'll say something—"

"You've got to listen to me. Let me at least explain. I don't know what you heard—"

"No. You listen to me. I heard more than enough. You went to 'meet up' with her at her place last night when you told me you had to go in to work."

"Charlotte, listen—"

"*You were with her in our own home, Sebastian! Our home!*"

Sebastian stared down at his empty palms. "I'm not saying it doesn't look bad, but you need some context. Shouldn't I have a chance to at least tell you what happened?"

Charlotte pinched between her eyes with her fingers and shook her head. "It doesn't really matter, does it. Whatever it was, you screwed everything up, Sebastian. *You have a family!* You had me..." Her voice broke as she slumped down into a chair at the kitchen island, closed her hands over her face, and began to weep in earnest.

Sebastian took a deep breath, and continued. "Listen. Stephanie works on my team. She was hired a few months ago to help out with some of our negotiations on this big deal I've been trying to put together, to get us back above water. We got to talking, and became friends. After a while, she started making excuses to hang out at work more often. I didn't think much of it at first. But she was very... forward. I didn't see the harm, since we were just talking."

He walked over to the sink, poured a glass of water, and pressed it against his forehead as he leaned against the counter. In the harsh overhead lights, he suddenly looked much older, wearier. "I admit, I was flattered. I think anyone would be. I guess it was the perfect storm. You know things have been a little...distant between us lately."

Charlotte's eyebrows shot up as she rose from her chair. Clenching her fists and controlling her voice carefully, she seethed through gritted teeth, "Surely, you're kidding me right now. Are you seriously blaming it on...*distance*? Like that gives you the right to destroy our marriage?"

Sebastian raised his hands and stepped back.

"No, of course not. I'm just saying, I think I was feeling a little...vulnerable. I mean, it felt good to get attention like that again. I'm just trying to be honest, Charlotte—"

Charlotte slammed both fists on the table hard enough that the glassware shook in the kitchen cabinets. "*You're pathetic.* I can't believe you're trying to make excuses here." She wiped her eyes with the sleeve of her dress and sat back down heavily as Sebastian ran his hands through his hair.

He bowed his head, closed his eyes, and pushed on. "Please just hear me out. After a while, we started to meet up for lunch, sometimes drinks. Yes, we met up here sometimes, and sometimes over at her place, but we weren't ever doing anything...just talking, a few drinks. I think I was becoming...I don't know. Maybe it was a little bit of an infatuation."

He paused, and looked directly into Charlotte's eyes. "It wasn't like we were...I'm not in love with her or anything like that..." He ignored Charlotte scoffing loudly, and continued. "Just listen. Last night, I did see her. And she kissed me."

The words spread throughout the room and hung heavy in the air. Charlotte's mouth went dry. "And then what."

He paused. "And then, nothing. Nothing else

happened. I told her that we needed to stop, and I left. I realized then how far things had gotten. I swear to you, Charlotte, I never meant for this to happen. I am truly, truly sorry, from the bottom of my heart. It was all a terrible mistake, and I will do whatever it takes to make it up to you."

"Did you kiss her back?" Charlotte asked.

"What?"

"You said she kissed you. Did you or didn't you kiss her back?"

Sebastian pressed his palms into his eyes. "Yes. I'm sorry, baby, but I want to be honest here. It was just for a few seconds before I came to my senses. I'm ashamed. I'm so ashamed..." Tears had formed in his eyes as he looked up at her in supplication. "Please, nothing like this has ever happened or will happen ever again. I was so confused...It's an awful thing for me to let happen and I take full responsibility. I'll do whatever I have to for you to forgive me. I know I don't deserve it, but please. We have twenty-six years together. Our children..." He trailed off. "I want you, Charlotte. No one else. Last night made me realize just how much you mean to me. I love you."

Charlotte closed her eyes as tears silently fell from her face. "If you loved me, you wouldn't have let something like this happen. I'm leaving, Sebastian."

The color drained completely from his face. "Charlotte, please, I'll do anything—"

"I'm going back to Marina Cove to stay with my family for a little while. I need to be away from you right now. You have no idea..." The words caught in her throat. "You have no idea what this feels like for me right now. I feel so stupid..." She shook her head as the hot tears continued falling. "I need to think about everything for a while. You need to respect that."

"Are you leaving me?"

She let the words hang for a moment. "I don't know what I'm doing yet. But we need a separation. I don't know what you thought would happen. I need to get out of Manhattan for a while and figure out what I want."

His eyebrows furrowed. "I thought you didn't talk to your family anymore."

"Well, that's my problem to deal with."

"When are you leaving?"

"Tomorrow morning. There's no way to call and explain this all to them, so I'm just going to show up and hope for the best." She laughed bitterly. "Won't that be a fun little surprise for them," she said to herself. She'd be lucky if Ramona didn't slam the door in her face.

Sebastian grabbed a nearby hand towel and dried his eyes. "Of course. I respect that. Take all the time you need. Charlotte, I need you to know that I'll do anything to make it up to you. It was inexcusable, and you deserve so much better. I hope from the bottom of my heart that you can give me another chance. If you do...I'll spend the rest of my life making sure you know what you mean to me."

Charlotte stood from her chair and looked deeply into his eyes. "You shouldn't have needed a relationship with another woman to learn that. I should've been enough. You were always enough for me."

With that, Charlotte turned and padded up the stairs to their bedroom. It would be her last night in this condo for a while. The last night forever, perhaps. Despite the twisting and writhing in her stomach, she felt a small spark of hope. Her whole life was in front of her. She was taking the plunge, finally standing up for herself, asking herself what she really wanted.

Whatever she was going to face returning to Marina Cove, at least now she would have a chance to figure that out.

6

The frigid wind burst into the living room as the front door swung open. A booming voice called in, "Okay, people, the guest of honor has arrived! Let the festivities begin!"

Charlotte dropped her hardback copy of *The Adventures of Tom Sawyer* as a grin spread across her face and rushed from her reading spot by the warmth of the fireplace to the foyer. The dulcet tones of Perry Como crackling on the old record player made their way through the inn as the aroma of cranberry lemon bread baking in the oven filled her with sweet, heady nostalgia. Her older brother Gabriel was waiting at the door with open arms. She rushed in to embrace him, inhaling the scent of sea salt and driftwood. Her eyes welled up as she whispered, "I missed you so much."

"I missed you too, little dove," he said, squeezing her tight. Gabriel was six years older than her and had been working in Boston as a fisherman for the last several years. She hadn't seen him since he left Marina Cove after dropping out of high school to pursue his dream of adventures on the open sea. "Guess who I found wandering around outside?"

Another draft of icy wind swept through the inn as the front door opened again and her oldest sister Diane made her way in with an armful of bags and an enormous suitcase in tow. "What, are you moving back home, Di?" asked Gabe, one eyebrow arching up, mock concern in his expression.

Diane grinned as she pulled them both in for a hug. "You know me. Always prepared for anything. Anyway, one of these gifts was for you, Gabe, but now I'm thinking maybe I want it for myself."

"Good, because I didn't get you anything this year. Wasn't feeling like you deserved one."

She punched his shoulder playfully, took off her coat, and put her arm in Charlotte's, guiding her toward the kitchen. "I don't know about you, but I'm starving. How's everything here been?" Diane dropped her voice to a whisper. "Mom tells me that you and Christian are getting pretty serious." A wicked grin spread across her face.

Well, no secrets were safe around here, apparently. Christian would be stopping by later, so it didn't really matter anyway. The truth was, she and Christian had become inseparable. They'd been seeing each other for a few months, and Charlotte was head over heels for his kind manner, his rumbling baritone, his strong arms around her. A memory glittered within her, sitting next to him on their first date at the movies, arms brushing against each other, Christian turning toward her and tilting her chin up for their first kiss.

She knew in her heart that she was a girl in love. No matter how many people told her otherwise, talking down to her and reminding her that she was only sixteen, she knew she had found her person.

"Everything's been good around here...same old," Charlotte said, unable to stop one corner of her mouth turning slightly upward.

"I notice you're dodging my question. Don't think you're getting away that easily." Diane winked as she turned into the inn's large kitchen. Charlotte's mother Ella and middle sister Natalie were hunched over the counter, spreading green and red frosting over a fresh batch of sugar cookies cut into the shapes of Christmas trees and reindeer. Ramona, two years younger than Charlotte and the baby of the family, was humming to herself as she stood in front of an easel in the corner, a beautiful watercolor painting of a wooden pier leading out to a sparkling ocean emerging from her careful brushstrokes. Ella was swaying her hips, singing cheerfully along with Andy Williams as she glanced up at her daughters arriving in the kitchen, arm-in-arm. With a squeal of delight, she dropped the gingerbread man she'd been frosting and put her arms around them, tears forming in her eyes. "Oh, my beautiful girls. Diane, we've missed you terribly."

"I've missed you too, Mom," Diane murmured into her hair, pulling them in tighter. "Thanks for putting all this together. I assume the cranberry and popcorn is standing by?" Every year they'd team up and see who could build the longest strand of popcorn and cranberries in ten minutes. Every year, Gabriel had won in a landslide, parading his strand around the room, belting out victory songs at the top of his lungs. Winner got to open the first gift Christmas morning.

"All ready to go, and I've got a new box of ornaments to finish putting up on the tree, so let's finish this batch of cookies and I'll get some cider on." Ella stepped back and looked Diane up and down wistfully. "It really is so good to see you, sweetheart. I wish they'd give you a little more time off over there." Diane was an account director at an advertising agency in Los Angeles, and had rarely made it back home since she'd graduated college a couple of years ago.

"Well, they technically give us unlimited vacation days, but no one takes them. Still paying my dues. But things should settle down in a few years. But enough about me—how's your first semester been, Natalie?"

Natalie was a freshman at the University of Maine and had arrived back home a week ago. She swept her long blonde hair back behind her shoulder and smiled sheepishly. "It's good. Still getting used to things. But my classes are fun. Finals were killer, though."

"I'm sure you did great," Ella said. "You're all so talented."

"You have to say that, Mom," Ramona said, a smile tugging at the corner of her mouth.

"No, I mean it. Your father and I have the most wonderful children in all the world. That's just a fact."

"Where is Dad, anyway?" said Diane. "Has he busted out Dancing Santa yet?"

They all laughed. The ridiculous plug-in figurine was a mainstay of Christmas, but every year, it needed serious repairs. It was at least half duct tape at this point. "Your father was still tinkering with it this morning. He's out shopping for last-minute gifts. He was supposed to be back an hour ago; I guess he got held up."

Ten minutes later, they made their way into the living room of the inn, armed with sugar cookies and hot apple cider. After a crackling pause on the record player, the opening notes of "White Christmas" filled the room, joining with the sound of Gabriel's rowdy shouts and cackling laughter. The heat from the fireplace was winning the tug-of-war against the cold drafts seeping in through the inn's ancient windows and doors. The guests of the Seaside House, the family inn and their home, were all visiting relatives or friends this close to Christmas, so they took full advantage of being able to be as loud and silly as they wanted.

"Mom, where do you keep the needle and thread?" Natalie asked as Ella headed into the kitchen for more cider. "Gabe upped the ante this year for the cranberry and popcorn contest. Winner doesn't have to clean up after dinner tonight."

Ella laughed cheerfully and said, "I'll grab it, honey, it's upstairs."

The popping and creaking of each step as she climbed the old staircase was in that familiar sequence, an old tune you knew by heart and could recite perfectly, no matter how long it had been. Sometimes, as she tried to fall back asleep in the middle of the night in the years to come, Charlotte would recall the next few moments with a terrible clarity: Bing Crosby's silky voice floating through the room, Gabe's devilish grin and wildly gesturing hands as he told some crude story, the air redolent of firewood and saltwater from the shore not twenty feet from the inn's front door, just as she heard her mother's wail piercing the air.

The Keller siblings clambered over each other up the stairs to their mother and father's bedroom. Charlotte was unable to draw a breath, and her legs felt encased in cement as she climbed up in what seemed like slow motion.

Her mother was sitting on the edge of her bed, shaking and shuddering, racked with sobs. A sheet of paper loosely folded into thirds sat facing the ceiling next to her. Charlotte recognized her father's scrawl before she could read the words.

It was short, just a couple of sentences. Bracing herself, she grabbed the paper and held it up as her siblings circled behind her.

Ella, I'm sorry to say that I'm leaving. This isn't working. I have no doubt that you'll be better off, and I know you'll take care of our children. I have to go and make some sense of some things now. Please don't try to find me.

"Oh my God," whispered Diane.

Gabe's eyes knitted together before he tightened his fists. "He just left us? He's just gone?" The pitch of his voice rose as the words sputtered out of his mouth.

Natalie turned to her mother, fire in her eyes. "Were you guys fighting or something?"

Ella was silent for a few moments before she firmly shook her head a single time. Tears splashed down onto the blue patterned fabric of her dress. "I don't understand. Jack would never do this to us. He would never do this to me."

A fresh sob broke from her lips as she fell back on the bedspread, pulling her knees to her chest. Charlotte hadn't taken a breath since entering the room. The floor seemed to tilt one way, and then the other, a wave of nausea plowing through her stomach and almost knocking her over. There was no way her father would be so selfish and just abandon them. To what, go make sense of his life, or whatever he had written? Was this some sort of midlife crisis? He and her mother had been so happy. She frantically scanned her mind like pages flipping in a book for some sign, something that would lend some sense of understanding to what was happening.

Gabriel was pacing around the room muttering to himself as Diane and Natalie stood in stunned silence, gazing into empty space. Ramona was stroking her mother's back, eyes swimming with tears. The gears of Charlotte's mind weren't turning properly, hitting against one another, cracking and crashing together. Gabriel slamming his fists against the wall broke through the haze, and Charlotte turned, ran down the creaking stairs, and pushed through the heavy wooden door into the freezing night.

AN HOUR LATER, Charlotte was rocking herself back and forth in the sand as snow began to quietly fall, her fingers and toes numb as she stared at the sea through tear-stained eyes. She had fled the inn and wandered around aimlessly until her feet had unknowingly led her to her favorite spot, the beach in front of Old Man Keamy's large empty plot of land on the southern shore of Marina Cove. It was her private place to think, to daydream, to imagine her future.

And now, it was her place to grieve. Something in the letter had registered a knowledge deep within her, his words locking an understanding into place. Her father was really gone. This wasn't just some idle running out after a nasty fight. She thought of the last time she had seen him, cooking pancakes on the griddle over the stove, winking at her with his twinkling golden eyes as she came down the stairs for breakfast.

The sound of someone calling her name made her leap up in terror. Charlotte made out the wavy light brown hair and the familiar angle of his face. She ran through the sand as fast as she could toward him. He'd known where to find her. Christian pulled her tightly into his chest as Charlotte wept loudly into his shoulder, tears streaming down her face, her entire body shaking like a leaf. He wrapped his coat around her, held her face in his hands, and lifted it to meet his gaze. "I'm so sorry, Charlotte."

He held her tightly against him as sobs racked her body, and softly hummed "Beyond the Sea" into her long dark hair, the song he would always sing to comfort her. The frozen wind whipped against them as the darkness deepened overhead and snowflakes collected on their skin. As Christian rocked her slowly in his arms, she tried to fathom the empty void in front of her as she felt the binding threads of her family snap in half.

Charlotte's eyes were closed as she stood on the passenger deck of the ferry on the way to Marina Cove, deeply inhaling the sweet saltwater air that washed over her, hair whipping in the wind. The sun beamed down from a cloudless sky and radiated across her skin, warming her from within, as birds squawked overhead and the gentle rocking of the ship across the cerulean waves of the Atlantic Ocean made her feel pleasantly drowsy. Ollie was bounding clumsily across the deck from end to end, sniffing the air like he was hot on the trail of something delicious, and happily accepting pets and ear scratches from other passengers. She took another sip from the cup of coffee that warmed her hands made stiff by the cool ocean breeze drifting across the deck.

She was exhausted after tossing and turning in her bed all night while Sebastian kept his distance downstairs. Well before the sun rose over the Manhattan skyline, she'd already packed up what she thought she'd need for an extended stay in her large hot pink suitcase. Sebastian had watched her movements like a sad puppy before she took the elevator down to their driver, who was waiting to take her to Hyannis Port to catch the ferry to Marina Cove.

Sebastian asked her to call him once she safely arrived, to which she'd tersely agreed. He called one last "I love you" into the elevator as Ollie gave him a low *harrumph* and a brutal dog scowl. She couldn't bring herself to respond as the elevator doors closed between them.

As the ferry pulled away from the harbor and she watched the mainland grow smaller and smaller, a small tug somewhere in her solar plexus urged her to call it off, to jump ship and paddle back to shore with Ollie and her pink suitcase for flotation. But she pressed her eyes shut and firmly shook her head. This was the right thing to do. Like it or not, her life was changing. There was no going back. So she might as well move forward.

As Charlotte stood and watched the endless crystal blue horizon in front of her, a chime from her pocket broke her concentration. A text from Allie.

Hey, Mom <3 Hope you and Dad are surviving without me over there ;) I'll call you in a few days. Love you.

Allie. The kids...In the crazy spiral of the last day and a half, it hadn't even occurred to her to fill her kids in on what had happened.

A punch of guilt hit her in the back of the throat. What on earth was she supposed to tell them? *Sorry, your father decided to have a fun little entanglement with another woman, so I've fled the city to see my family, whom I abandoned almost three decades ago. How've you been?*

That task could wait a bit. She fired off a quick text to Sebastian. *Let me talk to the kids about this.* First, she wanted to clear her head and try to brace herself for what was to come as she returned to the place she never imagined she'd see again. She sat back in one of the deck chairs and let the sea breeze wash over her as she drew Ollie closer to her and wrapped her arms around his furry chest.

Charlotte's stomach clenched as Marina Cove

slowly swam into view. Great jagged cliffs of rock shot up from the sea, ending in sprawling emerald forests and fields of wildflowers painted in a stunning kaleidoscope of colors. Long, untouched coves of golden sand punctuated the bluffs, violet and azure water lapping placidly against the shoreline. A few small boats hummed lazily to and from long wooden docks stretching out over the water.

Her breath caught in her throat as she took in the sight in front of her. She'd completely forgotten how stunning it was after all her years away. A tiny flicker sparked somewhere within her.

As the ferry pulled into Hightide Port, the echoes of distant memories carried over the saltwater wind, making her shiver despite the warmth. She finished her coffee and went inside to retrieve her suitcase. As she and Ollie made their way to the stairs leading down to the dock, a deep voice called out behind her, "Charlotte? Is that you?"

Charlotte turned. Walking down from the upper cabin was a handsome older man in a captain's uniform. He had wavy salt-and-pepper hair, a thick beard, and dark blue eyes that seemed to sparkle with amusement. She'd recognize him anywhere; this was the same man who'd ferried her to the mainland when she had left Marina Cove.

"Mr. Sutherland!" He pulled her in for a warm embrace as she was transported back to her last day on the island. "I can't believe you're still here! Aren't you ever going to retire?"

He chuckled heartily. "Me? Retire? Never. I need the open sea. Besides, after my Martha passed, rest her soul, I need something to do all day. And by the way," he added with a wink, "I think you're old enough to call me Leo now."

Charlotte smiled. "I'm so sorry to hear about Mrs. Sutherland, ah, Martha. She was always so sweet. We loved perusing her bookstore."

The ghost of a smile crossed his mouth. "She was one of a kind." He cleared his throat. "Anyway. I never thought I'd see you back here...it's been so many years. I remember the day you left like it was yesterday." He turned to her, a look of concern knitting his eyebrows. "You looked like you were sort of...hightailing it out of here."

Charlotte opened her mouth to respond, but no words came out. Leo shook his head quickly. "It's none of my business, I'm sorry. I was just worried about you. I know things were a little hard for your family after your dad..." The unfinished sentence hung in the air between them.

"It's completely fine. I just had to get away, start

over is all," said Charlotte. It would be impossible to explain everything, how her father leaving had set certain events in motion that would ultimately lead to her leaving Marina Cove a year and a half later. "Everything all worked out. I wanted to come back and see my mother. And Ramona. It's been a long time. Do you know how they're doing? How's the inn doing?"

Something flashed across his eyes, so fast she nearly missed it. "Well, I, uh...I haven't really seen much of Ella in a while. Or, ah, Ramona, for that matter..." He shifted on his feet, looking uncomfortable. "I'm sure they'll be happy as clams to see you, though. It's good to have you back. Marina Cove hasn't changed one jot, you'll see. The best-kept secret this side of the Mississippi, I've always said." He smiled as he turned to gaze out over the harbor with a look of pride. "Just don't go posting about it all over your social media and what have you; don't want to go opening the floodgates all at once," he said with a wink.

After giving Ollie a few well-earned scratches behind the ears, they hugged, and Leo made his way back up to the ferry cabin. The interaction had unsettled her; he'd deftly dodged her question about her mother and sister. And the inn, for that matter.

Her stomach roiled as she carefully descended the steps to the dock. Something told her that this might not be as simple as she'd hoped.

CHARLOTTE GRIMACED as she crossed the sand. Heels had been a terrible choice. It occurred to her how ridiculous she looked, her diamond-encrusted purse and a form-fitting navy blue designer dress, enormous pink suitcase, and an over-excited chocolate lab in tow. She had to get to Ocean Avenue, and then walk west toward Main Street and the inn, a mile or two down Seaside Lane.

Because Marina Cove was only about nine miles at its longest, people mostly traveled around on foot or on one of the many bicycles that were stationed all over the island, free for anyone's use. Cars were uncommon on the island; some residents owned electric scooters or golf carts to get around. As much as Ollie would love nothing more than to share a bicycle seat with Charlotte and cruise the streets together, she had no choice other than to walk the two or so miles to the Seaside House. Ignoring the blisters already forming on her ankles, she wiped the sweat from her forehead and trudged along.

Nostalgia burned through her as she crossed Ocean Avenue and turned onto Main Street. Everything was exactly as she'd left it all those years ago. The single-lane streets lined with towering pine and spruce trees, the brightly painted houses and businesses in every color stacked closely together around little cobblestone plazas, residents milling about in friendly conversation. Marina Cove had always been a tight-knit community; everyone knew everyone else and neighbors looked out for one another. It was the sort of place where no one locked their doors and crime was virtually unheard of.

Charlotte turned right onto Seaside Lane as a painful familiarity struck her. This was where her father had taught her to ride her bike; an image of her mother watching from the front porch of the inn as she rode back and forth and her father cheered along filled her mind, a soreness and longing forming in the pit of her stomach.

The inn was at the end of the lane, the last house before the southwest shore of Marina Cove. She saw it emerging as she approached the end of the road, the familiar wraparound porches encircling the inn on the first and second floors coming into view.

Something scuttled up her spine as she approached the inn, and she picked up her pace.

Something was wrong, off about the place. From a distance it held its shape that was etched permanently into her mind, but now, as she got close, it was like a twisted imitation of the inn she had known, an upside-down nightmare version standing before her.

Her eyes welled with hot tears as she took in the hanging shutters, the missing railing, the shattered windows. The beautiful white exterior paint with blue trim was peeled and whole sections of bare wood were exposed. The second-story wraparound porch had an entire section missing that had been hastily boarded up, and it appeared as though someone had taken a gigantic sledgehammer to most of the roof tiles. Broken wooden furniture lined the first-story porch, lying on a thick coating of what looked like years' worth of dirt, sand, and driftwood.

Pain slashed through her gut as she recognized one of the broken wooden rockers, that baroque pattern so delicately carved into the wood trim that she remembered so clearly from her childhood, sitting cross-legged next to her mother while she rocked away, Ramona in her lap and a cold glass of lemonade in hand, mesmerized by the crystal waters. It was on this porch that she'd shared countless hours with Christian on the large wicker double chair, her head on his shoulder, nothing but the endless summer stretching before her.

Charlotte thought back to the last time she'd spoken with her mother. It had been a couple of years. A short and terse conversation, her mother mostly grunting responses. Charlotte had given up and hadn't called back since. She thought her mother still lived at the inn, but no signs of life came from within. The front door was firmly locked as she turned the knob. A few knocks; no response.

Wiping the tears from her eyes, she marched down the porch's three wooden steps around to the side garden. Or what used to be a garden. Her father had built it one summer, a glorious vegetable garden bookended with trellises of ivy and circled with roses and sunflowers. Now, it was a tangled mess of weeds and thickets, sage brush and rotting driftwood overflowing against the inn, the trellises nowhere to be seen. She lifted the rock next to the garden where they'd always kept their spare key, not that they ever locked the place. The ground under the rock was empty.

She walked back to the front of the inn and sat down on the steps with Ollie. Her heart was broken. The inn had always been bustling with people, even during the winter months, as tourists came to enjoy the beautiful Christmas season on the island, to relax in front of the hot fire with cups of hot chocolate and look out through the large bay windows as the snow quietly accumulated on the sand. Tourists were an important part of the island's economy, but it never got so crowded that the soul of the island had changed. It was still a tiny piece of paradise, somewhere to escape the hustle and bustle of the outside world. While the Keller family had never been rich, or anywhere near it, the steady flow of travelers provided them with everything they had needed to get by. It was enough.

Maybe her mother had moved in with Ramona? As far as she knew, Ramona still lived in a small bungalow around the corner; she'd moved there when she'd gotten married to her long-time boyfriend Danny. Not that Ramona had told her that; anything she learned came in broken bits and pieces from Diane or Gabriel. Or her mother, when she was feeling up to it. Charlotte always had the sense that her siblings knew little more than she did.

Steeling herself, she gathered her purse and suitcase, and she and Ollie turned the corner onto Bay Street. Evening was closing in; the sun was dipping toward the horizon, casting sparkling rays of tangerine light across the deep blue waters. Even though summer was just ahead, the temperature of the air had dropped a bit, and she rubbed her arms in an effort to warm herself. She was woefully underprepared.

She was at her sister's tiny bungalow in just a minute or two. Lights shone through shuttered blinds and out onto the meticulously kept postage-stamp yard squared by neat driftwood picket fencing. Someone was definitely home.

Charlotte rolled her suitcase up to the front door, shared a look of uncertainty with Ollie, and knocked on the front door.

8

Ramona sighed heavily as she stared at the stacks of dishes piling up on her kitchen sink, the ever-present aromas of mildew and old dust emanating from seemingly everywhere in her bungalow, lazily creeping around the place in tiny tendrils and snaking their way into her nostrils. The muffled sounds of some game show floated in from the closed door of the lone bedroom. She had just enough time to cook something for the two of them before she headed out to her second job at the restaurant for her nighttime shift.

Quickly shuffling through the contents of the cupboards above the sink, she decided on beans and rice, again. There wasn't enough time for anything else. Her mother would just have to accept it.

Ramona listened to the water boiling as she looked out the window above the sink to the small break between the treeline that provided her with a fractured glimpse of the shoreline, and the dark waters that extended endlessly toward the horizon. The familiar popping and crackling of panic and fear roiled in her stomach for a brief moment, threatening to rise to her chest, before Ramona quickly slammed a lid on it, forcing it back in a well-practiced and almost rote manner.

Just one day right now, today, today. Just the next hour. Get through the next hour.

She could manage that. Ramona knew that looking any further than that was the quick train to despair.

The stove timer went off, graciously kicking her out of her thoughts. Ramona dumped the rice and beans into two bowls and sprinkled cheese over everything. She walked to her bedroom and hesitated outside the door. Ramona took a breath, closed her eyes, and exhaled slowly.

"Hey Mom, I have some dinner. Sorry it's not something better...I'm running late for work."

A long pause, and then the sounds of contestants cheering cut off. Her mother slowly opened the door. "This is fine, Ramona, thank you. I'm not that hungry anyway." Her hair, once curling and waving gracefully around her like she was walking through a perpetual ocean breeze, was now matted and sticking out at odd angles. Ramona remembered how her mother's eyes always crinkled at the edges with a smile, always sparkling, but something had long clouded over them, now framed by rings that never seemed to go away.

Ramona's heart swelled painfully with love for her mother as the needling of helplessness that had plagued her for almost as long as she could remember began poking at the base of her spine. They made their way to the tiny wooden table against the kitchen wall and began eating wordlessly.

The sounds of silverware scraping were punctuated only by the steady *tick tick* of the cuckoo clock mounted on the wall behind her. Ramona hardly ever knew what to say to her mother anymore. At first, when Ella had moved out of the inn to stay in her bungalow, Ramona had seen it as a welcome change, something to spur her mother out of her funk. She'd long felt her mother was just languishing away at the inn, waiting for change to happen. It was only supposed to be temporary, until they got the inn back up to snuff enough that people would start booking rooms again, but that was two years ago.

No. Her stomach turned and flopped as she thought about it. It had been four years now, maybe five. Time had an unreliable quality to it now, every day sketching out a rough facsimile of the one before it. It was hard to remember when exactly she'd realized just how badly things were actually going for them.

The Seaside House had once been booked out for months in advance, a popular place for tourists and locals alike to stay with its quiet waterfront location and walking distance to Main Street and the ferry port. For several generations the large property had been in their family. Marina Cove was something of a hidden gem, not too far from the much more popular attractions of Nantucket and Martha's Vineyard, but not nearly as well-known. So while they'd never been rich, they always had enough. It was enough.

Until, suddenly, it wasn't. After her father had abandoned them, the majority of the care and upkeep of the inn had fallen on her mother, Charlotte, and Ramona. Diane and Gabriel were already living away from home, and had kept their distance, and Natalie went off who knows where, always someplace new, whenever she deigned to call.

Charlotte up and leaving them out of nowhere not even two years later had really broken her up. That one, she hadn't seen coming.

As she pushed down the fire beginning to burn in the back of her throat, she looked up at her mother. Ella had done her level best against the odds, that much was true. Ramona admired her. After having the rug completely pulled from under her, Ella had gone into survival mode. She'd done everything. Learned to handle all the maintenance, repairs, bookings, on top of the accounting and cleaning she'd already managed. They were going to make it without Jack after all, it seemed.

But somewhere along the way, it had become too much. Ramona suspected that her mother had taken everything on as a way to distract herself from the pain of her father leaving. They all had their own ways of dealing with it.

Paint had started to chip, small things started to go unrepaired. Complaints from guests here and there, nothing dramatic. Ramona started to notice a room or two unoccupied one summer, a true rarity. Then, half their rooms.

What had become a terrible catch-22 ensued,

with no apparent solution. They needed more bookings to pay for upgrades, maintenance, repairs, everything. But without the upkeep, the bookings were dropping, and so the well was drying up. Ramona didn't have the full scope of their financial problems until they were so far underwater that Ella, for all intents and purposes, had thrown in the towel. They didn't have the money to get things back up to where they needed to be. Without any apparent recourse and the family sinking deeper and deeper into debt, Ella had frayed, stretched beyond her breaking point.

With her ex-husband Danny long gone out of Ramona's life and her bungalow feeling painfully quiet, she had asked Ella to stay with her while they figure out what to do, together. Her siblings had no real way of knowing what had happened, and as far as Ramona was concerned, they didn't deserve to know. She wasn't about to go groveling to her siblings to rescue them. They'd gotten this far without their help, and she'd wait until the Atlantic itself dried up before she asked for it.

So Ramona took the money they needed for the inn out of her home equity. She got a second job as a waitress in addition to her job as a freelance bookkeeper to stay on top of it all, determined to pay it back as soon as humanly possible. Which had worked, for a while. After a promising summer of renewed interest in the inn, more fundamental issues began to crop up. The inn was old, very old, and despite the efforts to rejuvenate the inn's surface, deeper fissures in its old bones began to appear, things that were going to require a lot more money than she had. For the first time in her life, she was truly at a loss.

Ramona silently watched her mother, her head down, eyes faraway, picking at her food mindlessly. The woman was a gem, a true beauty of a person, and deserved so much more than this. Ramona would do anything to make the vibrant woman she'd once known come back to her.

As Ramona hastily finished eating and tried her best not to let her eyes wander to the overflowing mail sorter on the kitchen counter that held countless unopened past-due bills, she heard a knock at the door. She glanced over at the cuckoo clock; she hadn't been expecting anyone. Ella shrugged at her as Ramona set her bowl in the sink and looked out through the kitchen window, leaning to see the small landing in front of her door.

Her heart slammed hard against the wall of her chest and a sensation of the room disappearing around her almost knocked her off balance. Ramona pressed her eyes shut and shook her head hard, as though to shake away what she saw in front of her. No. There was no way.

After all the long years that had passed, just standing there on her porch facing Ramona's small front yard, with her ridiculous hot pink suitcase and overpriced clothes like she owned the place, was Charlotte. Charlotte, her sister, her partner and companion and best friend when their father had left them. Charlotte, who had left her all alone with her mother and never looked back.

9

C harlotte held her breath as she turned to face the street, thrumming her fingers nervously against the hem of her skirt. A hot sweat had broken out all over her body; her clothes suddenly felt too tight, her shoes too small, constricting her. What had she been thinking turning up at the door, unannounced? Why hadn't she just called?

Because, the rational part of her brain reminded her, you were afraid they'd tell you no. Then you wouldn't have anywhere to go. Then what?

The door swung open hard, hitting the wall behind it and causing the glass of the front window to shudder.

"What are you doing here, Charlotte," a voice seethed at her.

"Ramona..." Charlotte turned to approach her, took a step, and halted in her tracks when she saw the look on Ramona's face. "Um...I'm sorry to just come here without calling."

"What are you doing here," Ramona repeated, her face a stone.

"Well, uh..." Charlotte stammered. This was pretty much what she'd expected, but it didn't soften the blow. Ramona looked older than her forty-two years, weathered, as though life had been slowly eroding her from the outside in. Beneath the expression of hostility and the dark circles under her eyes, her baby sister faintly glimmered, someone swimming frantically to the surface of the water for a gasp of air. Charlotte's face was flushed with heat, her throat thick, leaving her unable to speak. Ollie panted happily next to her, wagging his tail.

"Charlotte, I don't know what's going on here, but you just show up after how many years on my doorstep...Out with it, because I have to get to work." Ramona looked into her eyes for what felt like the first time since she'd been speaking, and her brows knitted together into a frown. "What happened?"

"Ramona..." she choked out as a lump formed in

her throat and hot tears brimmed her eyes. "I didn't have anywhere else to go. I'm sorry..." Charlotte felt her face crumple as she began to weep, tears falling down her cheeks and onto her dress.

Ramona watched her for a few moments, expression unchanged, before turning and going back through the screen door into her house. She'd left the front door open; Charlotte debated for a moment, and decided to take it as a grudging invitation inside.

The entirety of Ramona's bungalow could be seen in one glance as Charlotte stood in the living room by the front door. The fastidiously kept exterior belied the disarray of the rooms inside. Clutter on every surface, frayed carpeting, old peeling wallpaper and water stains on the ceiling. It wasn't dirty, exactly, just unkempt, someone who either didn't care or didn't have the time to bother. Ramona had gone into the kitchen and was busying herself with a stack of dirty dishes in the sink. Her mother was sitting at the table, gazing out through a small window above the sink, a faraway look in her eyes.

"Mom..." Charlotte said as she made her way to the kitchen. Ella seemed to snap to, looking up at Charlotte, a blank expression on her face as though she didn't recognize her. "Hey, Mom...It's been a long time," Charlotte said, unable to keep the tremble out of her voice.

A brief moment passed, and a tight smile formed on her mother's face. "Charlotte. What a surprise. We weren't expecting you...were we?" she asked in Ramona's direction.

Ramona didn't answer, silently scrubbing away at the sink. Charlotte leaned down and wrapped her arms around her mother, burying her face in her hair like she'd done when she was a little girl, inhaling the lilac scent of her hair, clutching her like she was a life preserver. "I missed you so much, Mom."

Her mother lifted one arm in a sort of halfway hug and patted her firmly twice on the back before pulling away. "Well. It certainly has been a long time." Ella motioned for Charlotte to sit at the table. "What brings you here?" she said evenly, apparently not noticing the streaks of tears on Charlotte's face.

While she'd spoken with her mother periodically over the phone, nothing had prepared her for seeing her in person again. Her mind was fractured with confusion. Part of her saw her mother as she was before her father had left, which was hard to square with the woman in front of her now. She was just as beautiful as ever, but the same shroud of tiredness and vague irritability she'd always heard over the phone seemed to blanket itself around her body.

"It's Sebastian..." Charlotte inhaled deeply and held it for a moment before slowly letting the air out, and found the words tumbling out of her like a dam that had just burst. "I just found out he's been having an affair. I don't know what to do. He says it's over and he says they just kissed but they had this whole ongoing relationship, an emotional affair, I don't know if I even believe his version of events, and... and I don't know what to do, Mom," she stammered through tears pouring from her eyes. She decided to leave out the part where she and Sebastian were going bankrupt. Ramona would probably just think she was here for money, which she wasn't. It was clear, at any rate, that she'd find no financial help here. "I've never been so hurt in my life. I'm sorry to just turn up like this. I didn't know what else to do." Charlotte held her face in her hands as quiet sobs racked her body.

Charlotte heard Ramona pause her scrubbing, but she didn't turn from the sink. Ella reached out and briefly placed a hand on Charlotte's shoulder before retracting it. "I'm sorry to hear that."

Charlotte swallowed hard, and asked the question she knew she needed to ask, dreading the answer. "I saw the inn…" She let the words hang in the air.

"We've done just fine without you here, Charlotte," Ramona said to the dishes.

Not sure what to say, Charlotte continued. "I didn't know you were living here, Mom. I was hoping to stay at the inn with you for a little bit while I figure out what I'm going to do next, but it doesn't look habitable over there…"

Ramona turned around suddenly. "I'm sorry, Charlotte, but you can't stay here. Look around you. We don't have any room as it is." She motioned to the blanket on the couch. "Mom's staying in my room, and I sleep out here." Charlotte felt Ramona's gaze linger on her diamond necklace, her expensive dress, her suede heels. "You can obviously afford to stay somewhere nice. Check into an inn, or whatever, if you're sticking around. I don't care. I'm sorry, but I have to get to work."

Charlotte knew that Ramona was aware there wouldn't be anything available on the island on such short notice. Ramona was right, though. There was clearly no room here, unless she wanted to camp out with Ollie on the floor next to Ramona. Charlotte had the feeling that her sister wouldn't be up for a slumber party.

Ella was glancing between Ramona and Charlotte. "I'm sorry, Charlotte, we just weren't prepared for you to...come back. Maybe you'll have some luck if you call around."

Ramona grabbed her jacket and purse from the hook on the hallway wall. "You can sleep at the inn if you want. Mom's room should be fine. It's not posh, like you're clearly accustomed to," she said, eyeing her up and down, "but it was always enough for us, anyway. I'd stick around, but some of us have to work for a living." She leaned down and gave their mother a peck on the cheek, and brushed past Charlotte. "I hope you find what you're looking for."

Ramona closed the front door hard as she left. Her mother was staring down at the table. "You're welcome to stay at the inn, of course. It looks worse over there than it is. Maybe we can catch up more tomorrow...I'm getting tired, and I'm sure you need to rest after your travels." Ella motioned toward a cupboard in the hallway. "There are some blankets in there. If I were you, I'd bring a flashlight, too."

Charlotte tugged at the hem of her skirt, unsure of what to say. At least her family would be nearby. "Thanks, Mom. I'll stop back over tomorrow."

"Ramona will be at work in the afternoon, so that'd probably be the best time." She kindly didn't elaborate. "Keys are on the hook. It is good to see you again, Charlotte." She paused. "I just wish you hadn't waited so long to come back."

A prickling heat crawled between her shoulder blades, and she felt the armor she kept around her chest clink back into place after her brief moments of vulnerability. Her mother couldn't possibly understand all the reasons she hadn't been back. She didn't even know why she'd left in the first place. She'd never tried to understand.

Charlotte collected a blanket and a large silver flashlight. Lingering at the front door for a moment, she turned to look back at her mother. She seemed so small and frail hunched over the table, like she might blow away with the first breeze. Nothing like the woman she once knew. The old flickers of anger reached out their long fingers from the dark corners of her mind, prodding her forcefully as an image of her father swam before her eyes. Gritting her teeth, she slammed her mind shut like a door, grabbed the keys to the inn, and left without another word.

CHARLOTTE GAVE A HARD SHOVE against the inn's front door as it inched open and a draft of stale, dusty air smacked her in the face. The last rays of sunlight were skittering across the water, the reflection glimmering faintly against the large bay windows on each side of the door. Ollie was dashing all around the yard, tail wagging frantically, sniffing all the sniffs and prancing around his new playground.

As she entered the foyer and surveyed the room, memories crashed against her like billowing thrusts of wind in a hurricane. Her favorite reading spot in front of the large fireplace in the common area; the expansive dining table where guests would gather, laughing and singing long into the night, her family frequently joining in; the enormous wooden staircase leading up to their bedrooms; the room she'd shared with Natalie and Ramona, the sound of whispers and giggles pulling at the edges of her mind. For a moment, she smelled cranberry lemon bread baking in the oven, heard fresh coffee percolating in the kitchen, felt the warmth of the fire spreading to her bones.

But it was gone in an instant, replaced with the heartbreaking scene in front of her. Thick dust coated every surface, drapes were tangled and falling around the windows, boards were missing from the hardwood floors that spread throughout the house, and wallpaper was torn away in whole sections, traces of glue and edging all that remained. A steady *drip drip* of water came from somewhere in the back of the house. She felt as though someone had punched her in the gut, the wind knocked from her, unable to draw a full breath. A feeling of vertigo washed over her as she grabbed the wooden railing of the stairwell for balance.

What had happened here? How had they let this happen to her home?

Charlotte went to the wall panel and flicked on all the switches at once, desperate to get some light in the room. The light fixture directly above her flickered and, with a large *crack*, flared and went out, making her cry out and jump nearly a foot in the air. About half the first-floor lights came on, a pale, orange-ish glow clouding the room, casting sinister shadows over the fraying furniture and stained area rugs.

A deep rumbling came from the pit of her stomach as Charlotte realized she hadn't eaten since this morning. Maybe there was still something in the cupboards here. At least she had thought to bring several days' worth of food for Ollie. Suddenly, exhaustion coursed through her bones, a feeling of carrying a pack of boulders arching across her back.

After finding nothing in the kitchen or the refrigerator to eat, she pulled down a dusty glass from the cupboard above the sink and flipped on the faucet. A pounding from somewhere down in the basement emanated through the floorboards, followed by a rushing sound in the walls and a quick bursting spray of water that splashed onto her arms and dress. A stream of dark brown water poured from the faucet. Charlotte gave it a minute, and the water eventually cleared. After a long day, she was parched. She'd take her chances.

After determining that the water hadn't poisoned her, Charlotte poured a bowl of water for Ollie and gave him his food from her purse. A loud scraping sound from the common area startled her; slowly craning her neck around the corner, she saw one of the shutters outside the window was being battered around by the wind outside. Letting her breath out slowly, she went to the foyer, wearily lifted the handle of her suitcase, and thunked it up the wooden stairs one by one. She still knew the creak and pop of each stair by heart.

With each step, her feet felt more leaden, her head beginning to swim. Charlotte had no idea where the nearest place to get food was, and she wasn't about to trek all over town this late. Her breath caught in her throat as she turned left at the top of the stairs and approached her parents' bedroom. A flash of Ramona as a little girl filled her mind, crouched next to Charlotte in the hallway as Natalie kept watch at the top of the stairs; giggling in hushed voices as they crept across the hardwood floor of their parents' bedroom on their hands and knees, avoiding the creaky boards, to get to the closet where their mother hid the large pillowcases filled to the brim with the Halloween candy they'd collected together.

Everything was exactly as she remembered it, only it was like looking at a room preserved in a museum somewhere. A patina of white dust covered every surface, and the windows that normally filled the room with bright, warm sunshine were shuttered. Most of the furniture was still there, but at the center of the room where the ornate mahogany bed should have been was an empty space with a rectangular indentation in the dust.

A loud *crack* from somewhere made Charlotte cry out as all the lights in the house went out. Panic gripped her as she reached out in the milky blackness for something to hold onto. She fumbled around in the dark until she found the handle of her purse. Dropping to her knees, she frantically ripped through its contents, feeling around for the familiar shape of her phone. A scream rose in her throat as she heard someone clambering up the stairs toward her. Her hands were shaking as she finally grasped the smooth surface of her phone, yanking it out and swiping to press the button for the flashlight just as something collided with her, knocking the phone out of her hand as the light scattered all around the room until it shone against the ceiling. A large, wet tongue against her cheek let her know who the intruder was.

"Ollie, you scared me to death," Charlotte whispered as relief washed over her. She pulled him in close, wrapping her arms around him. He gave a sloppy grin and lay on his side next to her, ready to accept a belly scratch.

No way was she going to venture all the way down to the basement in the dark to find the breakers. That basement had terrified her as a child, and that was with the lights on. She'd just have to make do up here in the bedroom.

Another tug of regret pulled at her stomach. She didn't belong here. It was naive to think she could just show up and hope her family would welcome her like nothing had happened, like she hadn't abandoned them all those years ago. Clearly, they were struggling.

But she was struggling too, Charlotte reminded herself. There was no more money, and her bastion of stability had ripped away her heart and her whole life. She hadn't asked for this. And she hadn't asked to feel like she had no one to turn to after everything that had happened to her, causing her to leave the island behind. It was a two-way street. They hadn't exactly been pounding down the doors to see her in New York.

Charlotte grabbed the bundle she'd brought up the stairs with her and laid the blanket down on the bare hardwood floor. She flicked on the silver flashlight she'd borrowed from Ramona's house; a weak light trickled out before it spluttered and died. How very fitting.

Sighing, she used her phone's light to pull out a few clothes from her suitcase to use as a makeshift pillow. Her eyelids were drooping as thick exhaustion pulled at her limbs. She lay down on the thin blanket, trying fruitlessly to find a comfortable position. Ollie curled up next to her, cradling his head in the crook of her arm, and fell asleep instantly, his steady breaths the only sound in the room.

Charlotte lay awake for a long, long time, curling into herself as the house creaked and shifted, unknown sounds creeping around her in the inky darkness. She pulled Ollie closer and stared at the ceiling, listening nervously to her own heartbeat and wondering how her life had gone so terribly wrong so quickly.

10

Charlotte watched through blurry eyes as the first thin slivers of light cast by the rising sun through the wooden shutters inched slowly down to her makeshift bed on the hardwood floor. The sounds of the gentle breeze swaying and waves lapping against the shore carrying in from outside were interrupted only by Ollie's loud dog snores.

Charlotte sat up on the blanket, wincing as the movements tore at her stiff limbs and the painful crick in her neck from lying on the floor all night. Rolling her neck around her shoulders, she reached for her phone to look at the time only to see that she'd drained the battery from using the flashlight so much overnight. Sleep had completely evaded her; every time her body gratefully succumbed to the wall of exhaustion that had been mounting all day, some creak or imagined scampering in the corners slashed its way into her consciousness, causing her to leap up in terror and grab her phone light to investigate. Ollie, who had once slept like a baby through a full-on earthquake when she had been visiting a friend in Los Angeles a few years back, house lurching up and down and shelves and plates crashing all around him, had been entirely unconcerned.

As Charlotte sat on the floor, listening to the steady rhythm of the waves, she carefully kindled the tiny spark of hope that had flickered to life within her sometime during the long, dark night, fanning the almost imperceptible flame until it caught and a small warmth began to spread into her arms and feet. She'd had an idea. The first inklings of an idea, a plan for what she should do next, but she didn't want to risk smothering anything by not thinking methodically, being rational and careful.

First, she needed to shower, then find someplace to charge her phone and, as a horrible growl escaped her stomach and woke Ollie from his deep slumber with a yelp, something to eat.

Then she'd head into town. Charlotte had some investigating to do today.

AFTER A FAILED ATTEMPT TO shower that involved lots of screaming and thrashing around under icy brownish water that felt like angry shards of glass all over her body, Charlotte decided that deodorant would have to do today. She pulled on another designer dress from her suitcase that was filled with clothes that, in retrospect, were wildly impractical for a comfortable stay in a small beach town. In her haste to leave Sebastian and the condo, she had also somehow forgotten to pack tennis shoes, a mistake that she knew was going to haunt her. She'd have to pick some up today when she went into town. And maybe a more comfortable outfit or two.

Charlotte's heel caught in between the wooden slats of the front porch, almost sending her flailing down the three steps to the grass. Her eyes darted around as she made sure no one was around to see her graceful demonstration, then she smoothed her skirt and hair as she recovered her stride. Then she whistled for Ollie, who'd been racing around the beach in front of the inn, kicking up plumes of golden sand in his wake.

Small, brightly painted buildings lining a cobblestone street appeared as she turned onto Main Street just a few minutes later. It was like coming out of a time machine into her own childhood. Mostly small businesses, a couple of coffee shops and bookstores, an antique shop. The quiet was scratching at the edges of her mind incessantly, needling her. After decades of the constant din of traffic and crowds all around her, the hush made her feel small, alone. Waiting a moment for Ollie to catch up, she took in the pattering of footsteps on the cobblestone, the floating aroma of freshly brewed coffee and something delicious baking, the gentle clicking of bicycle wheels as people lazily glided by her, whistling to themselves.

A small, pale yellow building sandwiched between a bookstore and a sewing and alterations shop emerged; a large wooden base underneath four flat turbines slowly twirling was perched on the roof. It was called "The Windmill," and Charlotte could see wait staff circling tables and booths through the glass windows as the delicious smells of cooked food poured out onto the street. Her mouth watering, she tied Ollie with his long leash to one of the bicycle racks out front, giving him plenty of room to explore the sights and smells of the restaurant front, and made her way inside.

A young waitress guided her to a booth by the window and laid down a menu. "Welcome to Marina Cove," she said with an easy smile.

"Actually..." said Charlotte, before realizing that she did indeed look like a visitor, and not the native she was. "Never mind. Thank you." The waitress smiled again and left for the booth next to hers.

A small laugh escaped her lips as she saw the pictures of the food throughout the menu, but she quickly swallowed it, heat rushing to her cheeks. This was exactly the sort of place her friends in Manhattan would have eviscerated, a place they'd never in a million years set foot in. Somewhere along the line, it seemed, that sort of judgment and superiority had settled into Charlotte's skin.

Settling on a stack of blueberry pancakes with a Denver omelet, toast, and bacon, Charlotte sipped from her cup of black coffee in front of her and looked around the restaurant. A prickling had been crawling across her chest since she'd turned onto Main Street, and she now realized what had been bothering her. She was terrified of running into someone she knew.

The past couple of days had been an incredible whirlwind, leaving her continuously unprepared. It was the feeling she hated most; she'd spent her entire adult life architecting everything in such a way that she wouldn't be caught off guard. And here she was, just dropping back into her hometown after twenty-six years, and had no plan for what she'd tell people if they asked. No idea whom she might run into from her past.

"Uh...Charlotte...?" a voice called out from somewhere behind her, as though the room had been listening intently to her private thoughts and playfully decided to add to her inner turmoil. A second later, recognition flooded her like dropping into a warm bath. She would know that voice anywhere, no matter how long it had been. "Is that really you?"

Charlotte whipped around and rose from her seat. Her childhood best friend Sylvie was rushing toward her, arms outstretched. "Oh, my God, Sylvie...it's been forever," Charlotte whispered into Sylvie's dark hair, the natural curls she'd always envied. She was suddenly twelve again, sunscreen and wide-brimmed hats and giant ice cream cones from Skip's melting all over their hands, skipping rocks over the turquoise water of the shimmering bay as the sun marched lazily across the clear blue sky. "I had no idea you were back...I thought you and Nick were still living in Cleveland?"

"We were, until a few years ago. An opportunity arose." Sylvie pulled back and indicated a pin on her light blue T-shirt, the words *Owner/Manager* next to a tiny old-fashioned windmill.

"You own this place?" Charlotte asked, her eyebrows arching. "Whoa, congratulations. I can't believe it...That's like your dream come true."

They broke their embrace, and Sylvie took a seat in the booth across from Charlotte. "I know. Being a sous chef and moving around all the time hadn't been great for the kids, and Nick and I really wanted to settle down." She reached across the table for Charlotte's coffee cup and took a long sip, sharing everything together just like old times. "My job at the restaurant I worked at appeared to be drawing to an end; for some reason, there didn't seem to be a strong market for high-end Brazilian/French fusion in the Ohio suburbs," Sylvie said through a laugh. "Nick hated his work in accounting...I brought him here one weekend—we needed to get away from everything—and he just fell head over heels for this place."

She drummed her fingers on the table thought-fully, looking out the window toward the street and the sparkling blue waters visible between buildings. "I'd never really wanted to leave in the first place, but I think the time away was actually a good thing. Helped me see this place in a new light... Anyway, there was a building for lease here on Main Street, and the rest is history."

Charlotte looked across at her friend uneasily. Guilt had been seeping through her as Sylvie was talking. "Sylvie...I'm so sorry I haven't kept in touch. I've really missed you."

A flash of sadness crossed Sylvie's face, but it was quickly replaced with a large grin, her eyebrows softening. "Oh, Char, I wasn't any better, was I? I was so wrapped up in my career, I basically put everything in my life on hold. I'm sorry too."

Sylvie reached across the table and took Charlotte's hand in hers. "Life happens to all of us. All that matters is that you're here now. It's a tragedy how long it's been since I visited you out in fancy-land. Ten years, give or take? How're the kids? How's Mister Sebastian, King of Manhattan? I want to hear everything. I can't even imagine how much your life has changed..."

Sylvie trailed off, looking at her as though seeing her clearly for the first time. Charlotte knew she probably looked the worse for wear; her eyes were still bleary from lack of sleep, and she felt weak and lightheaded from not eating for almost twenty-four hours. "What happened, Charlotte?" she asked in a lowered voice, a line of concern creasing her eyebrows.

Her waitress came up to the table, pen and pad in hand. "Morning, Mrs. O'Connor. So what can I get you, ma'am?" she asked Charlotte. Thankful for the distraction, Charlotte placed her large order, ignoring the automatic calorie tallying that was second-hand nature after years and years of slaving away to maintain a trim figure and keep up with her image-conscious friends.

"I'll have waffles, a large side of home fries, and all the coffee you have back there," said Sylvie. "Thank you, Ashley."

Charlotte felt tears forming in her eyes as Ashley left. Sylvie watched her tentatively. "Tell me everything, babe."

Charlotte took her through the events of the last few days, leaving nothing out. The words came spilling out, each sentence falling from her like emptying a sack of bricks she'd been carrying, one by one, each leaving her feeling lighter. Sylvie simply held Charlotte's hand in hers, eyebrows furrowed and sadness etching the lines of her face.

Before she knew it, she found herself telling Sylvie everything about Sebastian burning through all the money, the debt, the despair she felt as she looked at her future, the fire underneath her to figure out what that future would look like now blazing with the uncertainty of having Sebastian in her life, threatening to consume her completely.

Silence hung over the table for a few moments as Charlotte wiped her eyes and took a long drink of water. Sylvie seemed to be weighing her words. Ashley approached their table, quietly setting down plate after plate of food. Correctly sensing the tone at the table, she left without another word.

Sylvie ran her hands over her face and let out a long breath. "I can't even imagine what you're going through right now." Her eyes welled with tears. "All I can say is that my heart is broken for you, Charlotte. I am so, so sorry..." Sylvie shook her head, her voice catching on the last word. "I want you to know that no matter what, I'm here for you, however I can help. You should come stay with Nick and me. You can't be sleeping on the floor of a broken-down inn."

Charlotte felt a surge of affection for Sylvie course through her, warming her to the core. She felt all the years between them evaporate in an instant.

"That means a lot to me, Sylvie." Charlotte

leaned back in the booth, rolled her neck around, and shook the tension from her arms. "And thanks for the offer, but I think for now I'm going to stay at the inn...even if I can't stay with Mom and Ramona, I'd like to stay close." She sighed. "I think that no matter what, I obviously can't be in a situation where I'm totally helpless if Sebastian's out of the picture. I'm going to need to start working if I want to be able to make it in New York by myself. I can't assume that he's going to figure out how to turn things around; I don't even know if we're going to be together again."

A pain slammed into the back of her throat as the words came out. "I was hoping that staying here with my mom for a little while would give me a chance to get some perspective, and come up with a plan, but after yesterday's chilly reception, I don't know if that's going to work out like I thought it would."

Sylvie held her gaze for a moment. "Not sure if Ramona mentioned it, but she works here. For a while now...she was actually here last night." Not sure how to respond, Charlotte nodded and looked around the restaurant idly. "We don't really talk. She sort of keeps to herself. Good worker, though," Sylvie said. "Guess you two are still on the outs, huh."

"I can't really blame her...she's angry that I abandoned the family. It isn't really that simple, though..." Charlotte looked down at her hands. It was way too late to explain things to Ramona. It had always been easier to keep hiding in New York. And based on how Ramona had acted, nothing Charlotte could say would matter anyway. "It was...complicated. Dad leaving was just the start of everything." A stab of guilt went through her gut; she'd never explained to Sylvie what had really made her leave. "I abandoned you too."

Sylvie considered her thoughtfully. "I don't know what all happened with you back then...I know things got bad after your dad, and it was really none of my business why you left." As Charlotte began to protest, Sylvie cut her off. "I mean it. I felt terrible that whatever it was made you feel like you had to up and leave. I had a few guesses, but I didn't need to know. Besides," Sylvie said while reaching across the table to grasp Charlotte's hand, "you've been my friend since I was nine years old. A lot of great years, and we were able to keep in touch for a good bit there after you left, anyway, before life got the better of us. That's better than most people could ever ask for."

Charlotte squeezed her hand hard, and felt the

sweet relief of a burden lifting from her shoulders. Her departure had always been an unspoken thing between them, a splinter in her heel poking her with every step forward, never really understanding how much it was impeding her.

Sylvie cleared her throat and leaned back in the booth. "Now, how about you eat something, huh? You look like you could use a good meal, or three." Charlotte grinned, and they began to eat. She had to physically stop herself from setting down her fork and knife, grabbing piles of food from each plate, and stuffing her mouth like a wild animal. "How was your night at the Seaside House?" Sylvie asked.

Charlotte gave a hard laugh as she remembered clutching Ollie for dear life all night. "It's funny you bring that up. Staying there gave me an idea."

If Charlotte wanted to return to her life in New York, she needed to turn an income. But she had no real job experience; being a stay-at-home mom had been wonderful work for her, something that she quickly took to and fit like a glove, but her options were limited without even a high school diploma. She wasn't going to move away from her roots; her entire adult life had been built in Manhattan, the home base for her and her children, and even if she moved to a nearby suburb as a last resort, it was going to be pricey.

Seeing the condition of the family inn had shattered her heart, but it had also formed the first inklings of a plan in her mind. She wasn't sure how things had gone downhill so far, but being in Ramona's home had shown her that money was clearly part of the problem.

"I think I want to restore the Seaside House." Hearing the words escape her lips somehow gave the idea a certain gravity; now it wasn't just something spinning around in her mind.

Sylvie raised her eyebrows and set down her fork. "Wow. That sounds like a...uh, sort of big undertaking."

"I know. It's probably a terrible idea. I just want to maybe reach out to a couple of contractors and get an idea of what it would take to turn things around. Even though we don't have any money, that's never stopped Sebastian. Every 'next big thing' never pans out. I have an actual idea here, and so going a little bit more into debt won't make any real difference."

She stared out the window down the cobblestone street, across the sand glittering in the sunlight and the deep blue expanse of the Atlantic stretching out to the horizon. "I know what the inn could be." A flash of flipping through the pages of the guestbook as a kid struck her, reading about everyone's travels, how much they loved discovering Marina Cove, the delight at finding such a gorgeous and charming inn to stay at right on the water. "Even when I was a kid, I never felt it was living up to its full potential. I think with some fixing up, some advertising, this could turn the tides for me."

It seemed like a perfect idea. There were no prerequisites, no education requirements, no qualifying work experience necessary. Sebastian would need to agree to it, but in Charlotte's mind, she had every right to use their finances, especially given how Sebastian still relentlessly fired cash from his money cannon all over the city. One of them had to come up with a way to make some money, and it didn't seem like Sebastian really grasped that. She didn't blame him, exactly; it was a simple byproduct of money losing its meaning through years of near-infinite abundance.

"I know that Mom and Ramona would have to agree to it, but I can't see why they wouldn't," said Charlotte, pouring another round of syrup on her pancakes. Sylvie listened and sipped her coffee thoughtfully. "I'd be fronting all the money for the restoration. Once things get going, I can move back to New York, and help manage things remotely. Ramona could be the boots on the ground. Mom can do whatever she wants, relax by the beach, take up some hobbies. Each of us would have a share of the business; everyone wins."

And, she thought to herself, maybe it could be just the thing to make up for her long absence. A penance, something to take away the guilt she'd been carrying for so long.

Sylvie turned her fork around on her plate idly, frowning slightly. "Well, that all makes sense, but it might take a long time, you know...even if you got things fixed up, the place has a sort of...reputation."

"I can imagine. And I know. I know it's a long shot. But I have to do something. Right now, this seems like my best chance to get my life back the way it was. Mom and Ramona clearly need some help. It's an investment...I really think it could work. I was going to look up some contractors once I find somewhere to charge my phone today, maybe give a few a call. You don't happen to know any, do you? Anyone you've used for your restaurant?"

Something passed over Sylvie's face; Charlotte couldn't quite make out what it was. Sylvie opened her mouth once or twice, seeming to second-guess what she was going to say. A thrumming began building in her chest for some reason.

"Well, the island is small, so most people use contractors from the mainland," she began, furrowing her brows. "But if you want my honest advice, the best person around...is Christian."

Charlotte's heart fell into the very bottoms of her feet, only to violently slam up again and lodge itself in her throat. It was a long moment before she could form words. "Christian...my Christian? He lives here again?" She gripped the table as she swallowed hard, her mouth feeling like it was stuffed with cotton and sandpaper.

"Yeah, he's back...I don't know when." Sylvie cleared her throat, avoiding eye contact. "He keeps to himself...he built himself a tiny cabin over on Old Man Keamy's lot. Sort of a recluse...from what I've heard, he's basically off the grid completely. But he works all the time. He's really a masterful carpenter..." She glanced up at Charlotte.

Charlotte could actually feel the color draining from her face. Christian. Thoughts pounded against her skull like a jackhammer. She had no idea that Christian was back in Marina Cove.

When social media emerged, one of the first things Charlotte had done was try to look him up, just to see how he was doing. She'd never found anything. After a few more tries in the ensuing years, she gave up. There was no sign of him. It made some sense; Christian had always been a private person. And Charlotte was a happily married woman, so she hadn't really dug much further. After everything, Marina Cove was the last place Charlotte expected Christian to end up.

"Uh...that's a surprise," Charlotte said lamely. She began gulping her coffee before she realized it was singeing her throat; spluttering and coughing, she grabbed her water and drained the full glass, spilling it all over her face and onto her dress. Sweat had formed on her scalp and was trickling down her back, sending shivers up her spine. Sylvie watched with a sympathetic expression. "He, uh...restores houses here?" Charlotte stammered.

"Well...he only takes on a few jobs a year, but he commits himself to them completely. He sort of becomes...obsessed," she said, leaning back in the booth and looking up at Charlotte, sighing. "I hired him to help when Nick and I first bought the building here," she said as she motioned around her. "I had another contractor as well, but Christian was relentless. Built the windmill on top of the restaurant of his own accord. He's incredible. A little eccentric, but the work speaks for itself."

"Well, I think I'd like to explore my other options first," Charlotte said suddenly, smoothing her hands over her dress. "But thank you for the recommendation."

They quickly moved on from the subject, and caught up on what had been going on in each other's lives. Charlotte found herself terribly distracted; her mind kept tugging her back to that stormy summer night a year and a half after her father had left, standing there with Christian on the shifting sands of the bay, the delicate strings pulling and reweaving around her by a force unknown, transforming the images in the tapestry of her life that she couldn't yet see. The night everything changed.

The idea of strolling up to Christian's house and asking him to restore their family inn stretched her willing suspension of disbelief past its breaking point. There was no way that was going to happen. Not after everything they'd been through.

11

Charlotte raised her face toward the radiant sun striding across the sky, inhaling the warm, fresh breeze as she made her way down Main Street toward Seabreeze Avenue. Even after a full night without sleep, she felt an extra skip in her step as she and Ollie carefully navigated the cobblestone streets. It was time to put the first part of her plan in motion.

A small bell atop the door chimed as she entered Haywood's Supplies. Aisles of paints, plumbing materials, and garden tools loomed in front of her. "Can I help you, Miss?" a voice called from the register to her left.

Ramona's ex-husband set down a thick novel he'd been reading on the front desk. "Hey, Danny," said Charlotte, a trickle of nervousness making its way through her stomach. "It's Charlotte, hi."

Danny's eyebrows pinched together slightly. "Hello," he said tentatively.

"Charlotte Keller," she added with a sheepish smile.

"Oh, geez, Charlotte! I didn't recognize you." He ran his hands through his silver hair as he came around the desk to greet her. "Whoa...blast from the past. What brings you back? Never thought we'd see you again around these parts."

"Just visiting the family for a bit." Charlotte fidgeted with the hem of her dress, eager to change the subject. "I was hoping to gather a few supplies for a little project I'm working on. Sylvie highly recommended your store."

"Well, sure, what'd you have in mind?"

Danny grabbed a cart for her and led her down the aisles as Charlotte mentally tallied what she thought she'd need. She had a lot of work to do today, and wanted to get as much of a head start as she could.

If she wanted to pitch the idea to restore the inn to her mother and, by extension, Ramona, she couldn't just hit them with it directly. She needed to ease them into the idea, show that she was serious.

Ramona was likely to shoot down any idea Charlotte had, and if she could just *show* them what she was thinking, even in some small way, she felt it would go further than just words.

As she lay on the hard floor of the bedroom last night contemplating how she'd approach them, an idea clicked into place. She would fix up her parents' bedroom as best she could; remove all the clutter, scrub every inch down, put up a few tasteful decorations, and give the room a fresh coat of paint it so desperately needed. Charlotte knew from personal experience the difference a new coat of paint could make; every so often, she'd surprise one of her children by giving their bedroom a makeover, not allowing anyone in the room until she was done, turning it into a big event and reveal. She recalled the squeals of delight as they walked into their new space, eyes wide and dashing from corner to corner to take in the new wallpaper, the repainted furniture, new knick-knacks on the shelves.

Once Ramona and their mother saw that what she was suggesting was possible, the potential the place had, she hoped they'd be more open to Charlotte swooping in and proposing something that felt more audacious to her by the minute. Preposterous, even, but she knew in the back of her mind that she was running out of time to figure some way out of the hole she and Sebastian found themselves in.

Now was not the time to be meek, to let the winds carry her where they may, as she had for so long. It was time for bold ideas.

After Charlotte pushed her loaded cart to the front register, Danny rang everything up while they chatted easily, carefully skittering around the subject of Ramona. He hadn't changed much since high school; he still had his easy smile and laid-back attitude that always made him popular with the girls. She could still remember the dreamy look in Ramona's eyes as she came home to the inn after spending the day with him, unable to keep the grin from her face. Charlotte noticed the gold band around his ring finger and wondered how soon he'd remarried after Ramona left him.

"Oh, that's not necessary," Charlotte said as she saw Danny punch in an employee discount, cutting her total in half.

"Nonsense. Just a little welcome-back gift," he said with a warm smile. He swiped her card, and frowned at his screen as it emitted an unpleasant *beep*. He swiped it again. *Beep.*

"Ah, I'm really sorry...it's saying your card is

declined." Danny winced on the last word. "I'll just put this on a tab, though. Don't worry about it."

Charlotte could feel the color rise to her cheeks as panic gnawed at her chest. "Oh, God. I'm sorry. Try this one." She handed him another thick golden card, hoping Danny couldn't see the slight tremor in her hands.

Beep. "Really, Charlotte, it's totally fine."

"It's just some sort of mistake, that's all," Charlotte said, carefully keeping the rising notes of fear from her voice. She grabbed her phone instinctively, and cursed herself inwardly as she saw the black screen. "I'm sorry, Danny, this is embarrassing. I just have to make a quick call to my husband, I'll clear it up. Do you have an outlet anywhere? My phone is dead," she said, fixing an exasperated smile on her face.

"Of course, you can plug it in back here in the breakroom," said Danny, leading her through a door behind the register to a large room with fluorescent lights overhead. "Coffee's over here if you want anything, and there are sodas in the fridge. I'll give you some privacy," he said, gently closing the door behind him.

Charlotte powered on her phone, tapping her fingers nervously against her palm as she paced in front of a small table against the wall. She had several missed calls and texts. Ignoring them, she rang Sebastian.

He picked up on the first ring. "Charlotte...hi," he said, sounding out of breath. "I was really worried about you. You never let me know you got there okay last night."

"Everything's fine." She paused, momentarily forgetting the events of the last couple of days at the sound of his voice. "I got here fine. My phone died last night."

"I miss you." Sebastian cleared his throat. "I'm sorry. I just...it's quiet here without you. I just want to tell you again how sorry I am."

Charlotte pressed her eyes shut and blew out a long breath, leaving the words hanging in the air. "I was just trying to buy something, and my credit card declined. Actually, two of them declined. Do you know what happened?"

Dead silence filled the line for several moments. She pulled her phone back to see if the call had dropped. "Sebastian?"

He cleared his throat again. "I'll take care of it right now, Charlotte. I'm sorry about that. Give me two minutes and I'll have it sorted."

Charlotte couldn't help but hear something in

his voice that she couldn't quite make out. If she didn't know Sebastian and his limitless well of brash confidence and self-esteem better, she would've sworn she heard an undertone of worry.

"Thanks. I actually wanted to talk to you about something that came up anyway," she said, brushing past the uneasy feeling pooling within her.

She filled him in on her idea to look into what it would take to restore the inn, and how she thought they might be able to get it up and running properly again. Sebastian listened without interruption. "This was my childhood home. I can't bear to see what's happened to it. And besides, we could use the money. There are more tourists here on Marina Cove than when I was a kid...I think it has a ton of potential."

Sebastian started a sentence, then abruptly ended it. "Well, I think that's a great idea, Charlotte... I just don't think we can swing that kind of money right now," he said haltingly. "I've been working on something, something big, it just needs a little more time...I think this is going to work out very well for us. We should really wait until we're a little less in the red."

She'd been waiting long enough for Sebastian to figure things out. "I don't think it's going to cost a fortune to restore it, Sebastian...and besides, I have a right to work on something myself. I know the idea of me working on something of my own is foreign to you," she said as he began to interject, "but you've been spending money like there's no tomorrow. What about that ridiculous children's squash league, huh? A dining terrace? A relaxation sauna? What did that set us back?"

He gave a sigh of resignation. "That was a mistake. I committed to that a year ago, and I didn't want to look bad. I should've pulled out. I admit, things are a little...tighter than I thought they would be. But don't worry," he said, the tone of anxiety suddenly lifting from his voice, "I feel good about things. They're looking up."

Sebastian hesitated for a moment, and took a breath. "I just want you to do what you need to do... to figure things out. I want you to come home. I love you, Charlotte."

Charlotte felt her heart flutter with his words; he'd always had a way of speaking to her that made her feel like she was the only thing in the world he cared about; special, loved. The feeling lasted for just a moment before the grief that'd been following her since she left swallowed it whole. Her throat constricted.

"Let me talk to my friend Alastair, okay?" Sebastian continued after several uncomfortable moments of silence. "I've got a few loans out from him...what's a bit more? Just let me know what you need and I'll make it work."

After they ended the call, Charlotte was unable to ease the panic simmering away in her stomach. She abashedly paid for her supplies and thanked Danny profusely. When she realized with further embarrassment that she'd bought far more than she'd be able to carry herself, he kindly offered to help her carry everything back to the inn. As he called on an employee to take over the register, they hoisted up the heavy bags, and Charlotte called for Ollie to follow them down the cobblestone streets.

As Charlotte mentally planned out the long list of tasks she had ahead of her today for getting the room ready, she kept hearing the tone of Sebastian's voice on the call reverberating in her mind. The first cracks in the veneer of the man she'd never seen worry about anything. Charlotte suddenly felt more afraid than she had in a long, long time.

12

For the tenth time since she'd received it last night, Ramona stared at the text from Charlotte, the anger welling inside her now masking something deeper, something she couldn't easily identify.

Hi, Ramona. I think this is still your number...Do you think you and Mom could meet me at the inn tomorrow morning? Maybe around 9? I want to show you something.

Who did she think she was, just showing up after practically a lifetime of being gone, and asking anything of her?

A fleeting memory of being curled up on her comforter in the room they all shared after Charlotte had first left filled her mind, crying and screaming into her pillow. She still remembered the gut punch when Charlotte told them out of the blue that she was leaving, moving in with an old friend who'd relocated to Brooklyn a couple of years earlier. Ramona was completely speechless as Charlotte hugged her goodbye.

It hadn't occurred to her to ask why she was leaving; it didn't matter. Their family was in shambles after Dad left, and instead of facing it with her, Charlotte had decided to take the easy way out, just like the rest of her siblings. Diane and Gabriel barely kept in touch already, and no one ever knew where Natalie was.

Charlotte wouldn't have known it, but Ramona had been clinging to her for dear life.

Nothing Charlotte could do was going to undo the fact that everything had fallen on Ramona's shoulders. Dealing with the inn and the guests. Watching her mother slowly wither away and withdraw into herself. Ramona was the one who had kept her head down, toiling away day after neverending day, year after never-ending year.

She tossed the phone back onto the kitchen counter and squinted out the window toward the small slice of water she could see. She'd tossed and turned all night, memories of Charlotte and her as children battering her, poking around in parts of her she'd long buried away.

A burning sensation formed behind Ramona's eyes, something she didn't even recognize at first. Something she hadn't felt in a long time.

No. Ramona was done crying. It hadn't ever gotten her anywhere, and she wasn't about to reopen the wounds, no matter how much they pained her through all the scar tissue.

Ramona thought she'd been clear last night that she wasn't interested in some sort of reunion, but she obviously needed to be a lot more forthright. She had to protect herself. Calling toward her room for her mother, she slugged down a cup of hot black coffee in one go, tied her hair back in a ponytail, and braced herself for an unpleasant but necessary conversation.

"THANKS FOR COMING," Charlotte said from the inn's front porch, not quite meeting Ramona's eyes. "I wasn't sure you would."

Ramona grunted noncommittally as she took in the woman in front of her. Charlotte was dressed ridiculously in some heavy designer dress and a pair of high heels. She stood out like a sore thumb. That necklace alone, she thought with resentment pooling inside her, would probably buy Ramona and her mother groceries for a year.

Ella was watching the water lapping gently against the shore just a few yards away, looking lost in thought. "I miss this place," she said to herself, barely above a whisper.

"I just want to say...I'm sorry again for just showing up here unannounced. And..." Charlotte hesitated, finally meeting Ramona's gaze. "I'm sorry it's been so long."

"Well, shucks, Charlotte. That fixes everything," Ramona said, marching up the steps and brushing past her, pushing her way through the heavy front door and into the inn. "What is it that you've asked us here for?"

Charlotte blew out a long breath. "Well, I wanted to talk to you about an idea I had. But I thought I'd show you what I mean first," she said with maddening elusiveness.

Heartache filled Ramona's chest every time she had to set foot in the inn. It was a constant reminder of what her family had lost. Over the years, she'd been conditioned to develop a certain blindness in the periphery of her vision that shielded her from seeing things in the inn too closely. She carefully kept her gaze on the hardwood flooring as Charlotte made her way up the stairs, Ella wordlessly trailing her, as Ramona sighed and followed.

At the top of the stairs, faint notes of paint cut through the usual dust and mildew aroma Ramona now associated with being inside the inn. When Charlotte went inside their mother's bedroom, Ella froze in the doorframe and brought her hands to her mouth. Ramona's stomach clenched as she came up behind her mother.

As she stared into the bedroom, she felt like she was being smacked hard across the face. Hot tears forced their way through long-forgotten passages into Ramona's eyelids.

She was suddenly eight, standing in the doorframe in her footie pajamas and whispering to her parents to wake them up, her tummy rumbling, Charlotte and Natalie whispering and giggling behind her. It was Sunday, and Daddy liked to sleep in. But Daddy made the best blueberry pancakes, and they couldn't wait anymore. Mommy stirring, wiping the sleep from her eyes, a single ray of sunshine through the window illuminating the warmth of her face as she grinned at them. Yelling "Boo!" in Daddy's ear as he yelped, the girls squealing in delight as they bombarded the room and jumped up and down on the bed, hollering for pancakes.

Before Charlotte could see her, Ramona frantically swiped away the tears with her sleeve in one fell swoop and forced back the lump that had formed in her throat. With the exception of the missing bed that had been moved to one of the guest rooms long ago, the room was exactly as it had been when they were children. Every surface had been cleaned spotless, and Charlotte had even managed to locate the exact shade of light blue for the walls that her father had chosen all those years ago. Candles burned on the dresser, gently filling the room with the fresh scents of lavender and lemongrass that their mother had loved so much. On the nightstand was a picture of their family. Before everything, when they'd still been happy.

Ramona froze as her gaze held on the picture, on her father. The nostalgia that had swept her away suddenly melted, replaced with the familiar feeling of pain, of betrayal.

"What is this?" Ramona asked, more danger in her voice leaking out than she'd intended.

Charlotte spun around, looking at them tentatively. "Uh...well...what do you think?"

Ella moved past her toward the window and gently brushed her fingers across the sill. The shutters had been wrenched open, and warm sunlight filled the room, sparkling on every surface. Ella turned to Charlotte and whispered, "It looks wonderful, Charlotte. What made you do all this?"

Charlotte let out a long breath, as though she'd been holding it. "That's what I'd like to talk to you about." She smoothed out her skirt and looked pointedly between Ramona and their mother.

"I think we should restore the inn."

A long pause coursed uncomfortably through the room. "If we could've restored the inn by now, Charlotte, don't you think we would have?" Ella said, her voice fringing with irritation.

Charlotte looked caught off guard, as though Ella had interrupted some sort of long speech she had planned. "I'm saying that I would like to help you restore the inn. I will pay for it. I've thought hard about it, and this is something I want to do." Charlotte started to pace the room. "You both know what this place is capable of being. When I came here and saw what...had happened, something just clicked. I want to help. I want to be a part of this. I'm so sorry that this happened to our home, Mom," she said, looking at Ella with sadness in her eyes, "but I think we can get things back to the way they were."

Ramona had heard enough. "Absolutely not," she interjected. "No. You can't just come back here and wave your checkbook around and expect to solve everything overnight. Do you even have any inkling of what it would take to get this place back up and running? Do you really think that waltzing in out of nowhere in your high heels and your diamonds and slapping on a new coat of paint is going to change anything? What in God's name gives you the right to come back here—" Ramona turned away hastily as the words caught in her throat.

"I know it's a lot of work," Charlotte said carefully. "It'll take a long time, I know. But I came here to figure out what I wanted to do next, and this feels right to me. My kids are all gone, and with everything with Sebastian up in the air..." Her voice wavered slightly. "I want to work on something that's mine, my own, that he can't take from me. This could help all of us," she trailed off in a whisper.

Ramona looked at Charlotte hard in the eyes. Out of sheer desperation, a few months ago, Ramona had begun tentatively reaching out to realty groups on the mainland, taking the temperature of those sorts of companies that bought up properties like hers to flip. With debt piling up and drowning Ramona and her mother, she'd started to realize she might not have much choice. She knew the potential of the inn, had lived it, seen it with her own eyes, and knew that it was a prime piece of waterfront property and a beautiful building.

To her profound relief, the only offers so far had been investors who'd come to see the old house and told her that they wanted to tear it down and put up something else in its place. They only saw value in the land; they wanted to erect chain hotels or expensive condos. One investor had drawn up impressive-looking plans for a strip mall. Each offered her an insultingly low amount, due to the fact that it would be a huge gamble on their part, the island not exactly being a hot tourist attraction and all. Not yet, anyway. You couldn't keep a place like Marina Cove a secret forever.

Apart from the intense local pressure from island residents against hotel chains and the like, not wanting to erode Marina Cove's quiet charm and small-town integrity, it killed Ramona to think about some out-of-town fancy-pants strolling in and taking a wrecking ball to her family's precious home, the home that had withstood challenge after challenge in its long history in the Keller family. It would mean defeat. The end of their family's legacy. And then what? She and her mother would have enough money for a while, maybe, but not enough to solve their problems. The debts piled too high.

So she'd kept her head to the ground, and worked. And worked, and worked, and maybe, she'd hoped, maybe someday it would be enough again. But it was too late.

Ramona realized that her mother had been staring in her direction for some time now. As she caught her gaze, Ella said, "I think this is a good idea, Ramona. I think we need to do this."

Charlotte visibly let go of the strain in her body. "I have a few calls out to contractors from the mainland. They're all booked out since we're headed into summer, but they assured me that in a few months—"

"We don't have that kind of time." Ramona closed her eyes and again crushed back the tears threatening to form. "You obviously don't have to worry about money, but we do. The time for fixing the place up has passed. We're in too deep," she admitted through gritted teeth. "It's too late. We can't wait any longer. I have a few offers from real estate investors who will buy this place for the land. It'll be enough to float us for a while, barely. I don't see any other option."

Ramona turned to her mother. "I'm sorry, Mama," she said, nearly unable to get the words out. "I'm so sorry."

Charlotte ran her hands through her hair and turned to look out the bedroom window. "They want the land? So I take it they're going to tear this place down. And put what in its place?"

"I don't know what they're going to do," Ramona lied. "But it isn't any of your concern, Charlotte. Look, I know you're trying to help here. But you've come too late. I'm sorry we wasted your time."

Charlotte stopped her pacing suddenly, then turned to face Ramona. "What if I could get things started right now?"

"You just said everyone's booked."

"I ran into Sylvie today...and she mentioned someone else who might be able to help," Charlotte said, looking at her hands. "I don't know if he can do it...I'd have to talk to him."

"I don't think you understand, Charlotte," Ramona said, eyes narrowing. "We need money, now. And unless you want to pay off all our debt and buy my bungalow back from the bank, this isn't going to work."

Ramona saw something flicker in Charlotte's eyes that she couldn't quite make out. "I could help with some of your debt in the short run," she said slowly.

"For God's sake, that was sarcasm, Charlotte. I don't need you to pay my bills for me, thank you very much. Some of us work for a living."

Charlotte's face flushed as she looked at the floor. "Can you at least give us all a chance here? If someone buys this land, you pay off some debt, but then what? If we get this place going again, and I mean really going, there would be an ongoing income. Something that wouldn't dry up. You'll make more in the long run." She hesitantly moved closer to Ramona, as though testing the waters. "I'm offering to pay for the restoration myself. I'll be able to help manage this place remotely from Manhattan. Don't you want things to go back to the way they were?"

"Things will never go back to the way they were," Ramona spat back.

"Ramona, she's right," Ella said in a quiet voice. "It can't hurt to see if we could get things back into good enough shape to at least start seeing some guests again...before we have to sell our home." She gestured around the bedroom. "Look at what she was able to do in one day."

Ramona considered Charlotte carefully. She wanted nothing more than to believe in the possibility that she could once again hear the warmth of the noise and laughter of guests filling the inn, but she'd long ago learned to stop believing that someone else would rescue her from her problems. Charlotte had no idea what she was getting into; she was just some rich city girl now, looking for something to fill up her empty life.

"No," said Ramona. "No. Absolutely not. We don't need your help. We'll figure it out."

"You don't speak for me, Ramona," said Ella, sighing. "I'm saying we're going to give it a shot, okay? We need help here." She dropped her voice to almost a whisper. "This might be just what we need to move on with our lives."

There was no way Ramona could unhear the spark of hope in her mother's voice that she so longed for.

Fine. Let Charlotte be the one to destroy that.

"I've obviously been outvoted here," Ramona said, gritting her teeth. "So just do what you need to do. But we're going to pay back whatever you put into it from our share of the profit, if we ever see any. We don't need your charity."

"What's the first step, Charlotte?" asked Ella, pointedly ignoring Ramona.

"Just leave that to me." An unreadable expression crossed Charlotte's face. "There's someone I'm going to have to talk to."

13

Charlotte tarried along the golden southern shore as she made her way toward Old Man Keamy's lot, heels in hand and happy to be in the daylight after another long, dark night of clutching Ollie for comfort. Rolling her neck and shoulders to ease the stiffness from sleeping on the hard floor, she inhaled the sparkling saltwater air and grinned as she felt the warm sand crunching beneath her bare toes. Seagulls circled overhead, and the sounds of harbor seals barking carried over the gentle breeze, perking up Ollie's ears as he splashed clumsily through the water, trying to bite the waves. The long sandy beach met up with the one-lane road the locals called the Loop, as it ringed the entire coastline of Marina

Cove. Beyond the road, the land rose into high forests and dramatic rocky cliffs.

A hammering in her chest reminded Charlotte of her mission this morning. Sylvie had completely caught her off guard when she told Charlotte that Christian was living here again, and she knew then that she'd inevitably run into him. But she never thought she'd have to ask him a favor after not speaking to him for all this time. She had no idea what to expect. Would he even want to talk to her?

No sense in delaying any further. Time to pull off the bandage.

As she turned past the bend in the land, Keamy's lot emerged, several acres of unused land overgrown with tall grass situated against a long, flat stretch of gold sand, surrounded on both sides by forest. The lot had been empty for as long as Charlotte had known. She'd never met Old Man Keamy, as he was known locally, but he lived somewhere inland and had never sold the land for some reason. Apparently he was a recluse of sorts and, according to some, totally off his rocker. But Charlotte had long loved this area; it was her happy place, her place to think and to get away from everything.

She'd introduced Christian to it after they'd been dating for what she felt was a sufficiently long time; it was her secret, and it was like giving him a piece of her heart. They'd spent a lot of time here soaking up the sun, strolling along the gorgeous crystal waters, dancing under the stars. When they'd talk about their future together, they'd daydream about convincing Old Man Keamy to sell them the lot and building a house on it. White picket fence, children running around, all of it.

Thwack. Thwack. A loud sound cut through the trees from the far northeast corner of the grassy lot, stirring Charlotte out of her thoughts. As she peered across the land, she could make out a small structure barely tucked into the forest. Squaring her shoulders and taking a long breath, she ventured toward the sound, sweat breaking out on her forehead and anxiety prickling across her skin.

Charlotte froze as she stood on the outer edge of the copse of oaks and maples that surrounded a small cabin. It was him; his back was turned to her, and he hadn't heard her coming yet. He held a large wooden ax and was swinging it down hard, logs splitting and flying apart into the surrounding grass. He wore a simple black T-shirt and a pair of blue jeans; the thick, roping muscles of his upper back strained against his shirt, and she could see a sheen of sweat covering the back of his neck. *Thwack. Thwack.*

Her chest pounded harder as she fought to hold back the tears. She couldn't believe she was here, right here, in front of him. Her first boyfriend, her first kiss, her first love.

The man she once thought she would spend the rest of her life with.

Ollie ran up from the beach and, upon seeing Christian, jumped in front of Charlotte and started to bark wildly. Christian whipped around, jumping nearly a foot in the air and holding the ax in front of him like a shield. Their eyes locked.

Charlotte's heart stopped beating as everything slowed to a crawl around her. The leaves ceased their fluttering in the trees; Ollie's barking was swallowed in the silence. Christian's wavy light-brown hair had whipped across his face mid-turn and froze in place, his golden-brown eyes slowly widening. Charlotte's limbs refused to respond, locking her in place like a statue.

Several horrible moments as they stared at each other, Charlotte frantically trying to draw a breath. All at once she was a teenager again. She remembered the light touch of his fingers against the nape of her neck, the firm grasp of his strong arms around her. The smell of his skin as she nuzzled against his chest, cedarwood and leather and saltwater. The gentle whisper of loving words into her ear, the hairs on her arms standing on end.

"Charlotte," he said, his voice hoarse, as though it hadn't been used in a long time.

All at once she was back on the forest floor again, standing in front of him as she inhaled sharply. His hair was longer now, rougher, and his face was covered in coarse stubble. There were tiny lines around his eyes that weren't there before. But otherwise, he was just the same, her Christian.

Brushing away tears that had begun to form, she placed a hand on Ollie's head to calm him, and he stopped barking and growling at once.

"Christian," Charlotte said, barely getting the name out. She cleared her throat. "It's good to see you."

He dropped his ax to the ground and started toward her before freezing mid-step, gazing at her hesitantly. He ran his hands through his hair, making it stand on end. "Charlotte...wow. I didn't expect to see you here." He shifted uncomfortably on his feet. "I heard you were back in town..."

"I'm sorry I didn't call first." Charlotte's mind was an empty expanse; she couldn't seem to locate the words she'd rehearsed on the way over. "Sylvie says you don't have a cell phone."

One corner of his mouth tugged slightly upward. "That's true. And it's okay, you just startled me a bit. I'm glad to see you. I was hoping I'd run into you."

Ollie had been sitting patiently in front of Charlotte, but apparently deciding that Christian was a friend, he suddenly leaped toward him, licking the front of his shirt and wagging his tail frantically.

Christian chuckled as he lowered himself to one knee and began scratching Ollie behind the ears. Ollie sprawled out on the ground in the pose that plainly asked for belly rubs.

"And who's this fine gentleman?" he asked, gazing up at Charlotte, amusement in his eyes.

Charlotte's whole body softened as the gut punch of first seeing him finally passed. "This is Sir Oliver von Burrows. Ollie for short."

Christian gave a loud bark of a laugh, the kind that came from deep in his belly and always made her melt. "Well, it's nice to meet you, Mr. Ollie."

Charlotte felt a smile curve her lips. The hammering of her heart had slowed a bit as she slipped into the easy comfort that she'd always felt around Christian. "So I'm dying to know," she said as he stood up. "How'd you convince Keamy to let you build on his land?"

"Well," he said with a grin in his eyes, "that is a very long story for another day." His expression turned more serious. "It's actually my land now."

Charlotte looked around. A simple wooden cabin with a small front porch was nestled among some birch and silver maple trees. The door was open, and she sneaked a quick glance inside. The cabin held just one room with a fireplace, a single bed, and a tiny stove and sink. A small table with one chair was piled high with books. There were two rocking chairs on the front porch, and a violin with a bow was propped up next to one of them.

Charlotte felt Christian staring at her and turned to look up at him.

"Where are my manners?" he said suddenly. "Let me get you something to drink. Please, have a seat."

Charlotte sat down in one of the rocking chairs and looked out across the lot. There were just a few trees in front of the house, beyond which the grassy expanse extended out to a panoramic view of the crystal blue waters. It was the kind of view people spent a fortune on.

Christian returned with two glasses of lemonade and handed one to Charlotte. She smiled as he lowered a bowl filled with water for Ollie. He groaned as he settled into his chair, stroking his stubble idly as he gazed out toward the water.

"So..." he started, sounding hesitant. "Uh. What brings you back?"

Charlotte paused as she debated again how much to tell him. "Well...things have been a little... chaotic in my life lately, and so I decided to take a break from things to get my head on straight. It's been so long since I've seen my family, and I thought..." She wrung her hands in her lap. "I just thought maybe I'd pay them a visit, see how they were doing. I always missed it here."

She felt Christian watching her out of the corner of his eye as he listened. The silence thickened uncomfortably around her as he waited patiently for her to continue.

"I saw the inn..." she said as she turned to him. "I had no idea it had gotten so bad."

He lowered his eyes to the ground and grimaced. "Yeah...I was really sorry to see what happened." He twisted his boots into the ground idly. "It was a beautiful place. It was a real shame to see it fall apart like that. I offered to help them with repairs a few times over the years, but..." He shifted so he could give Ollie a few head scratches. "I don't think Ramona likes me very much," he said with a wince.

Charlotte gave a small, humorless laugh. "Well, don't take it personally. It's because of me, of course. Things are a little...complicated between us, after..." She trailed off, letting the sentence linger unfinished in the air, unsure how to continue.

A few long moments passed. Charlotte felt her mind starting to spin. How on earth was she supposed to handle this? The idea of asking him for help made her feel absurd. She knew she had no right to ask anything from him. Maybe this was all a bad idea. She'd just have to figure something else out.

As thoughts tumbled around in her mind, she looked up and saw that he'd been watching her. "You know, I don't know how long you're back for," he said, "but maybe I could still help you guys a little, if you wanted...maybe you could convince Ramona or something. I always thought that house was a thing of true beauty...true potential."

Relief swept through her body like a warm bath. "Oh, my God," she said breathlessly, unable to stop the words from pouring out. "Christian, I was so heartbroken to see my home in tatters like that...I wanted so badly to help but Ramona and my mother are in debt. I know what that place can be, though, what it can really be if someone could just give it the love it deserves, but Ramona wants to sell the house and the land to pay off their debt, and I think that if I could just have a chance to fix it, everything could go back to normal." Heat rose to her cheeks. "I wanted to help, but there are no contractors available for months, and that's too long. They can't wait that long. I didn't know what to do."

He considered her carefully. "So is that the reason you're here? To ask me to help?"

A sinking feeling hit her stomach. "I do need help, yes. And Sylvie told me that you sometimes take on projects. I didn't want to ask that of you, of course, especially since we haven't spoken since..." She took a large breath. "I don't want you to get the wrong idea, but I also want to be honest. If I don't find someone to help, Ramona won't have any choice but to sell our home."

Ollie darted out to chase a duck that had wandered onto the property but was unable to keep up with it. "I can't let that happen. I know I don't have any right to ask anything from you after so long, and I totally understand if you can't."

They rocked in silence for a few moments as

Christian watched the waves roll in and every nerve ending in Charlotte's body seemed to spark.

"I'd love to help, Charlotte. It's really the least I can do, after everything that happened."

Wave after wave of sweet, precious relief poured through Charlotte's body, and before she could stop herself, she started to weep.

Christian jumped up and ran into his cabin, emerging seconds later with a box of tissues. Charlotte took one without looking up, dabbing at her eyes as Christian politely gave her some space to compose herself.

He continued softly. "I haven't seen the inside, obviously, but from what I can see, I can almost guarantee it's going to be a massive job. I love a challenge, though." He took a long drink from his glass. "I like to stay busy. It keeps me...anchored. I don't take jobs for the money...I live a pretty barebones life, as you can see," he said, gesturing around him. "My labor is free, but"—he raised a hand as Charlotte interjected—"if you're pressed for time, I'll need some outside help, and even with my discount from Danny and his connections, materials will probably be expensive too. Just so you know."

Before Charlotte knew what she was doing, she rose from her chair and pulled Christian into a tight hug. "Thank you," she whispered into him, his familiar scent filling her with butterflies against her will. "You have no idea what this means to me."

Christian had one arm around her awkwardly, and after clearing his throat, he put a second arm around her, gave one quick squeeze, and gently pulled away. They returned to their rocking chairs, watching the waves crash in for a while. The ring on Charlotte's third finger suddenly felt very heavy as her mind served up images of Sebastian and what he had done to her. But sitting there on the porch, rocking and sipping lemonade with the cool breeze on her face and sunlight streaking through the trees warming her skin, she felt the edges of calm settle into her for the first time since she overheard the words in that stairwell that set off this whole chain of events.

Things were finally looking up.

14

T he next day, Charlotte found herself in Sylvie's kitchen, swaying her hips to Elvis on the record player, the counter covered in flour and her hands sticky from kneading dough. Sylvie had the day off and had invited her over, and Charlotte was teaching her how to make pain au chocolat, something she'd learned from Amélie during that summer in Paris. After a couple days of hopping around in the icy shower at the inn, she felt wonderfully cozy after a long, hot bath and borrowing a T-shirt and fuzzy pink piggy slippers from Sylvie.

Conversation came easily as they recounted the many things that had happened in the years they'd been apart. A salty breeze carried in through the open windows, and Charlotte could just make out the crystal waves rolling gently over the shore out on Decker Beach a few hundred yards away. She was struck over and over with waves of nostalgia, memories of her time in Paris with Amélie mingling pleasantly with childhood memories of baking brownies with Sylvie, preparing for one of their weekly Friday night movie nights, where they'd rent a stack of tapes and talk about boys until the sun came up. It left her feeling light on her feet after days of inner turmoil, and she welcomed the reprieve from suffering.

"I'm so glad you were able to connect with Christian," Sylvie said, carefully pressing dough with the heel of her hand the way Charlotte had shown her. "He's so talented. If anyone can get things going, he can."

"I'm just so relieved that he was able to help on such short notice," Charlotte said. "He came to the inn yesterday afternoon with a few contractors he knows, and they're already getting started." He'd walked through the house, taking copious notes, and told her that he'd have a better idea of the true extent of things as they got working and made sense of the old electrical and plumbing work. Charlotte was glad to be out of the house, as things remained awkward between her and Christian, and she wanted to give him space to work.

"So I had a little surprise for you," Sylvie said, grinning. "It was something I'd totally forgotten, but when I told Nick about you restoring the inn, he reminded me. When we started the restaurant, things were super slow at first. We were trying everything, advertising, reaching out to websites and newspapers, all of it. Anyway." She stopped to wipe the sweat from her brow with her forearm. "One night, this really well-dressed guy with a bow tie comes in and orders, like, half the menu. We didn't think much of it, but a few weeks later, things picked up. We started getting customers from all over, from the island and the mainland, too. We learned that they'd heard about the restaurant from a review in the newspaper. That guy was Felix Caldwell, and they apparently call him 'The Tastemaker.' Lame, I know. But he's some huge hotel and restaurant critic. He'd written a glowing review of us in the paper. It totally made our business."

She stopped kneading and turned to Charlotte. "So I reached out to him and told him a bit about your inn and how you were restoring it. He was interested, and said that once you're ready to open, he'll stay the night and write a review for you. All you have to do is let him know when."

Charlotte felt a surge of excitement course through her as she gave Sylvie a bear hug, practically lifting her off the ground. "That's incredible, Sylvie! I can't believe it. Things are really coming together." A genuine laugh of happiness escaped her, and she felt a huge smile on her face. "How can I ever thank you enough?"

Sylvie grinned. "You can keep teaching me. Those chouquettes you made this morning were to die for. I think I might add some of these to our menu, if that's okay with you."

"Are you kidding? I'll do anything for you, Sylvie, you've been so wonderful. I feel good for the first time in a long time."

Charlotte's phone chimed from Sylvie's dining room table, where Charlotte had plugged it in after it had died again last night. Letting Sylvie take over the kneading, she washed her hands and picked it up.

She beamed as she saw a text from Brielle. *I hope you're doing okay over there. Things aren't the same without you. Duchess and Princess are making me crazy, lol.* Charlotte's mouth quirked into a smile at the thought of Brielle having to roll her eyes at Kylie and

Riley to no one. *I miss you, girl. Hope you'll be home soon. <3*

Swiping the text away, she saw she had missed calls from both Allie and Liam. She was surprised to get a call from her son; she didn't hear from him that often anymore, with his crazy hours working on Wall Street as an investment banker. Listed under their calls were seven missed calls from Sebastian. Her heart twisted, heat rising in her throat. Couldn't he just give her some space? What was the point in coming here if she was going to have to talk to him so much?

Charlotte excused herself to one of Sylvie's bedrooms and dialed Allie. It went to voicemail; she was probably in class. A moment later, a new text arrived.

Sorry Mom, I'm in class. Just wanted to say hi :) Everything's going really well here. Just a quick FYI though, I tried to buy a textbook this morning, and they declined my card. Liam texted me too, same thing. Any idea what happened? No rush, just wanted to let you know. Love you!

She hadn't even known they were still financially supporting Liam. No way was Charlotte going to let her kids find out about the bankruptcy. A lurch of nausea punched its way through her stomach.

Charlotte tried to take a few steadying breaths while she dialed Sebastian. No answer. She tried again. Nothing. Pacing back and forth in the room, she tried to shake the dread forming at the base of her spine.

She yelped as the phone came to life in her hands. Sebastian. Trying to stop the tremble in her hands, she lifted the phone.

"Sebastian?" she asked, her voice a higher pitch than she'd intended.

"Hey, Charlotte..." Sebastian said, his voice low. "You got a minute?"

"What's wrong?"

He blew out a long breath. "I'm so sorry, Charlotte. This is a hard call for me to make." Several horrible moments passed as Charlotte felt her vision starting to tunnel. "I'm so embarrassed..."

"Just tell me what happened," she said, panic rising in her throat.

"It's sort of a long story, but I'll give you the short version." He cleared his throat. His voice wavered slightly, shooting Charlotte's pulse through the roof. "I told you I was working on something, it was a new investment. Sort of hard to explain; we were buying patents, biotech and pharmaceutical patents from a couple of bankrupt firms, and then we were...sort of enforcing them against competitors. It's complicated. We sank a lot into it. Me, Alastair, and a couple of the boys. Anyway, it didn't work out." His voice caught on the last word. "I'm so sorry. We're in a little bit of trouble, Charlotte, and if I had any way to shield you from this, I would. I wouldn't normally even tell you about it. But I know you had some sort of plan to restore that inn over there...That loan doesn't exist anymore. Alastair's in Fiji licking his wounds and I can't get any more money at the moment." He paused. "You're going to have to wait on your project until I can figure something out. I'm really sorry."

"Oh, my God..." Charlotte felt her whole world crashing down. Christian had committed to the project, had hired contractors. "We already started, Sebastian...work begins today. What am I supposed to do here?" She was starting to sound frantic.

"Can't it just wait a while?"

"We need someone around here to make money, Sebastian," she seethed. "It obviously has to be me. This inn could generate good money, but not if I can't restore it..." Charlotte's clothes felt too tight, restricting her breathing. She opened a window to let air into the room. "What are we going to do?"

No response. After a few moments, she checked

the phone to see if he'd hung up. "Can we sell the condo?" she asked desperately.

"The condo's underwater. If I had some rabbit I could pull out of a hat, I would've done it. I never saw this coming." Charlotte could hear the fear rising in his voice, and it sent ice down her spine. "I'm selling the Rolls and the Mercedes, so we have a little bit to live on for now. It isn't dire straits quite yet, exactly. But I will figure this out, Charlotte. You have my word."

"Sebastian, you keep saying that. *I'm* trying to figure something out here, something that has actual potential instead of bankrupting us further." She hadn't meant the words to come out so harshly. "My sister is threatening to sell the inn to an investor so she can pay off their debt. Someone is going to buy up the land and destroy the house, and there goes the plan. If I can't restore it, I don't have any claim on anything. And then there won't be any money. *What am I supposed to do here, Sebastian?*" she asked wildly.

"I will think of something, okay? I just need more time."

"*There is no more time!*" she yelled into the phone, not caring if Sylvie heard her at this point. "*I'm* going to have to think of something. You've somehow managed to strip everything away from me, Sebastian! In case you've forgotten, you've cheated on me, and now you've left me with *nothing*! I'm tired of waiting for you to figure things out. *I* will figure something out, since you haven't been able to."

She hung up the phone and threw herself on the bed, ignoring the buzzing from Sebastian calling her back. She clenched her fists and shut her eyes tight. The sensation of freefalling knocked into her, bile rising in her throat.

It was the exact feeling of being out of options that she had when she left Marina Cove all those years ago. And here she was, twenty-six years later, and she'd come full circle. Nothing had changed. Those years had just been a reprieve from the inevitable. Charlotte clenched her whole body tight as her mind reeled with panic. She had absolutely no idea what to do next.

15

Still trembling, Charlotte turned from the front door of the inn, squeezed Christian's hands, and leaned up to kiss him lightly on the lips. He pulled her in for a long hug. "It'll be okay, sweetheart," he whispered into her hair. "Are you feeling any better?"

Charlotte squeezed her eyes shut and clenched her arms and legs in an attempt to stop the shaking. "I'm so scared, Christian...What if it's something really bad?" She swallowed the large lump that had formed in her throat. "What am I going to do?"

"Whatever it is, we'll figure it out together," he said, his steady voice providing a life preserver as Charlotte felt like she was thrashing around in the open sea, unable to tread water. "I'm here with you

no matter what. The doctor said it's probably nothing, they just want to be sure."

EARLIER THAT MORNING, Charlotte had been walking
with Christian along Snowfall Haven, named
because of the unusually white sand that covered its
beaches. It was a beautiful summer morning, the
crisp air filling her lungs, golden sun warming her
skin. Suddenly, she felt the world tilting around her.
It was another of what she'd taken to calling her
"episodes" where her vision narrowed into a tunnel
and her arms and legs went numb. The world
swirled around her as she dropped to one knee,
Christian grabbing her around the torso to steady
her. Then, nothing.

She woke up to the crystal blue sky. She registered a voice, far away. It sounded vaguely familiar.
Her ears were ringing. After a few moments, the
darkness receded from her vision, and she looked
around for Christian. He was running toward her
from the Loop behind them as a blue sedan sped
away down the road.

"Charlotte, I flagged down a car. They're going to
call for help. Just hang tight and relax, help is on the

way." Charlotte could tell he was working hard to keep his voice calm; his eyebrows were knitted together in concern as he leaned over her and stroked her hair gently, holding her hand in his like it was made of glass, as though the slightest move would shatter her.

AFTER SEVERAL HOURS of waiting at the emergency room, she'd finally met with the doctors. Shaking like a leaf, she described the symptoms she'd been having over the last few months. Dizzy spells. Sudden numbness in her arms and legs. Headaches. How symptoms seemed to come from nowhere, and ended after a terrifying few minutes, sometimes more. But they were getting worse. And now, she'd fainted when walking along the beach.

After checking her vitals and a brief neurological exam, the doctor couldn't determine anything for her. He wanted to send her for an MRI to get more information.

Charlotte had always closely watched Christian's face when she was anxious, a sort of barometer, like watching flight attendants' expressions during heavy turbulence. As the doctor mentioned the further testing, she saw Christian's skin blanch, and while he'd carefully set his face without expression, she saw tiny beads of sweat forming at his brow.

WAVING GOODBYE TO CHRISTIAN, Charlotte entered the inn. The common room was much emptier than usual. She waved politely to a few guests reading and conversing before she went upstairs to the room she shared with Ramona. Despite the way things had been at home, right now she needed her family with her, to know what she might be up against.

As she grabbed the first post of the railing on the way up the stairs, it wobbled and cracked at the base. She shoved it back in its place, annoyed, and noted the inn's peeling wallpaper and chipped paint as she took the steps two at a time. The place seemed to be decaying in the last few months. She opened the door to find Ramona's back to her as she stood in front of an easel, slashing the canvas with black and violet streaks. Her headphones were on, and Charlotte could hear heavy metal music blaring in Ramona's ears.

Charlotte paused as she looked at the painting in front of Ramona. What used to be beautiful seascapes and soft portraits in bright colors had recently evolved into unrecognizable masses of dark, swirling colors, like painting a memory of a nightmare upon waking.

Since their father had left six months ago, everything had changed at the Seaside House. Their mother trudged through her tasks each day like a zombie and spent most of her time in her room. Charlotte couldn't count how many times she'd sat on the floor outside Ella's bedroom, back against the wall after pounding on the door repeatedly just to see her mother's face before finally giving up. She'd strain her ears just to hear signs of life; it was always silence, punctuated by the sounds of soft crying. Charlotte had no idea what to do. It was like she'd lost her mother as well as her father.

She hadn't heard a peep from her older siblings. Natalie apparently dropped out of college and, depending on the rumor, was either backpacking through the Icelandic wilderness or motorcycling with a much older boyfriend across Europe. Diane and Gabriel had already been gone and had kept their distance.

Ramona had been her lifeline at first. They stuck together, spent long nights talking to each other in the dark of their bedroom, sharing their pain, their anger, their sadness. Memories of their father. Questions about why he had abandoned them so suddenly, without a true explanation.

But the effort to maintain their bond slowly frayed over the passing months as it became clear that their father wasn't returning and their mother was withdrawing from the world. Ramona's grades slipped, and Ella hadn't ever returned the many phone calls from her teachers. Charlotte had dropped out of high school entirely, finding it impossible to pay attention, especially when her "episodes" started. When Charlotte told her mother, she'd responded with a single nod and returned to her bed. Charlotte grieved all over again as she watched her relationship with Ramona slowly crumble into ashes, until Ramona barely spoke with her at all.

Christian was the only one who knew about the episodes. She hadn't wanted to burden her family any further. But now, as she faced the prospect of something possibly being very wrong with her, she needed them to be there for her. A lifeline.

"Ramona, can I talk to you?" she called. Her sister either hadn't heard or was ignoring her. "*Ramona!*" she yelled, tapping her on the shoulder.

"*What?*" she spat, whipping her headphones off and scowling at Charlotte.

"Can I talk to you?"

"I'm busy, Charlotte."

"It's important..." Charlotte tried to keep the fear out of her voice. "I could use someone to talk to."

Ramona sighed, dropping her paintbrush on the desk, smearing paint everywhere. "Look, I can't deal with it right now, okay? I have enough going on. Why don't you just go talk to your boyfriend."

She turned and put her headphones back on, resuming her slashing at the canvas. Charlotte fought hard to keep the tears from her eyes. She turned on her heel and left the room.

Fine. If Ramona wouldn't be there for her, Charlotte would just have to talk to her mother. Marching over to Ella's room with her fists balled up, she knocked on the door and was met with steely silence, as usual. She pounded harder, until she finally just opened the door and went in.

Her mother was lying in bed, her back turned to Charlotte. "Mom, I need to talk to you."

Ella stirred, keeping her back to Charlotte. "Not now, Charlotte."

"No. I need you to listen to me. I'm asking you. Please." The fear rose in her throat as a vision of lying on a cold table being slid into an MRI machine filled her mind.

"Please, Charlotte. Go talk to your sister."

Charlotte clenched her fists as hot fire coursed through her, making her heart slam painfully against her ribs. A brief sense of vertigo came over her as she felt the familiar tingling in her forearms and legs.

"*Mom, please!*" Charlotte begged as the tears began to flow. "*I have a serious problem! I think there's something wrong with me! I need you right now!*"

Ella's shoulders rose with a sigh before drooping again. A long moment passed as Charlotte wept silently, terror creeping across her skin.

"Charlotte, you're seventeen. You have no idea what a serious problem is."

The words hung in the air, filling all the dark corners of the room and brutally squeezing against her chest. She stood there, stunned, feeling as though she'd been cracked across the face.

She'd long felt it in her bones, her body aware well before it had finally registered in her mind, but now everything had finally clicked into place.

Charlotte was alone; truly, desperately alone in her family. They were no longer there for her. Couldn't be. She strained hard against the sudden desire to run up to her father and bury her face in his chest, feel his strong, protective arms around her, like she'd always been able to do. She ran out of the house to the front porch, squeezed her eyes shut, and screamed into the endless sky until the gut-wrenching feeling passed.

The only person in the world she had now was Christian.

"TELL ME AGAIN. Everything. What it'll be like for us," said Charlotte, looking up into Christian's eyes.

A week later, Charlotte was sitting in a small wooden sailboat with Christian as the fiery streaks of sunlight shimmered across the calm harbor, the water like glass. She ran her fingers along the solid oak and cedar of the boat that Christian had built with his own hands, dipping over the copper rivets on the gunnel, watching the barely reflected glimmer of the setting sun against the oil finish that she'd watched him rub lovingly into the wood. She listened to the low thrum of his voice against the wind through the trees on shore and the birds singing above, taking in every detail as he described the plans for their future together.

Charlotte had received a phone call from her doctor that morning. Her results were all fine. When she asked him what had been happening to her, what the episodes were, he responded simply, "Panic attacks, most likely. The body responds to panic like it's an illness. But the panic is almost always masking something deeper." He'd asked her if anything had changed in her life recently. Charlotte was so relieved that she barely answered, muttering something about things being a bit difficult in her family at the moment. The doctor gave her some suggestions to manage her panic attacks, ways to stabilize and to ground herself when she felt them coming on.

Christian was almost giddy when she'd told him she was okay. To celebrate, he had suggested they take an evening picnic to Seashell Harbor.

They had composed their life plan over the course of their time together, note by note, until a beautiful song had emerged. Christian was set to take over his father's business; he was old and in poor health. Christian's older brother Elliott was in the Marine Corps fighting overseas and had no interest in returning to Marina Cove; Christian had always said his brother was going to be career military and so it was up to him to keep the family business alive. Not that it was out of pure obligation; Christian had been working in his father's woodshop helping him to make custom furniture since he was a child, and had a true passion for it. Charlotte would help him with the accounting, something she'd be able to keep up until her real dream of having children came true.

"And after we get married," Christian said as he adjusted the sails, "we build a beautiful three-story house on Old Man Keamy's lot, and fill it with music and books and art, and we laugh on our front porch swing while our children chase each other on the front lawn as the sun sets, and we clink our lemonade glasses together. We grow old together. We're happy, and in love."

Charlotte sighed happily, feeling at peace for the first time in a long time. Darkness had settled into the sky as the sun disappeared over the horizon. Christian steered them upwind so they'd drift slowly across the harbor, and motioned for Charlotte. She sat in front of him, and he wrapped his arms around her as they leaned back and stared up into the sky.

The darkness deepened, and before long, the expanse slowly passing above them was bright and sparkling, billions of pins of light glittering against the infinite black sky. Charlotte's heart caught in her throat. It was like swimming in starlight.

There was so much Charlotte wanted to tell him.

But words failed her as she lost herself in the vast blanket of stars swirling all around them, so she turned up to him and gave him a soft kiss on the lips, and contemplated the vastness of the future ahead of her, filled with love, and hope.

Seagulls circled and cried overhead as Charlotte made her way down the wooden planks toward the end of Shannon Pier, needing to get away from the inn for a bit. The sounds of the waves crashing against the tall pillars below mingled with children's peals of laughter as they whirled around The Rocket, an old roller coaster that had been an attraction since Charlotte was a child. People milled around holding large sticks of puffy pink cotton candy, and the aroma of powdered sugar filled the air as she passed a man selling funnel cakes. A large Ferris wheel loomed in front of her, its old, brightly colored cars creaking as it carried on its endless rotations.

A few weeks had passed since she'd gotten the

call from Sebastian that stripped away her funding. She spent a brutal night on the hardwood floor, staring at the ceiling, her mind racing through her options.

Ramona and her mother obviously were out. She couldn't ask her Manhattan friends for money— none of them knew about their financial predicament, and word traveled so fast in the city that Sebastian's reputation would be ruined, something he'd reminded her of time and again over the last few years when things had started to plummet. It could affect his ability to do business, and Charlotte still held out a glimmer of hope that he would find a way to save the day at the last minute. She was also smart enough to know that asking Sylvie for money would likely end badly; more friendships were ruined by money than anything else, and all that. Rekindling that relationship had been the only thing keeping her standing since she'd been back on the island.

So she'd spent hours on her phone researching other options. Desperate, she'd signed on for a no-credit-check short-term personal loan with interest rates so exorbitant that she'd actually broken out in hives reading the terms. It would be enough for the down payment to the contractors Christian had hired and some basic supplies and living expenses, but not much else.

It was a major gamble; she had very little time before she had to pay it off, but the ball was already rolling with the restoration, and it was her best bet to start making money. Charlotte had tried to broach the subject of time with Christian on a couple of occasions, but he stubbornly maintained that he was going to do the job right, and that he and his contractors would work as fast as they possibly could. She hadn't pressed the issue further.

At any rate, if Sylvie's experience with Felix Caldwell's critical review was any indication, Charlotte would have no problem booking guests quickly once it was published, and the summer months were upon them, meaning tourists would be looking for places to stay.

Still, a horrible feeling in her gut followed her everywhere she went, coloring her day and making her feel leaden, exhausted. What had she gotten herself into? How did she get here? It seemed like only yesterday her life had been happily rolling along, her most serious concerns where to eat lunch that day or what dress to wear to the next fundraiser.

Charlotte walked up to one of the vendor carts and paid for a large vanilla ice cream cone. She headed over to one of the benches toward the end of the pier, the one she always came to as a child. As she stared out over the water, the breeze whipping at her hair, she was suddenly struck with a feeling of loneliness. She missed her children. After a great deal of debating, Charlotte had finally called them, only saying that she was staying with her family in Marina Cove for a while, leaving out the details of her separation from Sebastian. They all had so much going on that she didn't want to burden them when she didn't even know what she was doing yet. She felt terribly guilty, but she had to simplify the chaos in her life right now, not add to it.

Rolling her wedding ring around her finger idly, she found herself missing Sebastian, too, despite everything. What he'd done hadn't simply erased the decades she'd had with him. Her whole adult life had been spent with him.

The worst part was, she still couldn't rid herself of the feeling that she'd somehow been responsible for it. She was ashamed to feel it; she didn't make him do what he did. But maybe if she'd tried harder over the years...It was complicated, and every time she allowed herself to think about him, her thoughts tangled and she felt worse off than when she started, so she tried to just block him from her mind. She hadn't been very successful.

AN HOUR LATER, Charlotte returned to the inn, scowling as she shoved her shoulder twice into the heavy front door that was always stuck. Ramona was in the dining room, scrubbing the far wall vigorously, a sheen of sweat on her forehead. Charlotte gave her a small wave, which Ramona didn't return. Irritation rose in her chest; couldn't Ramona just try?

She started up the wooden steps, and as she grabbed the first post of the handrail, it shifted and broke off at the base, like it had ever since she could remember. She angrily slammed it back into place. The sudden sound of a table saw being run by one of the contractors in the common room made her yelp, and then grimace with embarrassment. The old stairs popped and groaned as she stomped up them, the sounds like splinters in her mind.

Cleaning products, rags, and plastic buckets awaited her as she sat down on the floor of the first guest room to resume her work. While Christian and his crew were laboring away on the restoration, she'd been doing her best to clean and manage the clutter that filled the house. No small task. But Ramona had shown up every day between shifts or after work to help. That was something.

Her knees cracked and burned as she scrubbed the filthy hardwood, losing herself in her frustration. She couldn't wait to get out of this old, broken-down house and back to Manhattan. The sooner they got the work done, the sooner she could leave.

The distant tinkling of piano keys drifted into the guest room from somewhere downstairs. She wondered who was playing. As she poked her head out of the room into the hallway, her breath caught in her throat as she immediately recognized the first chords of "Clair de Lune."

Padding softly down the stairs, she crossed through the common room and stood with her back against the library, which housed the old upright piano. It had been a gift from her mother to her father; he'd always wanted to learn to play.

She held her breath as the increased agitation of the first section swept into four gentle rolled chords that reverberated into the common room. A pause, and then the gorgeous arpeggios of the second section that had always felt to Charlotte like chasing the moonlight over rolling hills of green grass by the sea, leaving her breathless and exhilarated. She pressed her eyes shut as the huge crescendo of the climax swept through her body, her heart skittering wildly, until the final glittering notes escaped, bringing small tears of emotion to her eyes. She heard the foot pedal release, and quickly composed herself as Christian turned into the common room.

"Charlotte—hey," he said, looking embarrassed. "Sorry about that. I haven't played in ages...I didn't know you were home."

She inhaled sharply to steady her breath. "I'm amazed you still know that song." Charlotte had a cassette tape of Claude Debussy that she'd listened to on the way to school, before she'd worn out the tape. While one of Christian's hobbies had been teaching himself how to play instruments, he hadn't ever played the piano and didn't read sheet music, but just a month later, he'd surprised her one night by sitting at that very same upright piano and playing the song in its entirety to her. How he'd managed to learn it by ear amazed her. After that, whenever she'd wanted to hear it, he'd play it for her. It had become one of their songs.

Christian shifted uncomfortably before lifting his head and looking into Charlotte's eyes. A long moment stretched between them as they stared at each other, tension twisting throughout Charlotte's body. He broke eye contact and ran his hands over his face before bending down to grab a hammer he'd left against the wall.

"Listen, Charlotte, I wanted to fill you in on a few things." He was looking everywhere around the room except at her. "We're making great progress, but we've found some underlying issues that we're going to need to address before you start having guests stay here. You've got some serious plumbing issues; I have a guy scheduled in a couple weeks to handle it. There's a good deal of electrical work that needs done, as I'm sure you've noticed with the power outages. Working on scheduling that now. And I hate to say it, but the heating system needs to be replaced." He motioned down toward the basement. "It's over forty years old and could stop working at any time. So try not to use it until we take care of it, okay? Shouldn't be a problem since we're headed into summer here." He looked up at her tentatively. "Is that all okay? It'll add a decent amount to the cost, but there's not a lot I can do about that since it won't be my guys working on it. It might take a while to get people scheduled, too."

Just perfect. The sinking feeling that the whole thing had been a bad idea bubbled to the surface of Charlotte's mind for the thousandth time. Ramona had been right, of course; Charlotte hadn't had any clue how much work it would take to fix up the inn. And now, she had put herself further in trouble with a bad loan just to cover the down payment, with no plan in place for how to actually afford all this work. The costs just kept on mounting, with no end in sight.

"Is that all absolutely necessary right now?" she asked, trying to keep the fear from her voice. "I mean, can we just get things looking nice enough to start booking guests again and tackle some of these things over time?"

"It absolutely needs to be done before anyone stays here, yes," he said firmly. Good thing she hadn't told him she was sleeping on the floor upstairs. "Some of these things are safety issues. I'm sorry, I won't compromise on that."

Charlotte silently dug her fingers into her palms to try to take the focus off the old familiar feeling of dizziness, of the prickling in her arms and legs. "I understand, of course. It's just, I'll need to talk to my, uh, lender. Since there will be some extra costs." She hated the feeling of bending the truth, but he couldn't know about her financial predicaments. Heat blushed her cheeks. "It might take a bit to get that sorted."

"Hey, that's no problem at all. I've worked with all these people before; I can buy you plenty of time, don't worry about that. They know I'm good for it." He flashed her an easy smile.

The tension eased in her limbs, the vertigo fading a bit. "Thanks, Christian. I just want to get things going is all." She debated her next words. "I know you're working as fast as you can, but if there's anything we can do to...speed things along at all..."

He bristled. "This is as fast as it can go. I'm putting my name on this job. I won't do shoddy work."

Charlotte's face flushed. "No, I know, of course not." She forced a smile and, without thinking, grabbed his hands. "I seriously appreciate everything you're doing here. Really. I know you said your labor is free, but I'm going to pay you."

His shoulders relaxed, and he gave her hands a squeeze. "It's my pleasure, Charlotte. And like I said, I don't do these jobs for the money. I basically have no living expenses, so I don't need much. I just love what I do," he said with a grin that made her heart flutter.

She felt the warmth of his strong hands in hers radiating up her arms. She opened her mouth to say something, but the words were lost in her throat.

Suddenly, a knock at the door broke the spell, and she quickly dropped his hands. "Be right back," she said sheepishly, turning on her heel.

The front door was stuck again; she grabbed the handle and yanked three times with the whole weight of her body before it scraped open. Charlotte felt the color drain from her face as she took in the figure standing on the porch, back turned, long dark hair so much like her own cascading down her shoulders and fluttering in the breeze. A small yellow suitcase stood next to her. Her oldest daughter turned around, eyes red and rimmed with tears.

"Mariah? What's wrong? What are you...how did you..." Charlotte spluttered as she pulled Mariah toward her. She buried her face in her mother's hair, her body suddenly heaving against Charlotte in silent sobs.

Charlotte clutched her for several long moments, trembling with anxiety at her daughter turning up unannounced all the way in Marina Cove. A pit of unease formed in her stomach as she felt the bones through Mariah's skin; she was much thinner than when she'd last seen her. Dark rings had formed under her eyes. "It's okay, it's okay, sweetheart," she whispered soothingly into Mariah's hair.

Mariah pulled away and wiped her eyes. Charlotte guided her down the steps and into the backyard. They went into the small white gazebo that Charlotte's father had built when she was a child. It was one of the places she used to sit and think when she was sad.

Mariah sat on the bench next to Charlotte and started to laugh through her tears. "I'm sorry," she said. "Everything is fine. Really. I'm okay. I just needed to see you. Dad told me you were here working on your family inn, he gave me the address...I tried to call this morning, but your phone kept going to voicemail."

Charlotte grimaced. Her phone had died again, and with the unreliable power in the house, she hadn't been able to charge it yet.

"Mariah, I'm so happy to see you, but...I know something's wrong. You can talk to me. We'll figure it out together."

Mariah paused as she seemed to weigh her next words. "I took a leave of absence from med school." She looked up at Charlotte expectantly, a look of shame crossing her face.

Charlotte nodded and gently tucked a strand of Mariah's hair behind her ear. "Tell me everything."

Mariah leaned back against the bench and

exhaled a long, shaky breath. "It feels so good to say that out loud. I'm embarrassed...I tried, Mom, I really did." She wiped her eyes with her sleeve. "At first, everything was fine, my classes were going well. But when we started rotations, actually working with the patients..." Mariah squeezed her eyes shut, and Charlotte saw her hands clenching. "At first, I just chalked it up to it being new, that things would get better...but things just kept getting worse."

She looked out across the backyard. A warm breeze was fluttering the leaves of the birch trees that surrounded them, and the sounds of waves crashing carried over from the golden shore. "I was losing sleep, just up all night tossing and turning. But I kept at it, studied harder, worked harder and harder. But weird things started to happen, like I would get horrible dizzy spells, or feel like I couldn't breathe." Charlotte winced, recognizing the symptoms of panic attacks. "I could barely eat anything by the end. I gave it everything I had in me, down to my bones. I think I just pushed myself way too far."

Mariah turned to face Charlotte, and looked into her eyes with a resolute expression. "I'll figure it out. I know you and Dad always said we didn't need to work if we didn't want to, but I needed something for myself. I don't want to rely on your handouts, you know? I want to do something meaningful. Something I can do the rest of my life."

Her shoulders slumped. "I just need a break, I think. To think things through."

Charlotte's heart broke as she thought about the suffering her daughter had gone through in her attempts to find her own way. Mariah had somehow been wise enough to avoid letting money and complacency rule her life, something that had taken the loss of everything to become clear to Charlotte. Unfortunately, it seemed her drive to create her independence had gone too far.

"Baby, I'm so, so sorry for everything you've been through," Charlotte whispered. "You did the right thing, and I'm so proud of you." She took Mariah's hands in hers and gave them a squeeze. "That was a very brave thing you did, taking a leave. Most people stubbornly stick with plans they've made, even when they know they're wrong, because they're a lot more afraid of the unknown than they are of suffering. It takes a lot of courage to consider your own happiness, even when it means facing uncertainty."

Mariah's shoulders fell back as the tension visibly left her body. "Thanks, Mom."

They sat there for several moments in comfortable silence, taking in the warm rays of sunshine cascading through the trees overhead and the scent of fresh-cut grass and saltwater.

"Why don't you stay here with me for a bit?" Charlotte asked. "I'll be running around a lot with the restoration going on, but we could fix up one of the guest rooms for you. It won't be much, but you get used to it. Give you some time to clear your head, soak up the sun, meet some cute surfer boys?" She wiggled her eyebrows ridiculously as Mariah gave a loud, genuine laugh that warmed Charlotte to the core.

"That sounds absolutely perfect, yes. This place is paradise." Her eyes crinkled with amusement as they followed Ollie bounding across the yard from the beach, ears flapping gloriously in the wind, eager to greet the new guest. "And I'm going to help you out with the inn while I'm here. It'll help me take my mind off things."

They sat together in the gazebo for a long time. Charlotte thought about what she'd told Mariah about how hard it was to face the unknown. How courageous Mariah was to push against the bands of tension that keep people passive, static, unchanging. Despite herself, she felt the hard pull of her old life in Manhattan, where everything was figured out, where every day, every month, every year was laid out in front of her in the clear light of day, organized and predictable and comfortable. She thought of Sebastian, his laugh, his arms around her.

Something had cracked inside her the day her father abandoned her, a crack that had spidered and spread until it finally shattered the night that everything changed for good. She'd fled the island seeking safety and certainty, and had never stopped chasing it. She thought about how she would do almost anything to get that feeling of certainty back, even if it meant sacrificing her own happiness.

17

"Are you sure you know where you're going?" Ramona asked irritably as she wiped the sheen of sweat that had formed across her brow, carefully climbing over a log that had fallen across the Redwood Canyon trail. Charlotte was a few paces ahead of her, looking uncertainly toward a split in the trail.

Ramona was already exhausted after a long shift on her feet at The Windmill but had reluctantly agreed when Charlotte invited her to go for a walk, telling Ramona that she wanted to "show her something." Ramona had deliberated for a couple of days about how to approach Charlotte about the phone call she'd received, and was grateful for an excuse to just be out with it.

"It's been almost thirty years," Charlotte said, wandering around the fork in the trail overgrown with scrub and tall grass. "Things look a little different."

Ramona had been struck with a feeling of déjà vu ever since they started the long climb up the trail through the thick forest, like she'd been here before, but was unable to place it. She had no idea where Charlotte was taking her, and was getting annoyed with the air of mystery and surprise her sister was attempting to cultivate. Over the weeks, Charlotte had been trying with varying degrees of subtlety to bond with her, as though a lifetime of distance and problems could be solved just like that.

Still, it was hard to avoid remembering how things used to be. There was a time when Charlotte was her best friend in the world, her mentor, her confidante. Sometimes she'd catch Charlotte with a crooked smile, or hear her laugh, and it was like they were kids again. It would hit her so hard she sometimes had to leave the room to catch her breath. It was powerful, and Ramona found herself constantly wishing Charlotte hadn't shown up, disrupting everything into a confusing mess.

Apparently seeing some clue that decided things, Charlotte chose the left trail, and motioned for Ramona to follow. "I promise, it'll be worth it. Just trust me."

Sorry, Charlotte. Trust went out the window a long, long time ago. Ramona swallowed the irritation and took a long drink from her water bottle. The sun had marched across the sky and was beginning to dip toward the horizon, the air now pleasantly cool, but the effort of the steep climb had worked Ramona into an uncomfortable sweat.

After what felt like another long hour, the tall white oaks and ash trees suddenly opened into a small clearing in front of a huge, nearly vertical wall of rock. Recognition pierced her like a bullet.

"Charlotte, I don't want to climb that."

"You don't have to," she said, looking at Ramona carefully. "But if you wanted to see what's up there...I can help you. There are plenty of footholds, look." She gestured to a crevice that ran up the center of the wall of rock.

Their father had brought Charlotte and Ramona here once, the summer before he left. His excitement had been infectious as he held Ramona's hand, leading them up the trail. But when they got to the clearing where she and Charlotte now stood, Ramona had been too scared to climb the wall of rock, and had rocked on her heels impatiently as

Charlotte and her father climbed to the top and disappeared out of sight. She'd asked Charlotte later what she'd seen, but Charlotte told her that Ramona had to see for herself and that she'd take her back whenever she was ready. After Dad left, the plan had been lost entirely, like so much else.

He had taken too much away from them, and Ramona was tired of it.

Grimacing, she dropped her bottle of water and let Charlotte take her hand as she carefully guided them up the recesses in the wall that had been eroded by years of rain and wind. A flash of her father's face crossed her mind, that broad smile and sparkle of mischief in his eyes. She swallowed the lump of sadness that had formed in her throat. Her stomach lurched as she cautioned a glance down; they were uncomfortably high, but Charlotte's grip made her feel more secure.

She waited an uncomfortable moment as Charlotte heaved herself up the last ledge and turned back around to grab Ramona's arms, helping to pull her to the landing at the very top of the wall of rock.

Ramona's breath caught in her throat as she looked all around her. She could see the entire island from this height, an incredible panorama sweeping around her, filling her with awe. Jagged peaks and cliffs jutted out into the water, and miles of untouched golden sand circled the island. She could see Hightide Port and the ferry making its way back to the mainland, several small boats dotting the bay, sails flapping in the warm breeze. Main Street crossed inland as people milled peacefully in and out of stores, or rode bicycles across the town square; children were eating ice cream cones, carefree and holding hands with their parents. Shannon Pier shot out over the water, and the bright, multi-colored lights that lined the spokes of the Ferris wheel rotated slowly as the distant screams of people riding the wooden roller coaster carried over the wind.

She could just make out the Seaside House, sitting right on the water, as seagulls circled overhead and a dolphin shot out from the waves only to disappear back into the stretch of sapphire and violet. The two sisters stood in silence as the last rays of golden sunlight reached plaintively across the water toward the coast for one last embrace before their final descent over the western horizon.

Ramona's throat constricted, and she suddenly felt like someone had dumped a bucket of ice water into her stomach. Her father had been right here with Charlotte as Ramona stood waiting at the bottom, having no inkling that she would never get to share this moment with him. That in just a few months, he would be gone, forever. That she'd never again have the chance to hear his bright voice, to feel his arms around her, to hear him say that he loved her.

Her eyes welled up with tears, and this time, she didn't stop them. Silent sobs racked her body as Charlotte took her hand.

"I miss him, Charlotte," Ramona whispered, her heart leaping in her chest.

Charlotte sniffled and wiped her hand across her eyes. "I miss him too."

They stood together for a long time, watching the sky darken over the horizon. Ramona stopped fighting it, and let the memories of her father wash over her as the tears streamed silently down her face.

THE SKY WAS black when they began their descent down the rock face toward the trail. Charlotte used the flashlight on her phone to illuminate the indentations in the rock ahead of them. Ramona let out a small yelp when her foot slipped, and started to slide down the rock. Charlotte shot out her hand and gripped Ramona's flailing arms, stopping her slide.

"Here, let me go first," Charlotte said, panting slightly.

"I'm fine," Ramona said, catching her breath as she dusted off her pants, flushing with embarrassment. "Just shine the light so I can see."

Ramona inched down the rock face, clutching on to pieces of the rock that stuck out from the wall for support, her sweating palms slipping on the smooth surface. Almost there.

She didn't even know what was happening until she was already falling, unable to get purchase on the rock wall, and for a moment she heard someone screaming from far away before she realized the sound was coming from her throat. She tumbled head over heels as her feet caught on something, and she landed hard on the pine needles covering the bottom landing, the wind knocked out of her and a sickening *crack* emanating from somewhere in her body. She gasped unsuccessfully for air as panic lurched through her. Charlotte's shouting became muffled as the stars overhead faded to blackness.

· · ·

Ramona woke with a start. Her eyes darted around frantically as she tried to make sense of her unfamiliar surroundings. She quickly sat up, and pain shot through her body, causing her to lie back down. There was a steady beeping and the whirring of some sort of machinery, and Charlotte was suddenly poised over her, eyebrows knitted in fear.

"Ramona?"

Her head felt like it was stuffed with cotton balls. Suddenly she remembered where she was. The long way back down the trail, arm wrapped around Charlotte as she half-carried Ramona for what felt like endless miles, stumbling in agony through the pitch-black darkness as Charlotte dialed her phone again and again, unable to get a signal. Flashing red lights, a turbulent and nauseating drive, and then precious sleep.

"Charlotte." Her throat felt like sandpaper, the words caught in her mouth as fear made its way through her body. She blinked back tears. "Am I okay?"

Charlotte reached for Ramona's hand. "Some scrapes and bruised ribs for the most part." Ella appeared next to the hospital bed, concern etched on her face. Charlotte looked at Ramona hesitantly, seeming to weigh her words. "You broke your leg.

That's the worst of it. Nothing permanent, though. I'm so sorry, Ramona. I never should've taken you there. It's my fault."

"No, it's my fault. I told you I didn't need help climbing down." Ramona pressed her eyes shut. "How long for my leg to heal?"

Charlotte winced. "The doctor said you'll need a cast and crutches, and that you'll have to stay off it for a while. He said it might take a couple of months to fully heal."

Ramona broke out in a cold sweat as she took stock of things, working hard against the quicksand of her mind. It could be worse. She could still do her bookkeeping from home. But if her leg was broken…

"I won't be able to work at The Windmill now. Charlotte, that was half of my income. I can't afford not to work there." She clutched her hands hard and pushed the panic that filled her back into the recesses of her mind.

Charlotte's mouth moved to say something, but no words came out. "We'll figure something out, Ramona," she offered.

Ramona looked into Ella's eyes. Over the long years together, they'd learned a sort of silent communication. Ella's mouth formed a thin line, and she turned her eyes to the floor. It was all ultimately her mother's decision, and she knew what they had to do as well as Ramona did.

"Charlotte," Ramona said as she exhaled all the air from her lungs. "Someone made an offer to buy the Seaside House, and we're going to take it."

The color drained from Charlotte's face. "What?" she choked out.

Ramona sighed as Ella turned to pace around the room, defeat in her eyes. "I was going to tell you on our hike. I got the call a couple days ago. Mom didn't decide anything...We wanted to see how things progressed with the restoration. But I told you that before you got here I'd been reaching out to realty groups, just to have some options if it came to it. Everyone always wanted to tear down the house and build something else in its place. We never wanted that, obviously, but I needed a backup plan if it ever came to it."

She shifted uncomfortably as a dull throbbing began to make its way through her legs, the painkillers apparently starting to wear off. "These guys reached out to me this time...some real estate group led by this guy Giovanni. MDRC, or something. They've agreed to keep the Seaside House, to restore it and manage it as a rental. It'll even be in the contract. They offered more than anyone else has yet. It's still an insultingly low amount, but it's better than nothing."

Ramona winced as pain shot up her leg and into her back. "We were already running out of time, Charlotte. We've been on a razor's edge. And now if I'm losing my waitressing money, I have no choice anymore." She avoided Charlotte's gaze. "I'll pay you back for the work that's been done so far with the money I get from the sale. It would've been nice to get the inn going again, but...I'm sorry. At least they won't tear down our house. It's something."

Cautioning a glance, she saw Charlotte looking out the window with a dazed expression. Ramona's chest tightened, but she quickly reminded herself that her financial issues long predated Charlotte's arrival. She couldn't help if she had to make certain choices with cold, hard logic. She was desperate.

After a long moment, Charlotte turned back to Ramona, tears in her eyes. "Sebastian and I are bankrupt."

Ella stopped pacing in her tracks. Ramona looked at Charlotte, stunned. In a flash, she replayed everything that had happened since Charlotte arrived, everything Charlotte had said and done, and it all clicked into place.

"That's why you wanted to restore the inn."

Charlotte nodded, her gaze on the floor and her cheeks flushed bright red. "I didn't have any other options, and everything Sebastian tries just puts us deeper in debt. I was trying to figure something out for myself. And when I saw the inn, I saw an opportunity."

Ramona's mind whirred as she decided if she should be angry or not. She thought maybe Charlotte had been back to try to make things right, a reconciliation of sorts. And last night, she'd felt something she hadn't in a long time, like she had someone in her corner, someone who could understand. Now it seemed Charlotte was only looking out for herself again.

But Ramona knew firsthand the particular brand of terror that came with being in serious financial trouble. It was impossible for those who'd never experienced it to understand. The sleepless nights, the way food lost its taste. It was a wretched helplessness, an existential desperation.

She looked at her sister, hunched over with her face in her hands. She looked so small. A wave of empathy rolled over her, dissipating some of the heat flushing through her body.

"I'm sorry, Charlotte." She blew out a long

breath. "I know what it's like. I don't really know what to say. I'm out of options."

Charlotte stared at the wall, wringing her hands. A thick silence filled the air as Ramona grasped for something to say, coming up empty.

Suddenly, Charlotte grabbed Ramona's forearm. "Wait. I have an idea."

18

A few days later, Charlotte trudged up to the inn's front porch and shoved her shoulder into the door three times before it budged. The smell of sawdust filled the air as a man operating a table saw waved to her from the common room. She waved back and walked into the kitchen, eager for a glass of cold water.

The wall next to the kitchen table was opened up, and a man in blue overalls was unrolling a tape measure and recording something in a small note-book. Mariah was crouching in the entry facing the dining room, finger poised over the shutter button of an old film camera that looked vaguely familiar. Her hair was tied back in a ponytail, and her clothes were covered in dust and paint. She looked up at Charlotte, her eyes brightening.

"Hey, stranger!" she said with a grin. "I've barely seen you the last few days. Want some macaroni?" She gestured toward a pot boiling on the ancient stove. "It's either that or sandwiches again."

Charlotte laughed. "I know this must be a little strange for you being here. I'm sorry we don't have better accommodations."

"Are you kidding? This is great. Honestly. It's sort of like camping," she said, snapping a photo of the dining room, which was currently halfway through repairs of the hardwood floor.

"Is that the old camera your dad and I got you when you were a kid? I didn't know you still had it."

"Oh yeah, I take pictures all the time. I'm so glad I brought it...this island is gorgeous. Anyway, I've been documenting the progress on the house between tasks. I thought it would be cool to see everything before and after." She snapped another photo. "How was work?"

Charlotte drank a full glass of water in one go. "Good. Exhausting, but good."

As Charlotte had sat in the hospital next to Ramona, feeling the world slip from her fingertips, a thought sprang into her mind. She offered to take

Ramona's place as a waitress at The Windmill; she knew Sylvie would go for it, and the money Charlotte made would replace what Ramona would be losing until her leg healed. Ramona would be able to continue paying her bills for the time being.

She begged her mother and Ramona to wait to take the offer on the house until she had a chance to finish work on it. She explained about the newspaper critic Sylvie had put her in touch with, and how it had put Sylvie's restaurant on the map. The inn would provide a lot more money over time if they were the ones running it than if they took a one-time offer.

If the opening failed, Charlotte said, then they could sell it. Ramona had reluctantly agreed, saying that she would do her best to hold Giovanni off for a few weeks but that she couldn't guarantee how long he would wait.

It was at least something. Everything was banking on the critic for a successful reopening. Once guests started rolling in, she'd have money to pay Christian's contractors and take care of the personal loan she'd taken out. A chill scuttled across her skin and settled between her shoulder blades. It was a long shot, but she was in way too deep to turn back now.

"I'm going for a walk, honey," she said to Mariah. "Need to clear my head a bit." She gave her daughter a hug and headed back outside, her head swimming after another full day of panicked thoughts grinding through her mind.

AFTER AN HOUR OR SO, she looked up and realized her feet had carried her to Seashell Harbor. It was a balmy night; darkness was deepening across the clear sky, the first pinpricks of light forming. The harbor was far enough away from anything that all she could hear were the sounds of crickets carrying over in the warm breeze.

She jumped as she suddenly heard someone cursing under their breath near the old wooden dock that stretched into the black pool of water. She froze in her tracks, squinting until she made out a familiar figure hunched over a small wooden sailboat, untangling thick rope from a dock post.

"Christian?" she called out as she made her way toward the dock. He whipped around, scowling, until he met Charlotte's eyes and his face softened.

"Charlotte, hey," he said, running his hands

through his hair. "What're you doing out here so late?"

"Just taking a walk to clear my head a bit. You?"

He smiled. "Same. Long day and all."

"Yeah, and again, thank you so much for everything you're doing." She shifted anxiously on her feet. "It means a lot."

He waved her off. "Don't mention it. I love the work. Keeps me good and occupied." He paused before gesturing toward the sailboat with a tentative expression. "Want to join me? For old time's sake?"

THE BREEZE FELT cool against Charlotte's skin as the expanse of starlight drifted above them. Her heart fluttered like a hummingbird.

"I'd forgotten how beautiful it is here," she said, her neck craned toward the sky.

"It really is." Christian turned the rudder in the water and sighed deeply. "It's amazing how we get so caught up in the day-to-day that we never think to look up."

It was true. Adjusting to the different pace of Marina Cove had been hard. There was a distinct lack of the sorts of things she'd long become accustomed to: fashionable clothing stores, high-end art galleries, restaurant after classy restaurant. She'd kept wondering what people did around here for fun.

She'd never noticed how little there was to do on the island when she was growing up, until she moved to New York. She'd fallen in love with the endless beauty and scale of the great city, but years and years of ingratiating herself into her social circle kept her constantly rushing. Always another show, another gallery opening, another renowned chef brought in from overseas to demonstrate his haute cuisine to the endlessly consuming masses, the social nobility devouring experiences for sustenance like a man dying of hunger. Charlotte had always been happy to hop on the merry-go-round, the endless loops providing a powerful distraction from the painful thoughts and worries loitering ominously in the dark recesses of her mind.

"It's definitely a far cry from the city."

He nodded thoughtfully. "That's what I love about the island. Things move a little slower. It isn't flashy, for sure, but it suits me."

Charlotte considered that for a moment. "What's it like, living off the grid?"

A thin line appeared between his eyebrows. "Well, I don't know if I'd call it off the grid, exactly..."

He looked out toward the shoreline, in the direction of his cabin. "I guess I've become a bit of a hermit...I just like my privacy. And I don't go for...things. Cars, clothes, fancy houses and all. They don't make people happy. I like being able to count all my worldly possessions on one hand."

"Isn't it lonely, though? Aren't you giving up... relationships with other people by cutting yourself off like that?" Charlotte immediately regretted her words. She didn't know Christian anymore and didn't have any right to ask something so personal. "Sorry," she quickly stuttered. "That wasn't really what I meant to say."

He dropped his gaze to his hands. "No, it's okay. It's...hard to explain. I need control...after some of the things I've been through." He closed his eyes, and Charlotte noticed his shoulders tighten almost imperceptibly. "Limiting everything keeps me steady. Keeping busy with my hands, working and building, it keeps me grounded. But it has its costs." He looked up at Charlotte, a rueful smile breaking his grimace. "I'm sure you can imagine that women tend not to stick around long for someone who shuns the material world the way I do. Someone who doesn't have a cell phone. Or a place big enough for two people," he finished with a low chuckle.

Charlotte returned his smile. "So I guess you've never been...married or anything?"

"No." He shrugged. "I've had a few good relationships here and there, but like I said, they don't really last. I don't seem to be cut out for them."

His smile disappeared, and he turned to look out over the water. The harbor was so quiet you could hear a pin drop. Starlight reflected all around them like fireflies on a summer night.

"What about you?" Christian asked, breaking the silence. "How's married life in the big city?"

Charlotte's stomach twisted. Sebastian had been out of her mind for almost the whole day, and she was thankful for it. Every time she felt the heavy wedding ring on her finger, she felt a stab in her chest, a horrible reminder of everything that had happened.

Before she could stop to think, the words tumbled out. "Sebastian and I are separated." She felt a burning behind her eyes, but willed herself not to cry in front of Christian.

There was a long silence. "I'm very sorry, Charlotte," he said as she looked up into his face. The man she once had planned her whole future around, now practically a stranger. Charlotte nodded, and didn't add anything further. She felt a heaviness settle into her stomach.

Christian let out the sails, taking them deeper into the bay. Charlotte watched the swirling patterns of starlight in the black sky, her hands running idly along the smooth finish of the boat's wooden edge.

"Did you ever try to find me?"

The words had escaped into the air before she knew what she was saying. The silence that followed threatened to pull them both underwater. Christian met her gaze, and she felt a shiver run down her spine.

He looked into her eyes for what felt like an eternity. "I did."

He ran his hands over his face, exhaling hard as though he'd been holding his breath for a long time. "A long time ago. A few years after I left. I came back to Marina Cove, and heard you were gone. I went to the Seaside House to find you, and Ramona told me you'd moved to New York. That you...got married. Already had a couple of kids with him." Charlotte's heart broke in two as she heard his steady voice crack ever so slightly on the last words. He looked at her with a serious expression. "I didn't want to intrude. You had moved on."

A heavy hush sat between them for a long

moment. "Did you ever try to find me?" he asked. Lines of sadness formed on his face as he watched her tentatively.

Thoughts tumbled relentlessly around in Charlotte's mind. All the plans they'd made together, everything laid out neatly in front of them. All they'd had to do was walk the path.

The naïve wishes of a silly teenager, she supposed. Nothing more.

"I did try. The first thing I did when social media came around was try to find you. I had been asking my family, until we weren't really talking anymore. No one knew where you were." She blinked back tears in her eyes. "And at any rate, I was married," she added, just above a whisper.

Another uncomfortable silence stretched between them as Charlotte avoided eye contact.

"Well," Christian said suddenly, clearing his throat. "No sense in dwelling on the past, right? You have your family, and a great life in Manhattan. You've done really well for yourself. I'm really sorry again about your separation...I hope you two are able to work things out, if that's what you want." He paused, placing a hand gently on her forearm. "And I'd love for us to be friends, even though you're going to be leaving again soon. You can always talk to me, Charlotte. I'm always here for you."

Charlotte smiled weakly and placed a hand over his, the warmth of his touch spreading across her skin. She couldn't help but notice the grief in Christian's eyes. The corners of her mind pulled horribly at her, the thoughts and memories of everything she'd lost, everything *they'd* lost, threatening to tear her apart.

There was no way to undo the past. She'd never imagined that things would turn out the way they did, everything falling to pieces, nothing like the life she'd dreamed of all those years ago, together with the man she'd loved with her whole heart.

19

Charlotte carried herself slowly across the shore toward the inn, her conversation with Christian ringing in her ears. It seemed like several long days had passed since she got up to start her waitressing shift at The Windmill that morning, and the heavy throbs pulsating up from the soles of her shoes into her legs reminded her yet again how utterly exhausting it was to work on your feet all day. At least she had her nightly dance under the icy shower to soothe her weary bones.

As she shoved open the front door with all her might and went inside, Ollie barreled down the stairs and pelted her with large, wet smooches. He was followed by Mariah, a sly smile on her face.

"Hey, Mom, I think there's something for you out on the shore," she said, wiggling her eyebrows.

Confused but intrigued, Charlotte turned back toward the shore in front of the inn and started walking through the sand. Through the darkness, she could make out a few small lights. She turned back to Mariah, who grinned and gave her a thumbs-up.

The shore was only a few yards from the front door, but the dark was penetrating without the moon to illuminate the water. She didn't see the huge white silk and velvet cabana until she practically tripped over it. It was open on all four sides, and underneath was an expansive wooden table, at least ten chairs, and an ornate display of high-end French cuisine on silver serving platters, surrounded by vases of flowers and hundreds of tiny white candles. Three waiters in all-white tuxedoes stood together with their arms behind their backs at attention, and Chopin's expressive sweeps across the ivories carried over the breeze from some speaker she couldn't see.

At the head of the table, looking up at her with hesitancy in his eyes, was Sebastian.

"Charlotte," he said, standing promptly as she came upon the cabana.

Charlotte was almost too stunned to speak. "Sebastian...what are you doing here?"

He looked at her in supplication. "I'm sorry to drop in on you like this...I called several times, but I think your phone died again...I wanted to speak with you about something important. I thought we could have dinner together."

A waiter approached her wordlessly and motioned a gloved hand toward a chair next to Sebastian. Another waiter poured her a glass of ice water. She became suddenly aware of her appearance: the food-stained uniform she wore during her shift today, the comfortable but ridiculous-looking pair of large white tennis shoes that Sylvie had lent her. She quickly tucked in the hair shooting wildly out from her ponytail and wished she'd had a moment to check her makeup in the mirror before she'd come out here.

Seeing Sebastian was too unexpected for her to make any sense of what was going through her mind. Some distant part of her registered anger, felt intruded upon. Before she knew what she was doing, she grabbed a croissant from one of the silver platters and took an enormous bite.

Sebastian smiled and waited patiently for her to finish chewing. "It's good to see you, Charlotte. I know we talked about keeping our...distance. And I'm not trying to encroach on your space. I have some good news, and I wanted to tell you in person."

The look in his eyes was so sincere that the shock coursing through her began to evaporate. "It's okay. I'm just...I'm a little surprised is all. I didn't expect this." She looked around at the wait staff, the exquisite dinner. "How did you..."

"I thought you could use a nice dinner. Mariah told me that you've insisted on sleeping on the bare floor of one of the rooms here, and that things are a little...rustic." His mouth twisted subtly at the word. "I figured you might like a brief return to the finer things. And besides...I missed you." He made a gesture toward the waiter, who Charlotte saw was poised with a bottle of champagne.

She waved him off. "Not for me, thanks."

He shrugged, and motioned for the waiter to pour him a glass. He took a long drink, closing his eyes and sighing contentedly. "Charlotte, our money troubles are almost over."

Without making eye contact with the wait staff, he raised a hand toward the silver platters. They promptly began to load plates of food and set them before Charlotte and Sebastian. Charlotte bristled as Sebastian seemed to stretch the moment out before them, building the anticipation. "Okay...? What happened?" she said, unable to hide the irritation in her voice.

He motioned for her to eat. "Well. Alastair and I just wrapped up a major investment deal, with several more on the way. Back to our roots, pharma and biotech and all that. It's what we know best and what we should've been doing all along. The ink has dried. A lot of our debt is already gone." He grinned at her. "We're not out of the woods yet, of course, but it's a done deal. After this first one, more will follow. I told you I'd figure it out."

Something tickled the back of her mind, something she couldn't place. Despite the great news, she was surprised that she was still filled with apprehension. "Are you sure?"

"I'm sure. It's done. We have a couple of other irons in the fire. And that's not even the best part." He set down his fork and looked deeply into her eyes. Charlotte felt a tiny flutter in her heart. Despite everything, she missed him dearly.

"I don't know how you're still restoring this inn without any financial backing, but I have a solution for you. When you left, I know you talked about wanting something...for yourself. I know you wanted to work on something. So, I have a job for you."

He leaned forward in his chair, the starlight glimmering in his eyes. "Alastair is heading an offshoot of Carter Enterprises, and he needs a business partner. An equal partner. Someone he can trust with our new direction. I can think of no one better than you."

Charlotte scoffed irritably. "Sebastian, I don't know the first thing about any of that."

"It doesn't matter. You'll be trained as you go. I have it all set up already. Alastair will get you up to speed, and you'll have a whole team of people under you. Your corner office is already set up; it has a gorgeous view of the city skyline, you'll see. And take a look at this."

He pulled out his phone, tapped a few times, and turned the screen to face her. It was a picture of a shiny, bright-red convertible, parked in a spot with a sign that had Charlotte's name already printed on it. It was a newer model of the same car Slater had bought Brielle a few years back, and she'd commented to Sebastian once how nice it was.

"It's yours. Brand-new company lease. I know how much you liked it." He grabbed her hand and clasped it in his. "It's a great opportunity, Charlotte. A fresh start. For both of us."

He lifted an index finger and reached into the inside pocket of his black tuxedo with his other hand. A small rectangular box of velvet emerged, and he set it on the table in front of her.

Charlotte's mind spun frantically. It was all too much information at once. She opened the box and pulled out a stunning white gold tennis necklace encrusted with brilliant crystal-clear diamonds that glittered in the candlelight. Sebastian rose from his seat and stood behind her, gently clasping the necklace around her neck. Charlotte felt frozen in her seat, unable to make sense of the jumble of thoughts slamming through her mind.

"Here's a small gift. I thought of you when I saw it. This is just the start of what's to come. I know we haven't figured things out between us yet...but I want you to have everything, Charlotte. I want you to be home in New York, and not stuck here mired in some project. You deserve only the best." He crouched in front of her, staring deep into her eyes, filling her stomach with butterflies. "I want you to be happy, and I will be forever sorry for everything I did. I hope that we can find our way through this. I love you."

Charlotte felt the throbbing in her feet and the weariness in her muscles. She was well and truly exhausted to her core. The last few weeks had taken everything out of her, and despite her very best efforts, she found herself so much worse off than when she'd started. Money due for the loan shark she'd been stupid enough to borrow from, a broken-down inn with no signs of being anywhere near completion, and no way of paying for the pool of contractors toiling away every day without a smashing success of an opening that would give her throngs of guests throwing money from their wallets. The odds were so remote. Everything was balanced on a razor's edge.

Sebastian's offer was the answer to all her problems. All she'd wanted was to get back to Manhattan, to her home, to Brielle and her friends and the knowledge that everything would be okay. She'd wanted something to do with her life, her future, and this could be it.

Maybe this could be their way back to each other.

But something was flitting around in her stomach. Some feeling she didn't want to shine a light on, but it persisted. She closed her eyes for a moment, inhaled the fresh saltwater air that cooled her lungs, and stilled the white noise in her mind.

Although she couldn't deny the strong feelings that ran through her in Sebastian's presence, he had broken her heart. She met his gaze, feeling ice water roll down her back as she recalled the words she'd heard in the stairwell that day a million years ago.

She was no fool. No matter what he said, his offer came with strings attached. This only seemed like a solution at first glance.

Besides, Charlotte had returned to Marina Cove to think about what to do next, to figure out how to make something of herself, to break her years of complacency. If Sebastian was the one lining up this job, he could also take it away. Charlotte had heard Sebastian's "solutions" many times before. She no longer trusted his plans.

"I can't." Charlotte closed her eyes, ignoring the cold sweat filming her body. She didn't want to feel obligated to get back together with Sebastian; she wanted to decide it for herself, for the right reasons. "I'm sorry, Sebastian. I can't."

Sebastian's face fell as his eyebrows knitted together. "I understand that you're trying to figure things out...Maybe you just need some time. Can you at least think about it? Please?"

Charlotte hesitated for a long moment before nodding once. Sebastian's face softened and he exhaled a long breath. They began to eat their dinner, the waiters scurrying around them, continuously dusting crumbs from the table with tiny silver brushes and bowing deeply. The diamond necklace Sebastian had given her felt heavy on Charlotte's neck as she forced back the familiar vertigo, the pins and needles in her arms and legs as panic coursed through her body, the expanse of uncertainty stretching endlessly before her.

20

The days after Sebastian's impromptu visit marched on relentlessly, a haze of scrubbing, painting, rushing around the restaurant taking endless orders, and crashing on the hardwood floor that Charlotte had eventually become accustomed to and now felt almost comfortable. Almost.

Each day, Charlotte silently kicked herself for not immediately jumping on Sebastian's offer, but reminded herself that he had given her false hope many times before, and it had only ever made things worse. They were still deeply in debt despite his windfall; he was assuming the success would continue. She had taken matters into her own hands for a reason. And she was in too deep now anyway; people were counting on her to see the project through. Ramona. Her mother. She couldn't abandon them a second time.

After another long shift at The Windmill, Charlotte kicked off her shoes and stared up the long staircase to the inn's second floor, where more endless hours of work awaited her. She sighed heavily and looked to the dining room, where she saw Ramona balanced on a stepladder, a crutch under one arm and a paint roller in her hands, her clothes splattered with white paint. Ever since their night at the overlook, sharing their grief over their father, Charlotte had felt a tiny shift between them. Ramona no longer openly scowled at her. It was something.

Charlotte raised her hand in a small wave. Ramona hesitated for a moment, and waved back. And if Charlotte wasn't totally mistaken, her eyes didn't communicate her usual disdain. It was practically a full-body bear hug.

Charlotte made her way into one of the guest bedrooms and got to work. As she dunked a rag into the bucket filled with cleaning solution and dragged it across the filthy floorboard, she couldn't help but replay memories from her life with Sebastian. Her hand in his as he whisked her down narrow cobble-stone streets in Madrid under the moonlight. Laughing and dizzy with elation while dancing a waltz at The Vienna, her elegant dress sweeping around her. Mariah's tiny fingers wrapped around his thumb on the night she was born, tears in his eyes.

Her entire adult life was wrapped up in his. They had children together. They'd been happy. Nothing he could do would ever erase that.

Perhaps, in the end, she'd be able to forgive him for what he'd done. He clearly regretted what happened and wanted her back. Did she really want to end everything over it?

Charlotte groaned as her back spasmed while reaching high into a corner with her wet rag, dirty water streaming down her arm. Despite all the efforts being put into the inn, even with Mariah and Ramona working relentlessly alongside her, it somehow still looked like very little progress had been made. Charlotte felt the heavy burden around her neck of the looming repayment of her personal loan. To make matters worse, one of Ramona's lenders had started hounding her repeatedly, calling her at all hours of the day and night, and virtually everything Charlotte made waitressing had gone to appeasing him. Her nights were spent tossing and turning, sweating profusely and snuggling with Ollie for comfort, making her feel like a frightened child.

Thankfully, Christian had continued to assuage his contractors—Charlotte told him her lender had "dropped the ball" again and that she would work it out, but she promised him she was good for the money. She hated herself for lying repeatedly to Christian, but she was desperate, and knew that once the critical review came in and guests started filling the rooms, she'd have no trouble paying everyone back. All she needed was time.

Her phone chimed in the corner as it powered back on after it had died again, followed by a second chime that meant she had a voicemail. Charlotte was usually connected at the hip with her phone at all times, but since she'd been staying on the island, she kept forgetting about it altogether for long stretches.

Eager for a break, she wiped her wet hands on the back of her shirt and lifted her phone to play the message. A man with an accent that was inconsistently halfway between American and British began to speak in a rumbling tenor.

Hello, Ms. Keller, this is Felix Caldwell. I hope you do not mind my calling you directly; Sylvie provided me your information. I wanted to inform you that next week

I will be leaving the country for a few months; my wife and I will be summering in Greece, you see, and we will be back at the start of autumn. I look forward to visiting your little inn when I return. Ciao!

Charlotte's heartbeat thundered in her ears as she dialed the number next to the message, her hands trembling. They didn't have anywhere near that long to wait. Ramona had said she could only hold off the investor who wanted the inn for a few weeks. Felix answered on the fourth ring.

"Felix."

Charlotte's mind suddenly emptied. Her mouth felt like cotton. "Hello?" she managed to choke out.

"Yes?" he said, a note of irritation in his voice.

Charlotte shook her head and closed her eyes to focus. "Yes, hello, Mr. Caldwell, this is Charlotte Keller. You left me a voicemail." Silence on the other end of the line. Charlotte looked at the phone, thinking maybe the call had dropped. "I heard you were going to be traveling for a few months."

A pause. "Is there something I can do for you?"

Charlotte blew out a long breath. "You had said you were leaving in a week; I was wondering if there was any possibility of you visiting us before you leave?" She decided to stroke his ego a bit. "I know it's a lot to ask, but we were hoping to reopen soon, and we greatly respect your work and your opinion. We would be eternally grateful for your...input before we begin having guests."

Another very long silence. She heard people talking in the background, then him speaking in a curt tone to someone. *"Ristretto macchiato. Doppio. Light on the foam, or I send it back."* She heard shuffling before he addressed Charlotte again. "I will be there in six days. Good day." *Click.*

CHARLOTTE BOUNDED down the stairs and asked a man who was holding a handful of electrical wires protruding from a large hole in the wall where she could find Christian. She pried open the front door and ran to the side of the house where he was leaning over a table saw, cutting through two-by-fours, sawdust spraying over his body as he grinned and swung his hips enthusiastically to Jim Croce playing from a portable speaker.

"Christian!" she shouted over the noise. He looked up in surprise, and a large smile creased his face. He turned off the saw and took off his safety glasses. "Charlotte, hey," he said, running a hand through his wavy hair. "It's good to see you."

Charlotte tried to ignore the fluttering in her chest as his eyes seemed to penetrate into hers. "I need to talk to you," she said breathlessly over the music.

He shut off the speaker, a small line appearing between his eyebrows. "Sure thing, what's going on?"

She explained about Felix Caldwell, and how crucial his review would be to a successful reopening. She recounted her phone call, how he would be staying at the inn six days from now.

He looked at her with an expression of incredulity. "Okay...Why didn't you just wait until he gets back?" He shook his head. "Nothing will be ready in six days, Charlotte."

Charlotte racked her brain as she tried to think of a way to steer clear of telling Christian about her financial issues and decided on a partial truth. It was better than completely lying.

"Ramona won't wait that long. She's talking to a real estate group who's offered to buy the inn and the property. She isn't as...confident as I am that we can do better by running the inn ourselves." She forced down the guilt churning in her stomach. "You and I know the potential for this place. But if we don't get things opened soon, she's going to sell. I obviously thought we'd have a lot longer than six days, but without a glowing review, it'll take forever to spread the word to guests and get this place profitable, and we don't have that kind of time."

He shook his head. "I'm really sorry, Charlotte, but it isn't possible. We're still sorting through electrical problems, you've still got major HVAC issues... I mean, we've got walls punched open and whole sections of old plumbing removed. I don't know what to tell you, but you'll have to cancel this guy's stay. It isn't ready."

Charlotte felt her face flush in frustration. "I can't let Ramona sell the Seaside House, Christian. This inn has been in my family for generations. We can't just let someone else take it from us." She ran her hands over her face, trying to keep her composure. "Can't we just get one of the rooms ready for now? He won't need to see any of the other rooms, we can just tell him we're still finishing painting or something."

Christian stared at her for what felt like a long time. Charlotte shifted uncomfortably, averting her eyes from the intensity of his gaze.

"Charlotte...It's really out of my hands. I understand what you're saying. But the issues...they're fundamental to the whole house. Even if we resolved those and only focused on one room...like we've discussed, it would still be weeks before it's even possible, and it won't be pretty. In my professional opinion, this place isn't anywhere near ready for guests." Charlotte winced inwardly; he still didn't know that she and Mariah had been sleeping in the inn every night.

"Please, Christian. I'm asking you as a friend. There has to be something you can do. I'm desperate."

"It isn't a matter of friendship, Charlotte...I want to help you. But I can't wave a magic wand. You asked me to help with the inn. I have no control over the extent of the damage...Whoever tried to open this place was going to have to deal with the problems before accepting guests. I won't have it on my hands, I'm sorry."

Charlotte clenched her fists and felt her lips form a thin, straight line. The words came out before she could stop them. "So that's it? You're just refusing to help me?"

He gawked at her. "Refusing to help? I'm working for free here, if you recall...I'm not seeing a cent from all the work I've put into it. You're not being reasonable."

"I'm not being reasonable? You have no idea

what I'm going through here, Christian. You don't understand."

He was suddenly upon her, and took her hands in his. "Then talk to me, Charlotte! Help me understand!"

A distant part of her mind registered that she wasn't being fair, that it wasn't Christian's fault that she found herself in such a desperate predicament. But the chaos and grief of the past weeks, the endless nights without sleep, the abject terror of being broke and having no idea what her future would hold had taken a serious toll on her. She felt unable to keep her head above water, the gravity of her situation pulling her down, deeper and deeper.

She pulled her hands from his. "I need this to work. I will make this work, with or without you."

Sadness etched his face as he lowered his gaze. "I can't compromise on this. I won't do it. I'm sorry."

Charlotte forced down the lump in her throat. "Then I guess I'm on my own."

"Charlotte..."

"I'm sorry. I know you don't understand. But I'm not going to let my family home be taken from me. I'll find a way. Thank you for your help with every-thing. I'll let you know as soon as I'm cleared to pay your contractors for what they've done so far. I'll take it from here."

Charlotte turned on her heel and made her way back to the inn, careful not to look back. She was afraid to see the look she knew he had on his face; there was no way she could handle it right now.

Now was the time for desperate measures. She had one final trick up her sleeve.

"Yeah, I'll have it ready for ya. Some drywall, coupl'a new pipes and wires, slap on some paint, we'll getcha goin'."

Charlotte stared at Gary, the contractor she'd dialed yesterday in a blind panic, who'd arrived three hours late this morning. In her initial search for contractors on the mainland, everyone was booked months out, but at the very bottom of the list was a company based in Boston that had mostly one-star reviews. She'd ignored them then, of course, but when she called after her argument with Christian, Gary had answered on the first ring. They could be there tomorrow, he'd said. Charlotte had sensed Gary was too eager, a note of something that sounded like hunger in his voice, but she needed someone now.

Charlotte watched him look around the common room, sucking on a wooden toothpick. "What about the electricity? And the heater..."

"It's June, doll. You run the heater around here in the summer?" He barked a quick, condescending laugh. "Electrical didn't look too bad from what I saw. Plumbing we can get going. Well enough, anyway."

A heady mixture of hope and guilt and fear washed over her. "Are you sure? My last contractor said..."

"Ah, I don't know why he's got his undies all twisted. Things ain't so bad around here. I mean, if you just need things open for one night..."

"Well, we'd want to open the other rooms as soon as possible after that...the person staying is going to be publishing a review..."

He cut her off. "It's no problem. My guys are quick, sweethaht, you'll see. And don't worry about those reviews, people just like to complain." He rubbed his hands together briefly. "I'll need a down payment up front, of course..."

There went the rest of her personal loan. As far as Charlotte was concerned, it was a small price to pay for the sliver of hope she now held. She forced back the alarm bells ringing in her head and motioned for him to follow her into the kitchen. "Let's get started."

THE NEXT SIX days disappeared in a flash of sawdust and paint, men lumbering around and yelling to each other over the loud blare of heavy metal music playing constantly. She hadn't seen Christian again after he called off his contractors. Any chance of rekindling a friendship now was pretty much ruined after how she'd handled things, insulting his work ethic and basically firing him, but she didn't know what else to do. Charlotte could barely contain the rising panic as each day passed, bringing her closer to Felix's arrival.

Ramona had been argumentative about the change in plans. She didn't see how things would be done correctly. But to Charlotte's surprise, she'd relented fairly quickly. She confirmed that there was no way to hold off the realty group until Felix returned from Greece. After first hearing about the critic arriving so soon, she'd called Giovanni, who had been pressuring her to come to his offices in Boston to sign the paperwork, and he gave her a deadline of a month for an answer before they moved on. Ramona wouldn't say it, but Charlotte sensed that she felt that the plan to reopen would fail and she'd be selling the inn. Her mother hadn't said anything at all, but Charlotte couldn't look her in the eye, afraid of what she would see there.

Charlotte and Sylvie had gone shopping at Danny's store and selected new sheets, pillows, a comforter, and some fancy-looking soaps and candles for the room Felix would be staying in. The giant holes in the drywall on the main floor had been patched up and painted over, and Ramona had helped Charlotte drag a wooden dresser to cover a hole in the wall with protruding cables that Gary and his contractors had missed.

Charlotte knew, of course, that the work being done wasn't the right quality, but she hoped that the inn's old-fashioned charm, the ocean waves splashing against the shore mere yards from the front door, and the surrounding natural beauty of Marina Cove would paint a picture of endless poten-tial in Felix's mind, even if things weren't quite perfect just yet. It was a long shot, but it was all Charlotte had.

Mariah pointed out that some sort of online presence would be necessary. She snapped and developed a few photos of the house and the surrounding beachfront, and worked with Charlotte and Ramona to develop an inviting description of the Seaside House. Mariah put together a barebones website in a flash that filled Charlotte with pride for her daughter. It was simple but very professional. Mariah helped Charlotte create a new profile on the leading review site for vacation rentals so guests could leave their star ratings and comments after their stay.

Sylvie had volunteered for The Windmill to provide meals for Felix's stay, promising that her cooks could whip up a few "fancy" dishes. At the last minute, she suggested that Charlotte bake some of the pastries she'd shown Sylvie how to make, saying that they'd be sure to knock his socks off. So one night before Felix's arrival, she found herself elbow-deep in thick dough with Sylvie and Mariah in the inn's kitchen, Dean Martin crooning from the old record player. They'd made homemade strawberry lemonade and ordered pizza, and had all the windows open, the warm, salty breeze coursing pleasantly through the house.

"What are these called again, Mom?" Mariah asked, dropping cubed butter into a processor filled with flour and salt and looking rather pleased with herself.

"Mille-feuilles. It's one of my favorites. I used to make these all the time with my friend Amélie when your father and I were staying in Paris before you were born." Her stomach clenched as she thought of Sebastian. How they'd been so in love then, a beautiful lifetime stretched out before them. "I learned to make all sorts of things."

"They're to die for, Mariah, you'll see," said Sylvie. They'd struck up a friendship of their own since Mariah's unexpected arrival on the island, and it warmed Charlotte's heart to have her best friend and her daughter there with her. It had gone a long way toward distracting her from her panic. Felix would be here in under twenty-four hours and Charlotte felt frantic, dread blooming in her chest and her body covered in sweat.

They joked around and fell into easy conversation as they continued with the array of delicious pastries that Charlotte hoped might place a finger on the scales for Felix. Maybe Sylvie could even give the recipes to her cooks to provide for the inn on an ongoing basis once Charlotte returned to New York. It would be a great way to add some value for the guests.

"Charlotte..." Sylvie began, but then she shook her head slightly, seeming to reconsider her words. "Are you sure this is the right thing to do?"

An awkward silence followed as Charlotte's heart sank. "I know it's a little slapdash. But I've said it over and over again...Ramona will sell the inn if we don't open it soon. I can't help that Felix will be gone for months. I don't see another way."

Sylvie furrowed her eyebrows and placed a hand on Charlotte's forearm. "I told you...I can help Ramona buy some time." Charlotte knew Sylvie was carefully skirting around the issue of her bankruptcy; Mariah still had no inkling of the hole Charlotte and Sebastian were in. "I'm concerned that Felix coming here might not...work out like you think it will."

Charlotte shook her head. "We're not borrowing anything from you, Sylvie. It wouldn't make a difference anyway. Ramona's investor won't wait long enough for us to do things differently."

Mariah stopped pulsing the butter in the processor and cleared her throat. "Why can't you and Dad just loan Aunt Ramona some money to tide her over? I don't trust Gary, Mom...He's a barbarian. I don't think they're doing the best job. Plus, he keeps calling me 'sweethaht' and I think I might smack him good the next time he does it."

Charlotte laughed despite the tightening in her chest as she thought about hiding the truth of the state of their finances from Mariah. Not to mention the separation...

"Ramona just needs to see that we can run the inn ourselves. I think we can do it." Charlotte ran her hands over her apron and sighed. "I appreciate your concern, both of you, I really do. I know things aren't ideal. But I have every hope that this will work out well. And if it doesn't, well, then Ramona can just sell the inn, and she'll be fine for now." *And I'll be fine too; I'll just lose everything I've worked for here and rely on Sebastian and his schemes again, which never help, and I'll be homeless before the summer ends and my life will be over, that's all.* "We'll be fine. It'll work out. It has to."

Charlotte just barely caught Sylvie and Mariah sharing a look before they both quickly returned to the tasks at hand. Charlotte blinked back tears as a fresh wave of nausea rolled over her body. One way or another, everything was coalescing, all the chaos of the last weeks converging to a single point tomorrow that would determine the course of her future. Her thoughts wandered to Christian, and the look in his eyes as she turned away from him yesterday. To Sebastian and the job he'd offered her back home. To Sylvie, and their rekindled friendship.

She thought of Ramona, and her mother, and the false hope she'd given them. Fire flushed her face as she thought of her father, and what he would've thought about Charlotte now.

21

C harlotte paced the inn's front porch the following night, pulling the blue wool cardigan that Ramona had lent her tightly around herself. It was past midnight; sleep would no doubt be elusive tonight. The air was unusually chilly; the distant rolling of thunder and the earthy smell of rain carried over the swift breeze that swept her long hair all around her. The full moon shone brightly and spilled across the expanse of sand and water, giving it a dreamlike midday quality.

Earlier this afternoon, a knock at the door revealed a short, bald man with black horn-rimmed glasses and a silk bow tie holding a tiny leather note-book and a small suitcase. Felix's manner was polite but terse, as though he had a hundred more interesting places to be. Charlotte's stomach clenched each time he paused while she gave him the tour, trying fruitlessly to read the expressions on his face as he jotted in his notebook. As long as he didn't go looking underneath or behind anything, or ask to explore the other bedrooms, they just might be in the clear. Once or twice her mouth went dry as Felix's lips seemed to subtly twist, an almost imperceptible furrow forming in his brow. Charlotte yelped out loud when the power went out for a moment, and tried ridiculously to cover it with a cough.

Still, Felix seemed to be enjoying himself. He sat at the head of the long dining room table and finished everything Sylvie and two of her employees brought him. He borrowed a Tolstoy book from the library and passed a few hours reading by the fire, sipping tea and devouring pastry after pastry they'd prepared for him, occasionally tapping his finger to his chin thoughtfully and scribbling a note. Charlotte and Mariah did their best to politely tend to him while keeping to themselves, Charlotte wringing her hands as she paced the kitchen and listened intently to his movements in the other rooms while Mariah did her best to calm her down.

She peeked through the window fretfully as Felix rocked in a wicker rocking chair, quietly watching the last rays of sunshine spread across the great sapphire sea, his bow tie removed and his notebook untouched on a side table. As the stars revealed themselves in the moonlit sky, he finally rose from his chair. Charlotte darted back into the kitchen and busied herself with some dishes when he poked his head in.

"Might I trouble you for a last spot of tea, Miss Keller? I will be retiring to my room shortly."

Charlotte's heart was thudding hard against her ribs, her nerves making her palms slick with sweat. "Of course, Mr. Caldwell, I'll be right up with it. Is everything...satisfactory?"

He gave her a knowing smirk. "You will see everything in my review. I will say, however, that the view from the porch is..." He seemed to struggle for the right word. "Magnificent."

Her cheeks flushed. "Thank you, Mr. Caldwell. Please let me know if I can get you anything else. Mariah and I will be right down the hall from you."

He nodded and started up the ancient wooden staircase. She grimaced as the creaks and pops reverberated throughout the house, ricocheting across the walls like firecrackers in a steel drum. There was nothing more she could do tonight; she closed her eyes and whispered a silent prayer that her home had left a positive impact on Felix, and gently held the hopes of her future in her hands like a dove with a broken wing.

SOMETHING PULLED at Charlotte's mind, tendrils creeping into her dreams and tearing her from the fitful sleep she'd finally fallen into. She blinked in the darkness, and wiped the sweat that covered her forehead. Confused, she sat up and listened carefully.

Her phone alarm was going off, muffled by the ocean waves crashing against the shoreline outside. The only other sounds were Mariah's soft snores from the pile of blankets next to her and the hard patter of rainfall on the roof.

As she rubbed the sleep from her eyes, she padded over to her phone to check the time only to find that it was dead. At that moment, she realized what had pulled her from her sleep.

The alarm wasn't coming from her phone; it was coming from the hallway. And all through the room was the strong smell of smoke.

"*Mariah!*" she screamed, feeling her body weaken with panic. She shook Mariah awake frantically. "*Wake up! I smell smoke!*"

Mariah jolted awake and shot to her feet. In a daze, Charlotte spun around frantically to get her bearings. She grabbed a T-shirt from the floor and pulled it to her face before bursting through the bedroom door.

The hallway was filled with smoke, and a wall of heat struck her with such force that it almost knocked her over.

"*The house is on fire!*" she screamed. Tears burst from her eyes as she struggled to catch her breath. "*Felix!*" She squinted through the smoke down the hallway and could see the wooden railing that led to the stairwell had fallen across the landing and was on fire.

Without thinking, she sprinted across the hallway and leaped over the flames, then crawled on her hands and knees to get beneath the smoke line, the sweat on her palms making her slip and slide on the hardwood. "*Mariah, cover your mouth with something and get outside now!*" she yelled behind her. She reached Felix's door and forced it open, hearing a sizzling from her hand as she quickly yanked it away from the hot doorknob.

"*Felix, get up! There's a fire!*" She shook him furiously and pulled him from the bed.

"What the...what is this?" he yelled irritably, tearing off his sleep mask and pulling out his earplugs. A sliver of moonlight shone through the wooden slats of the blinds, and Charlotte could see Felix's nose scrunch up and his eyes go wide, his face blanching.

Charlotte tore off her cardigan, rolled it up, and pressed it against his face to stop him from inhaling the smoke. "*Hold this and follow me!*"

They crouched together across the hallway landing, and Charlotte motioned for him to jump over the flames of the fallen railing as the smoke detector blared through the hallway. Mariah was on the other side, screaming and beckoning Charlotte. Felix shook his head once, his eyes saucers as they darted around, searching for another way out. She grabbed him by the shoulders. "*We have to go now! Jump!*"

She clutched his hand, and they both took a running start and jumped over the burning pile of wood, flames licking at her bare feet. Mariah grabbed Charlotte by her shirt, and they all bounded down the stairs toward the front door. The smoke wasn't as thick down on the main floor, but she could feel a wall of heat emanating from the center of the house near the library, and blue and red flames flickered on the wall next to the staircase. She grabbed the front door with all her might, but it wouldn't budge. "*Come on, not now!*" Charlotte shrieked. Mariah pulled with her, and on the third try, the door burst open, almost knocking them over. Charlotte grabbed Felix by the collar of his silk pajamas and pulled them out into the pouring rain.

Charlotte fell to her knees and gasped for air as Mariah came up next to her, her body shuddering and racked with sobs. "Is everyone okay?" Charlotte yelled, inhaling the glorious cold air that poured into her lungs.

"I'm okay," Mariah choked out. Felix sat hard on the ground and wiped his face with Charlotte's cardigan. "I'm okay," he said, staring at the ground and shaking his head.

"*Charlotte!*" she heard someone shouting from the shoreline. "*Charlotte!*" The rain fell hard around them, making it hard to see anything beyond a few feet in front of them. Suddenly, Christian was on his knees next to her, pulling her and Mariah into his arms. "Is everyone okay?" he yelled, glancing up at the house.

Charlotte and Mariah nodded shakily as Charlotte burst into tears. "How did you..." Charlotte spluttered.

Christian tore off his coat and wrapped it around them. "I was out sailing, I couldn't sleep...I was coming in as the storm started when I saw something orange flickering in the trees down here. I ran here as fast as I could—"

The sound of barking came from the house, interrupting Christian. Charlotte shot to her feet. *"OLLIE!"* she screamed at the top of her lungs, her vision narrowing to a tunnel as she felt her heart stop. *"Ollie! NO NO NO no no he's still in the house!"* She sprinted back toward the front door before something pulled her back, stopping her in her tracks.

"You can't go back in there, Charlotte!" Christian yelled. He dragged her back a few feet, her arms flailing wildly as she screamed. Christian went over to Felix and grabbed him by the shoulders.

"You see that house over there?" He pointed to Ramona's bungalow around the corner. "Go there and call 911. *NOW!*" He pulled Felix to his feet and shoved him in the direction of the house. Felix stumbled and dropped the cardigan, wiped the rain from his eyes, and started running toward Ramona's.

Christian's eyes bored into Charlotte's. "No

matter what, *do not come inside the house!*" Before she could respond, he took a deep breath, grabbed the sopping wet cardigan from the ground, and pulled it to his face before barreling toward the front door and slamming himself through it.

"*Christian, NO!*" Charlotte screamed, sobs racking her body as Mariah reached around her chest with her arms and held her in place. Red and yellow tendrils of fire escaped from the backside of the roof, flickering against the rainfall and pouring black smoke into the sky.

Charlotte's throat was hoarse from screaming, and she was trembling all over. In the panic and chaos of fleeing the house, Ollie had completely slipped her mind. He'd taken to sleeping down in the dining room since Mariah had moved into the bedroom with her, and she hadn't seen him during their escape. And now Christian had gone into the house to find him.

She would never, ever forgive herself if something happened to either one of them. It would be her fault.

Charlotte wept as Mariah pulled her tight, rocking back and forth, her eyes darting frantically around the house. Flames had spread to the front door. *What was Christian thinking?* She heard sirens in the distance, and closed her eyes against the pouring rain. Every second stretched out into an eternity.

Suddenly, one of the side windows shattered, and she saw a pair of hands tearing away shards of glass and wood before laying a tablecloth over the broken glass on the bottom of the window frame. Christian's legs swung over the edge, then he hopped out of the frame and ran toward Charlotte. In his arms was Ollie, his huge frame wrapped against Christian's chest, panting happily and wagging his tail as though he was taking a fun ride somewhere.

"*Ollie!* Oh my God, Christian..." Charlotte cried as she threw herself against Christian, embracing him and burrowing her head into his chest. Ollie licked her face wildly, and a loud laugh escaped through Charlotte's sobs as she stroked his head. "Oh, Ollie, I'm so sorry, I'm so so sorry..." she whispered into his fur.

"Christian," she stammered, gazing into his eyes for a long moment. She was unable to finish the sentence. Mariah put her arm around Charlotte's waist and whispered a quiet thank you to Christian, her hand on his. Christian pulled Charlotte in tighter and stroked her hair soothingly as the firetrucks arrived and the hard rain poured down on them from the black sky.

RAMONA RUBBED her eyes and stretched her back in the uncomfortable folding chair that she'd pulled up to the hospital bed. Her leg throbbed painfully in its cast. The room was completely silent save for the steady beeping of the heart rate monitor and the whirring of dry, frigid air being pumped in from a ceiling vent. Ella was pacing near the window, wringing her hands but not saying a word.

Ramona's heart skipped a beat as Charlotte's eyes blinked open. "Charlotte?"

Ella ran to the bed and grasped Charlotte's hand tightly in hers. Charlotte closed her eyes, and two tiny trickles of tears fell down her face. "Is everyone okay?" she asked.

Ramona blinked back the tears threatening to form. "You're okay, and everyone else is fine. We just spoke to the doctor when you fell asleep. No one who was in the house shows any symptoms of smoke inhalation. The fire had just started when you all escaped. Christian, Mariah, and Felix were all monitored and have already been discharged;

they're just resting in their rooms. Ollie is okay; my neighbor took him to the vet to have him examined. All things considered, we were lucky."

Charlotte brushed the tears from her eyes. "We're going to have to stop meeting like this," she said, a small smile quirking her mouth. Ramona laughed, and felt a tear steal down her cheek.

Charlotte exhaled slowly and shook her head. "This is all my fault. Everyone warned me. I'm so sorry, Ramona..." She looked into Ramona's eyes, her face etched with guilt. "I'm so sorry."

Ramona shook her head. "It isn't your fault. No one could've predicted the furnace causing a fire, even if it was old." She gripped Charlotte's forearm. "Mom and I knew the issues just as well as you did, and we didn't stop you. We just had the furnace inspected a few months ago, and he said it was running fine, it was just on its last leg."

Charlotte grimaced. "Felix must've turned the heat on. It was pretty cold last night. I didn't even have the contractors look at the heating...it's June..." She closed her eyes and shook her head again, and Ramona saw her clench her fists. "I'm sure the house is ruined."

"All that matters is that everyone is okay." Ella's voice was hoarse and trembling slightly. She cleared her throat. "But the damage wasn't as bad as it could've been. The firefighters told us that we were lucky it was raining so hard; the foundation and most of the rooms are fine. The fire went straight up from the furnace room through the far guest rooms to the roof, which opened up enough to get dowsed from the rainfall. It could've been a lot worse."

Charlotte stared out through the window. The sky was just beginning to lighten, but the clouds were dark and the rain continued to pummel down relentlessly.

"Everything's over, obviously. Even with insurance covering the fire damage, the house will take forever to fix now. Felix's review is going to be horrible, which tanks our reputation before we've even begun." Charlotte pulled Ramona's hands into hers and gave her a look that made the hair on Ramona's arms stand up. "You have to sell the inn, Ramona. I never should have gotten involved. I will do whatever I have to do to help you convince them to buy it."

A pit formed in Ramona's stomach. One of the first things she'd done as soon as she heard that everyone was okay was to call Giovanni. To her relief, he was an early riser. She barely finished explaining the situation before he cut her off and told her he wasn't concerned, that he was ready to move forward and that his group would handle the restoration even with the fire damage. Part of her was surprised, but she didn't want to press further.

"The realty group is still interested," Ramona said, not meeting Charlotte's eye. "I'm going to meet with them in Boston next week to sign the papers. It's still an insulting offer, but it'll keep me and Mom afloat for a while, until we figure out what's next."

Charlotte put her face in her hands. "I am so sorry. I really wanted this to work out for us."

Hot tears formed in Ramona's eyes, and this time she didn't stop them. She clenched Charlotte's hand. "The deck was stacked against us before you ever got here. We wanted this to work as much as you did. It would've been nice, but..." She was unsure what to say as a thousand different feelings coursed through her all at once. She knew this meant that Charlotte would be returning to New York. Despite the flickers of anger that still threatened when she looked into Charlotte's eyes, a significant part of her felt something else. Ramona closed her eyes, and instead of pushing the feelings down, she tried to listen to them for a change. A heaviness had settled into her bones.

It was grief. Something had shifted between

them in the weeks since Charlotte arrived. It was subtle, but Ramona had never forgotten that little girl she'd looked up to, who had her back and helped guide her through her young life until everything had changed.

And now, Charlotte was leaving again. Everything would go back to the way it was. Charlotte could never undo leaving Ramona with their mother for all those years, but Ramona was exhausted from holding onto the anger for so long.

After a long silence, Charlotte sat up, her mouth forming a thin line and a look of resolve in her eyes. "Mom...Ramona...I have something I want to tell you. I'm done holding everything in. I'm done keeping secrets. Life is too short, and I don't want to run anymore."

Ramona's pulse hammered in her temples as she looked at her mother. Ella nodded once, grabbed a chair, and pulled it up next to the bed. Charlotte reached for their hands, closed her eyes, and exhaled slowly, fresh tears falling down her cheeks and dappling her hospital gown.

"I want to tell you the truth about why I left Marina Cove," she whispered.

22

Charlotte closed her eyes and basked in the warmth spreading across her skin from the day's last rays of sunshine, inhaling the fresh, warm saltwater air and listening to the sea birds fluttering their wings in the orange and lavender sky. Today was her day, the day her future began, the day she would escape from the lonely confines of the Seaside House and begin her life with Christian.

She'd called him earlier and asked him to meet her on the shore in front of Keamy's lot when he was finished with work, saying only that she wanted to go for a walk. He'd been working constantly lately; his father's health had declined further over the months, and Christian was busy learning the ropes of the custom furniture business he hoped to take over. Charlotte had really gotten to know his father's kind manner, his meticulous nature as she watched him slowly carving ornate details into the furniture that people from all over the island and the mainland paid handsomely for. She listened intently as he guided her through managing the books, the business side that she'd be handling alongside Christian. Every day she spent learning with them was another step closer to her life with him.

But time crawled at the Seaside House. Her mother ignored her completely and rarely left her bedroom, refusing Charlotte's endless pleas to see a counselor. Ramona hadn't spoken more than a handful of words to her in months; she spent most of her time with Danny. When she was home, which was rare, she shut herself in her bedroom with her angry painting and blaring music. Charlotte knew deep down that Ramona was hurting as much as she was, and had no idea how to deal with her own life, let alone maintain a relationship with Charlotte, but that didn't make it any less crushing every time her sister scowled and turned her back when they crossed paths.

She was horribly, painfully alone in the Seaside House, and every day her father didn't return to them was another nail in the coffin. She'd read and re-read his cryptic final note thousands of times, each time the gulf between her and the man she thought she'd known widening. The part of her that continued to believe he'd come back home had eventually diminished to nothing. Life had been irreparably altered, whether or not Charlotte accepted it.

It was time for a change. When Charlotte's eighteenth birthday had passed without any mention from anyone besides Christian, she'd known then that she'd have to move on. With Sylvie away at college, Christian was all she had left in the world. It was time to take matters into her own hands.

Charlotte watched the great expanse in front of her as dolphins crested and splashed back into the violet waters, taking a deep breath to steady the anticipation crashing around inside her. She looked around to make sure he hadn't arrived yet, then put her hand in her coat pocket. A pale gold ring emerged. She grinned and held it in front of her, the sunlight glimmering against its smooth surface.

It wasn't traditional, sure, but she didn't care.

Christian wanted to wait to get married until he'd gotten on his feet with the business, when he was earning enough for them to make it. They'd gone over their plan for their life once they were married a thousand times: how they'd visit Old Man Keamy in person to try to convince him to part with his empty lot; rent a small apartment on Main Street; get the ball rolling with the long process of building a home on the lot, right on the water, with a wrap-around porch and huge windows to let in the sunlight and a garden, and someday, a handmade crib for the nursery.

Charlotte couldn't wait any longer to marry the man she loved, and she knew that even though he'd never expect her to be the one to propose in a million years, he would say yes. They were soul mates, destined to be together, and she knew he loved her entirely, unconditionally.

Her nerves sparked as she reviewed the words she planned to say when she asked him the question. Excitement coursed through her body, making her weak in the knees. But she felt no dizziness, no pins and needles, no weight pressing on her chest. With Christian's help, she hadn't had a panic attack in months. All she felt now were butterflies in her stomach and a burning in her heart to be close to him for the rest of her life.

As the shimmering sun inched closer to the horizon, Charlotte began pacing the length of the shoreline. Christian had been done with work more than two hours ago. The first inklings of worry fluttered in her chest. Maybe he'd gotten held up with a customer? He wouldn't have wanted her worrying here alone on the beach, so it was unlikely...

By the time the sun had fully disappeared and the first pinpoints of stars dotted the dark sky, Charlotte wondered if Christian had misunderstood her. Maybe he thought she meant another night. She didn't want to leave now in case he turned up, but if much more time passed, she'd have to go home and try to call him, or go straight to the woodshop.

Thunder rumbled in the distance, and a quarter of an hour later, rain began to patter against the sand. The air was warm, but Charlotte felt herself shivering. For a brief moment the world seemed to spin, but she clenched her fists and willed the panic away. She wasn't going to have an episode, not now, after all this time. It was time to leave.

Charlotte turned and headed toward the Loop across the long expanse of sand. The rain was falling hard now, pelting her across the face. She raised her arm against the downpour and continued trudging across the sand.

In the corner of her eye, Charlotte spotted movement. Her heart shot up into her throat. "*Christian!*" she yelled. Down the coast to her left, she could just make out a figure, but the rain was falling too hard to see if it was him. She began to run toward the figure, and as she got closer, she spotted the familiar wave of hair.

A flood of relief filled her, and Charlotte grinned as she finally got to him. But as she saw his face, a cold shiver ran all the way down her spine.

Something was wrong. His eyes were rimmed with tears, and he wore a grim expression. His shoulders were hunched forward, and he refused to meet her eye.

"What happened?" Charlotte breathed, her voice shaking. When he didn't respond, she pulled him into her and wrapped her arms around his back. Christian leaned down and buried his face in her long hair, and tears sprang to her eyes as his body became racked with sobs.

"Talk to me, Christian!" she yelled over the rain pummeling the sand all around them. A flash of lightning cracked in the distance, illuminating the dark sea. Christian spluttered and pulled away from Charlotte, meeting her frantic gaze.

"My brother died," he choked out. "He was killed in action...Oh, God, Charlotte..." His hands were shaking as he raised them to cover his face and began to sob again.

Nausea sloshed through Charlotte's stomach as she pulled him close and stroked his hair, drenched by the cold rain. It was a nightmare come true. Elliott had been stationed overseas for several years, and Christian and his father had long worried something would happen. "I'm so, so sorry," she whispered into him. Words escaped her as her heart broke trying to imagine what he was feeling right now.

Suddenly, Christian shook his head and disentangled himself from Charlotte's grasp, swiping away the tears from his face. His eyebrows knitted together, and his mouth formed a thin line.

"Charlotte," he said loudly over the rain, his eyes locked on hers. He took a deep breath. "I'm going to enlist."

The words plunged into her like a hot knife through butter. Charlotte felt all the color drain from her face as the shoreline spun dizzyingly around her. No. No no no no. The sound of the rain faded into the background as her ears rang and she gasped for breath.

His eyes were wild as he reached up with both hands and gripped her shoulders. "I'm going to take his place, Charlotte. I know you're going to hate me for it. But I have to do this for Elliott. For my family."

Charlotte shook her head violently. This wasn't happening. Everything had a slow quality to it, as though she were trapped inside a terrible dream.

He gripped her shoulders tighter, and the pain in his eyes broke her heart all over again. His face was clenched, and she could see the muscles in his jaws tighten. "I know you don't understand. I'm sorry, Charlotte." He closed his eyes, and his body shivered once. "I can't be with you."

Charlotte shoved his hands off her shoulders and put both her hands on his face. Her throat was so tight she could barely force the words out. "Christian, we can talk about this. We need to talk about this. I know you're devastated, I can't even imagine, but—"

"My mind is made up. I'm sorry." He pulled her hands from his face and took a step backward. "I have no idea what's going to happen. I could be killed." His face hardened. "I don't plan on coming back, Charlotte. You need to move on with your life. You deserve better. I'm sorry."

"*You don't get to tell me what to do!*" Charlotte screamed at him. "My future is with you, Christian. If you need to go, then you should go. Of course, go. But I'm going to wait for you."

"You're not hearing me. *I'm not coming back*." He shook his head and looked at her, agony flickering across his eyes. "I love you, and this is killing me. I hope you can forgive me someday."

"What about your father?" she cried. "What about his business? You're just going to abandon him?"

Christian shook his head. "He's selling the furniture store. He supports my decision. He wants me to go."

Charlotte felt a horrible lurch in her stomach, and couldn't catch her breath. "*Just stop it!* We can figure this out! Please, Christian—"

"*I'm not asking you, Charlotte! I'm telling you!*" he screamed through the sound of the rain. "It's over! I don't expect you to understand. I will not put you through this. Goodbye, Charlotte."

A horrible sob escaped from Charlotte's throat as Christian's eyes met hers. Something lined his face that she didn't understand, couldn't. She knew at that moment that it was really over.

A numbness crept over her entire body as she felt her whole future being ripped from her fingertips. Her love, her wonderful, gentle, beautiful boy, was leaving. A terrible white-hot anger suddenly flared within her like a furnace. She couldn't help but feel betrayed. He stood silent for a moment, his eyes wandering over her face as though he was committing her features to memory, before he turned and walked away into the pouring rain.

Charlotte stood with her feet cold in the wet sand, clothes clinging to her drenched skin, stunned out of her mind. Now she had no one. First her father, then the rest of her family, and now the man she had her whole life planned with had abandoned her too. Gone. She was painfully, frightfully alone. And she always would be.

Her mind reeled as the dark abyss of her new future threatened to swallow her whole. The expanse of it struck her with such force that she rocked on her heels and fell to her knees in the sand. As the world spun around her, Charlotte pulled out the ring she'd planned to give him and let it drop into the sand. Hot tears streamed down her face as thunder roared all around her and lightning lit up the sky like white fire, icy rain stabbing at her skin like thousands of needles.

Asking Christian to marry her had only been part of her plan tonight. There had been more. Charlotte squeezed her eyes shut against the terror in her heart, reached deep into her pocket, and clasped her shaking fingers around the positive pregnancy test.

R amona stared at Charlotte as she finished her story, stunned. Old memories somersaulted through her mind, reconfiguring themselves into new patterns, revealing new images. She vaguely registered the sounds of her mother sniffling beside her against the light pattering of rainfall outside. Tremors ran all over Ramona's skin as Charlotte closed her eyes and a single tear beaded and fell down her cheek.

"So Mariah..." Ramona managed, her voice sounding small and far away in her throat.

Charlotte opened her eyes and met Ramona's gaze. "Is Christian's daughter, yes."

Ramona hesitated. "Does she—"

"Mariah has always known Sebastian isn't her

biological father. I would never keep something like that from her. She just doesn't know it's Christian."

Charlotte sighed and leaned back in the bed. "I've always told her that if she was ever ready to know, that I would tell her about him, but she's never wanted to. I think it's because she's always been so close with Sebastian..." She gave a single humorless laugh. "I don't mind telling you, it's been a relief to not have to open that can of worms with her. Despite everything between Sebastian and me, he's been a good father to her. He always wanted children and was there from the moment Mariah was born."

Ramona's mind spun as she took in everything she was hearing. "Did you ever tell Mariah that her biological father doesn't know about her?"

Charlotte blew out a long breath. "Yes. I've always just said it was complicated. She's never pressed me on it...she said she respects my decision." Charlotte's shoulders slumped and fresh tears rolled down her face. "My heart was shattered when Christian left. I spent years wondering what might have been. What had happened to him. I didn't even know if he was alive. He told me he wasn't coming back, and I believed him. I was completely stuck...I knew if I told him I was pregnant, he wouldn't leave.

I knew that enlisting was something he needed to do, and I didn't want to force his hand." She shook her head and dropped her shoulders. "I was angry that he left, but not with him as a person. He was only doing what he thought was right. I got married and moved on, and tried to leave the past in the past. I was happy with Sebastian...I never expected Christian to come back to Marina Cove. I'll never know if I did the right thing, not telling him, but I can't change it now."

Charlotte turned and looked between Ella and Ramona. "When Christian said he was leaving me, I was beyond terrified. I was pregnant, and I had no idea what I was going to do." She brushed away fresh tears pooling in her eyes as the pitch of her voice rose. "I felt like I had no one in the world, no one to turn to. I know you were both grieving in your own way. But I had a baby on the way, and no support. I needed money, stability...so I called up Diane's friend who had moved to Brooklyn a few years earlier and asked if I could move in with her. I got a job as a waitress at a small café, met Sebastian, and the rest is history. He was good to me. He loved me."

Ramona closed her eyes and shone a light on the dark parts of her memories, the ones after her father left that she'd always thought would go away if she avoided them. The ache that had been building in her chest thrummed as she recalled spending all her time either with Danny or by herself in her room, thrashing paint across the empty canvas and denying Charlotte and anyone else around her, trying to ball herself up into a tiny cocoon so no one else could hurt her like her father had. A horrible pain punched her hard in the back of the throat.

Charlotte reached for Ella's hand and then Ramona's, squeezing them tightly. "I am truly sorry for leaving," she said, her voice wavering. "I was a scared teenager and I ran away looking for safety. Yes, I was angry with you both...angry and hurt and sad, but I should've tried harder. I was afraid to come back here, and I never knew how to explain myself. I'm done hiding, though. I'm sorry for everything, for leaving and for coming back and making everything so much worse. I love you both. I hope you can forgive me."

Ella reached up to Charlotte's face and wiped the tears from her cheek with her hand. "Charlotte..." she started, and immediately closed her mouth. She shook her head once, her eyes glistening. "I should be the one apologizing to you. After your father left us...I couldn't be there for my children." Ramona closed her eyes, forcing back the lump forming in her throat. "Charlotte, I'm so sorry you felt like you couldn't come to me. I should have done better. I could have gotten help like you asked, but I didn't. I was lost, and in many ways I'm still lost. But I want things to be better."

She turned to Ramona and laid a hand on hers. "That goes for you too. My heart breaks for everything that's happened. I'm sorry, Ramona. I'm truly sorry."

Ramona couldn't hold back any longer. She felt her face crumple as the years of anguish forced their way to the surface, racking her body with hard sobs. Charlotte leaned over and pulled Ella and Ramona close to her, wrapping her arms around them.

"I didn't know what you were dealing with," Ramona whispered to Charlotte. "I know I ignored you after Dad left. I wanted to be there for you like you'd always been there for me, but..." Her voice broke again.

"I know, Ramona. Dad leaving changed all of us." Charlotte squeezed them tighter. "I wish things could've worked out differently."

Ramona's skin felt cold as the events of the last day crashed through her again. Charlotte was going back to New York. Ramona and Ella were selling the

Seaside House. Her money troubles would be gone, for a little while, at least.

It was a hollow victory.

"So what now?" whispered Ella, leaning back and tucking an errant strand of hair behind Charlotte's ear, making Ramona's throat constrict. It was a small gesture, but it had been ages since Ramona had seen Ella do anything so tender.

Charlotte wiped the tears from her eyes with the sleeve of her hospital gown. "Sebastian has a job lined up for me...I didn't want to take it, but we still need money, and even though I don't really trust him, he seems to think we're on the right track." She laughed humorlessly. "I didn't want to go back like this, but I guess I was headed back to New York eventually anyway."

A long silence ensued as Charlotte leaned back against the hospital bed, staring at the ceiling, looking deep in thought. Ramona longed to say the words that filled her heart, that although part of her would always be hurt that Charlotte had left her with her mother, she wasn't ready for her to leave now. She felt like a little girl again, longing to bury her head in Charlotte's hair and cry freely, to share the pain of all the years with someone who could understand her. But she came up empty, unable to form the words, and instead just turned her head and listened to the gentle pattering of rain on the window.

A heavy weight settled deep in her stomach. Ramona had thought over the weeks that she and Charlotte might be able to find their way back to each other...but she knew in her bones that the rocky foundation they had just started to build wasn't enough. They hadn't had enough time. Ramona's heart folded as she felt the relationship with her sister dissolve in her hands, just like it had when they were teenagers.

24

"Can I bring you anything else before I leave for the day, Mrs. Carter?"

"Actually, it's Mrs. Keller...never mind. I'm okay, thank you, Giselle," said Charlotte. She'd never taken Sebastian's last name; it'd been the one thread from her past she'd clung to when she married him.

Charlotte's young assistant smiled meekly and quietly closed the door. The sound echoed throughout Charlotte's cavernous corner office on the 74th floor of the high-rise that housed Alastair's new company. She sighed, and turned to look out the wall of glass windows behind her. The sun was beginning to dip over the city skyline as Charlotte sipped her tea thoughtfully.

She had started the job Sebastian had procured for her a few days earlier, and it had been a whirlwind of meetings, paperwork, and more meetings with a slew of fancy suits whose names she'd been entirely unable to remember. When she took the job, not knowing what else to do, a cynical part of her had assumed that her title as "partner" was a formality; she and everyone she worked with would know it was nepotism, plain and simple.

But she was pleasantly surprised that Sebastian had arranged for her to have real power, real responsibilities. She'd barely scratched the surface of the company's investments over the days, but she leaned into the work and strove to make sense of the array of irons they had in the fire, with enormous assistance from the large team Sebastian and Alastair had gathered over his many years as Manhattan nobility. The components of the business ranged from researching and purchasing certain patents from companies that were in financial trouble (presumably to take advantage of when the companies went under; it was difficult for Charlotte to get a straight answer), to funding small pharmaceutical companies that would somehow acquire and develop older drugs and resell them at higher prices. As Charlotte poked around, it seemed that the branches of the investments they worked on fed into each other, funding parts of the company that were in debt, all of which were used to raise more capital and appease investors.

It was a tangled mess, and large parts of it didn't make sense to Charlotte, but she didn't know nearly enough yet to truly understand what went on under the hood. "Just get the lay of the land for now; Alastair will help you dive into things for real in a few weeks," Sebastian had told her. Nevertheless, she persisted, and appreciated having enough power to make decisions for where the money would be spent. She could tell that the other high-level employees were more than slightly disgruntled to have to report to her and didn't respect her. Alastair was clearly unhappy with the arrangement, and made no attempt to hide it. But Charlotte decided to focus on what she could actually control, and gave things her best effort.

Her mind drifted to Marina Cove, as it did all the time, and to Christian. He'd been visibly hurt when she told him she was going back to New York, but had told her he understood that she was trying to do the right thing. "I'm sorry I didn't try harder to convince you not to open yet," he said, his hands in his pockets as he shuffled from foot to foot. "If I ever thought a fire was at all possible..." Charlotte reassured him it was entirely her fault for letting her desperation cloud her judgment.

He hugged her tightly in a way that sent shivers down her spine. She promised to be back at some point, but Charlotte knew that whatever thought they'd had of getting to know each other again was essentially over. Her throat constricted as her mind was filled with images of what might have been before she forcefully pushed them away. They stood in the sand in front of the Seaside House, looking at each other for a long moment. Christian's mouth moved as though he wanted to say something, but he closed it and looked at her with an expression of such pain that Charlotte had to avert her eyes, blinking back tears. He squeezed her hand, gave her a small, sad smile, turned, and left.

Felix's review was about as damaging as she'd expected. It was more than enough to destroy the reputation of the Seaside House. The article was titled "The Seaside House: Come For the Pastries, Stay For the Near-Death Experiences." Despite Charlotte feeling that Gary and the new contractors had gotten the place in decent enough shape, Felix's keen eye hadn't been fooled in the least. He detailed every slipshod bit of work that had been done by them, somehow seeing things Charlotte had never noticed. He recounted in excruciating detail the house fire, painting himself as a heroic figure who'd been to the very brink of death, saved only by his quick thinking and a bravery worthy of songs. He'd somehow left out the part where Charlotte had been the one to notify him about the fire and get him out of the house before the smoke had been a real issue.

The only upside of the review was two full paragraphs where he raved about the pastries and desserts Charlotte had made with Sylvie and Mariah's help. Felix ended with vague threats that he might consider investigating damages for "emotional distress," and an unkind suggestion that the owners seek another field of employment. He'd kindly been thorough enough to paste his article as the very first review on the Seaside House profile page they'd set up, the single lonely star condemning them into oblivion.

In the days since Charlotte had been back in New York, she'd noticed that something had changed within her. Claustrophobia consumed her as she sat in wall-to-wall traffic to and from the office (the red convertible Sebastian had arranged as her "company car" was more than useless, as Sebastian had retained their personal driver). She felt a tug somewhere in her solar plexus for the wide-open skies bursting with endless sunshine and starlight, for the expanses of golden sand and crystal blue waters she'd become accustomed to. After spending her leisure time listening to the seagulls cry over the crashing ocean waves or watching the glittering sunset over the horizon, the treadmill of fancy restaurants and gallery openings didn't have the same luster. She couldn't comprehend spending even a single afternoon listening to Kylie and Riley prattle on endlessly with their gossip and comparing jewelry and purses and men.

Charlotte gathered her things and shut off the lights to her office. "Goodnight, Pete," she called to the night custodian, who gave her a friendly wave.

The traffic was unbearable as Charlotte's driver made his way back to The Windsor. Charlotte had decided to move back into the condo with Sebastian, partly due to convenience and partly because although she hated to admit it, she'd been softening to him.

Her time away had made her miss their routines, their old lives that had become like a comfortable pair of shoes, broken in and fitting in all the right places. He'd maintained a careful distance, but they'd taken to eating dinner together, conversation coming more easily by the day. Her heart broke anew each time she remembered Steph, but time had already begun to file away at the sharp edges of the betrayal.

The best part about coming back to New York was Brielle. They'd fallen right back into their friendship, spending their nights talking about Charlotte's adventures and troubles in Marina Cove, and all the ridiculous things Kylie and Riley had been up to. Charlotte had missed her terribly when she was gone, and the time away had actually brought them closer together.

Charlotte checked her phone, which she'd taken to keeping on silent after she'd gotten used to it dying all the time in Marina Cove; she had learned to appreciate disconnecting from the world for a while. She had a new text from Brielle.

Wanna meet up tonight? Wanted to talk to you about something.

Something flickered at the edges of Charlotte's mind. Last night, they'd been at her house watching bad reality TV and eating ice cream when Charlotte took a deep breath and shared everything about her and Sebastian's financial crisis. When she'd explained her new job with Alastair, Brielle was supportive, but Charlotte couldn't help but notice that something was off. After several inquiries, Brielle assured her that she was just tired, but Charlotte wasn't totally convinced. Her mind raced as she typed back.

I'm headed back to the condo, Sebastian's away for work until tomorrow. Meet me there in half an hour?

Charlotte quickly made a pot of coffee, gave Ollie a bear hug, and paced around until finally Brielle arrived and she buzzed her in. She felt sweat breaking out on her forehead as the elevators opened to the penthouse.

It was unseasonably cold out; Brielle was shivering as she took off her coat and rubbed her hands over her arms. Charlotte poured two cups of coffee and motioned from the couch. Her throat was dry as Brielle sat silently for several long moments, wringing her hands.

"Charlotte," she said, her voice wavering. Charlotte noticed Brielle's hands were trembling slightly. A prickling sensation scuttled across her skin.

"What is it?" she asked, impatience coloring her tone as she wiped her slick palms on the front of her business dress.

"Okay." She let out a breath. "When you told me that you were starting this new job Sebastian set up for you, I thought hard about it last night, and there's something I think you deserve to know." She smoothed her hair and straightened her back. "A long time ago, Slater actually worked for Sebastian. Slater and I had been married for a few years, and when we ran into some financial problems, Sebastian hired him. We were very nearly broke, but Sebastian saved us. Set Slater up with a great opportunity. But a few years later, Sebastian fired him. He took everything away. It took us years to get afloat again." Brielle's voice cracked as tears began to fall down her cheeks.

"Charlotte...Slater was fired because I decided to end my relationship with Sebastian."

The room began to spin as ice plunged through Charlotte's body. She grabbed the arm of the couch for stability.

Not Brielle. Not Brielle.

"How long," Charlotte managed to choke out. Her voice sounded a thousand miles away. She felt as though someone were sitting on her chest.

Brielle's chin dipped to her chest as she squeezed her eyes shut. "Six years."

All the air was sucked from the room, and Charlotte gasped for breath. Boiling sweat trickled down her forehead as the walls closed in on her, trapping her. Brielle started to weep quietly, her hands clasped over her eyes.

"There's nothing I can say other than I'm so, so sorry, Charlotte," Brielle said, the pitch of her voice rising. "It was before we were friends; I barely knew you...it's no excuse. But I needed to come clean. When Sebastian and I started...seeing each other, he gave Slater the job to keep me around. He used his money to keep me bound to him. I was grateful. But as the years went on and I got to know you, I broke things off. He tried to buy me nice things, he even bought me that red convertible you liked."

Charlotte idly fingered the diamond necklace that Sebastian had given her. It felt suddenly heavy, iron chains shackling her in place. Brielle's words were muffled and faraway, like Charlotte was underwater.

"When that didn't work, he dangled Slater's job in front of me. But I refused to be pressured into staying with him...so he fired Slater. A lot of the money we had was tied up in company shares that Sebastian dissolved. We lost everything because of that. It was years before we recovered."

Brielle turned to Charlotte, her face twisted in pure anguish. "Nothing I can say will undo what I did. When I first heard about Steph, I told you to consider giving him another chance because I didn't want you to lose everything, like I did."

Some very distant part of Charlotte was screaming at her to react to the betrayal, to throw her friend out of her home and out of her life forever, but she was too stunned to do anything at all. She couldn't form words. She was completely and hopelessly blindsided.

"Why didn't you tell me until now?" Charlotte whispered.

Brielle ran her hands over her face and through her hair. "I never wanted you to lose everything you two had. You had your money, your children...and the selfish part of me didn't want to lose our friendship. But when you told me yesterday that he lined you up a job with Alastair...You're still working for Sebastian. I couldn't let what he did to me happen to you too. Sebastian uses his money to control people. He's trying to buy you, Charlotte."

A long silence ensued while Charlotte's mind broke like shattered glass. Behind Brielle was a picture of Sebastian and her with Mariah, Liam, and Allie...their three beautiful children. It was all a lie, her whole adult life. Everything was a lie.

She wanted to seize Brielle by the shirt and scream endlessly in her face until all the poison was leached from her body. But she was frozen in her seat, a deer in headlights. It was all just too much.

Brielle spoke suddenly, yanking Charlotte from her reverie. "I know it won't make up for anything, but there's something else you should know. It's about your family's inn...the Seaside House."

Charlotte sat up straight on the couch and stared at Brielle, her whole body trembling. Sitting across from her wasn't her friend; she didn't know this woman.

Brielle took a deep breath. "You were telling me about your sister selling it to a realty group...that guy, Giovanni. And they would restore it? I told Slater about it when you got back. Slater's company does some real estate investing all across the Eastern Seaboard. They've had run-ins with Giovanni over the years. He hates him with a passion; I guess Giovanni's taken clients away from him left and right, has some shady business practices." She looked up at Charlotte. "Slater poked around, and he found out that Giovanni isn't going to restore the inn. He's going to tear it down. He made a deal with a property group to build some gigantic commercial retail center, big-box stores and whatnot. Slater says Giovanni somehow made some under-the-table deals with people in high places who will approve the re-zoning."

Brielle lowered her eyes to the floor, her cheeks flushing. "I guess they've already done it with a few other family inns on other islands. He puts clauses in that allow the property group to override the contract if they deem the inn 'unsuitable' for restoration or something. It's in the fine print and impossible to understand if you're not a lawyer."

She moved a little closer to Charlotte and lowered her voice to just above a whisper. "I know you said you and your family never wanted to tear down your home, so I thought you'd want to know. I know it doesn't make up for anything, and you probably never want to speak to me again. I don't expect you to forgive me. I'm so sorry, Charlotte. I'll let myself out." She brushed the tears from her eyes, reached for her coat, and padded silently across the carpet and into the elevator.

Charlotte sat frozen on the couch, paralyzed. She felt curiously empty, like she'd been hollowed out. Part of her wanted to tear the room apart in a cold fury, to scream at the top of her lungs until her voice gave out, to cry hard to let out everything that was boiling inside of her, but she was too stunned to do anything. She registered that hours had gone by, but she could do nothing. Everything she thought she knew was wrong. Again, she found herself all alone in the world.

As the first weak rays of sunlight broke over the Manhattan skyline, Charlotte felt like a stone, heavy and unmovable. Her eyes burned with the lack of sleep, and she was dehydrated. An image of a wrecking ball being taken to her family home played over and over in her mind, destroying generations of legacy and the last ties she had to her past. A pit of despair had formed in her that now felt permanent.

A memory of her father sitting at the upright piano, hair wild and laughing, struck her so hard it left her gasping for air. She shot up from her chair, grabbed the framed wedding photo of her and Sebastian that sat on the end table, and slammed it over and over again on the coffee table, screaming and sobbing, shards of glass flying everywhere and slicing into her palms.

Charlotte sat down hard on the ground, holding her head in her bleeding hands, when an idea speared its way into her mind.

She suddenly knew what she would do.

25

Ramona crinkled her nose at the faint smell of smoke as she meandered through the main floor of the inn. The first thin rays of sunlight were just making their way through the large bay windows, casting long shadows against the ancient hardwood flooring. A heaviness had settled into her limbs, and as she stared across the rooms of the inn that had been her family home, she fought back tears.

It was the last time she would ever be inside the Seaside House.

She checked her watch. Her meeting with Giovanni was set for noon, where she'd sign whatever paperwork she needed to hand over the inn.

She sighed and shut her phone off. No distractions today.

Before she left for the ferry, she'd wanted to take one last walk through the inn. Ella had declined to join her; ever since they'd decided to take Giovanni up on his offer, she'd been mostly shut away in the bungalow, and Ramona didn't want to push her. She couldn't imagine how hard it must be for her mother to know her home wouldn't belong to her anymore. Even though it would be restored properly by someone else, it was a false victory. For generations it had been in her family. Ramona felt like a failure, like she'd let her mother down in the worst possible way.

As she hobbled into the kitchen on her crutches, a memory sparked in her mind, Natalie wildly hosing the room down with a fire extinguisher after she and Charlotte had popped a full pizza box in the oven to reheat it; every wall and surface but the oven had been blasted with white foam. Their mother had run in from the yard after hearing the fire alarm, calmly removed the lightly smoking box from the oven, and then doubled over with laughter as her eyes followed the wayward trail of dripping foam that made them feel like they were inside a snow globe.

Ramona limped through the dining room, where countless holiday dinners had been served on their mother's finest china from the cupboard, Diane regaling them with tales of bad first dates and laughter echoing against the walls, the heat from the vent warming their feet and counteracting the cold draft from the windows. She passed the ancient wooden staircase, where Gabriel had once duct-taped flat sheets of cardboard all the way down the stairs; the Keller siblings took turns sitting in a card-board box at the top and sledding down wildly, straight through the front door, across the porch, and tumbling into the sand, laughing hysterically. Ramona smiled as she remembered the look on their mother's face as she came home early from the store to find Gabriel shooting out the front door like a cannon.

Her heart stopped as she brushed her fingers across the keys of the old upright piano in the library. A memory punched through her of her father's fingers sweeping across the keys, playing something discordant as her mother sang along, laughing that loud laugh he had that always made her feel light and free and safe. Leaving the inn was like being forced to say goodbye to him all over again.

Ramona stood in the landing, surveying the house one last time. She blinked back tears, took a deep breath, and pulled open the heavy front door. As she closed it for the last time, she could swear she heard her father's laughter again echoing somewhere within the house.

CHARLOTTE PACED AROUND the condo as she dialed Ramona's number again and again. It kept immediately going to voicemail. After the tenth try, she called her mother.

"Ella Keller," she answered after the fourth ring. Her voice sounded lifeless, defeated.

"Mom? It's Charlotte. Do you know where Ramona is?"

"Oh, hi, Charlotte...you missed her. She stopped at the inn before she was headed to catch the ferry... she has her meeting with that realty group in Boston today."

Charlotte's stomach folded over. "Oh, no. Oh, Mom, we can't have her sign that paperwork. I have a way we can keep the inn. But I need to get through to her. Can you give me the address of where she's going?"

There was silence on the line. "Hello? Please...I need to get to Ramona and stop her. They're going to tear down the house and put up a freaking retail center in its place!"

Another long moment passed. "What does it matter? We tried everything. Our home is gone...it's too late, Charlotte. We all need to move on."

Charlotte blew out a frustrated breath. "Mom, I don't have time to explain. I know things look bleak now but if I can stop Ramona from signing that paperwork, we still have a chance. Please give me the address, I'm going to leave for Boston now!"

Charlotte jotted down the address her mother grudgingly rattled off, hung up, and punched it into her phone. On the way down to the garage, she called Ramona again and left a message.

Ramona, it's Charlotte. I hope you get this. Please don't sign anything today. Please. We can keep the inn, I have a solution. I'm coming to you...at least wait for me and hear me out. I know you don't have any reason to, but I'm asking you to trust me one last time.

Charlotte pressed a large button, and the engine of the fire-red convertible roared to life, blasting the parking garage with thick, black exhaust. At least she'd get some use out of the ridiculous vehicle Sebastian had leased for her.

The tires pealed as she swung out onto the street on her way to Boston.

Already stuck in traffic, she dialed Mariah from the car phone. "Mom?" she answered, her voice bleary with sleep.

"Mariah! I need your help. Do you have a pen?"

Charlotte briefly explained that she needed to stop Ramona from signing the paperwork. "I'll tell you everything later. I need you to keep calling her until she answers, since I'll be driving."

Since Mariah was on leave from med school, she'd decided to stay back in Marina Cove for another week or two and try to relax. She'd fallen in love with the island, and when Sylvie had offered Mariah her guest bedroom, she jumped at the chance. Charlotte was thrilled at their blossoming friendship; it would be a link to Sylvie until she could see her again, whenever that would be.

"Why don't I meet up with you? I can be there for moral support."

Charlotte hesitated. "Are you sure? We could meet near Providence...I'm still probably four hours away..."

"That's perfect. I'll catch the ferry as soon as I can and just get a rideshare. I'll look up a café and text you the address. In the meantime, I'll keep calling Aunt Ramona."

Charlotte grinned. It would be nice to have someone in her corner. Despite having a concrete plan this time for keeping the inn, she still had to convince Ramona. It wasn't going to be easy.

The blazing sun sliced through the thick exhaust hovering over the highway like a blanket, piercing Charlotte's eyes and breaking her body out in a sweat. She did her best to take calming breaths as she crawled through the Manhattan traffic, feeling the cars pressing in on her, trying to trap and suffocate her as she dialed Ramona's number again and again.

RAMONA CAREFULLY CLIMBED out of the taxi balancing on her good leg, paid the driver, and hobbled through the revolving doors of the ominous-looking MDRC Realty Group building in downtown Boston. A frigid blast of air hit her as she passed through the doors, followed by a wall of sweltering heat that had settled into the reception area. A security guard in sunglasses stood poised by the entry, furrowing his brow at her. She walked meekly up to the receptionist, thrumming her fingers against her purse. She was more than an hour early. "Hi...I'm here for a meeting with, uh, Giovanni Romano?"

She punched a few keys. "Ah, yes, Ms. Keller," said the receptionist brightly. "Mr. Romano might be running a bit late today; let me take you to our client lounge. Can I offer you anything to eat or drink?"

Ramona shook her head. The receptionist led her down a long, narrow hallway, barely wide enough to walk down. The hardwood creaked loudly under her feet. The hallway was dark, illuminated every few feet by flickering fluorescent lights high above her head. It felt strangely like the walls were closing in around her.

The receptionist pushed open a thick wooden door and led her into a tiny, windowless room. Sweat trickled down her face as another wall of heat struck her like a blow.

"Cassie will be in shortly to take your lunch and drinks order. There's an espresso machine right there, and alcoholic beverages on the table there. Might I offer you a glass of champagne? Or something stronger?"

"No, uh, no thank you...It's a little hot in here, is it possible to turn on the air conditioning?"

She plastered a tight smile on her face. "Of course, Ms. Keller. Anything you need." She turned on her heel and closed the door a little too hard, the sound immediately swallowed by the stifling silence.

Ramona sat down hard on the low couch and set her crutches aside. She tried to steady herself by taking long, slow breaths, but the air seemed to press harder against her lungs each time.

There was no other way, she reminded herself. She thought of her mother, and how heartbroken she must be. Of Charlotte. How hard she'd tried. How much she admired her courage for finally talking about her reasons for leaving Marina Cove. How much it hurt to think about her returning to her old life in New York, and how alone Ramona felt again.

She wiped the sweat from her forehead again as she pushed away the flickers of doubt forming at the edges of her mind, a steely resolve taking their place. No matter how much you fought it, sometimes life simply didn't work out how you wanted it to.

Ramona was in too deep. There was no turning back now.

CHARLOTTE CRANKED up the air conditioning to no avail as she pulled up in front of the coffee shop. Mariah hurried over to the car. Charlotte's mouth dropped open as she spotted two familiar faces behind her.

"Mom! Sylvie! Oh, my God! What are you doing here?" Charlotte exclaimed as Sylvie slid into the backseat, followed by Ella. Mariah sat down in the passenger seat, grinning widely.

"Oh, you know, just felt like a little adventure today." Sylvie's mouth curved up in a sly smile. "We thought you could use a little support. And some sustenance." She reached into a paper bag, and the delicious smell of doughnuts filled the car.

"You're an angel." Charlotte reached back and squeezed her mother's hand, catching her eye in the rearview mirror. "I'm so glad I'm not alone today."

Ella smiled wistfully. "After you hung up and I had a chance to think about it, I realized I didn't want to just sit back if there was any chance of saving our home. We have to try. And just as I was heading out for the ferry, Mariah and Sylvie showed up at my door."

Charlotte was smiling wide and filled with a new resolve as she swung back onto I-95. She did her best to ignore the hot sweat trickling down her back, making her squirm in her seat. Mariah leaned over her phone, redialing Ramona over and over, eyebrows furrowed in frustration.

"So, are you going to tell us why we're doing this yet? The plan you have for keeping the inn?" Mariah set the phone down in her lap and looked up at Charlotte eagerly.

Charlotte hesitated. A gnawing feeling from deep within her gut scratched at her. It was the same feeling she'd had in the hospital bed before she'd told Ramona and Ella the truth about why she'd left. She was tired of all the spinning plates, tired of the secrets, of being too afraid or ashamed to let the people she loved in on the truth, no matter how ugly or difficult it would be.

Charlotte took a breath. "It's a long story, honey, and for it to make sense I need to start from the beginning, I'm afraid. I'm really sorry I didn't tell you about this sooner. Sylvie and your grandmother already know some of this; I hope you don't mind if they hear this too."

Charlotte did her best to explain the financial crisis that she and Sebastian had, the incredible debt and all the false starts and how she'd been trying to get the inn open in time to start paying back the personal loan she'd taken out, all the contract work, and Ramona and her mother's debt. She explained the new job, and how they were trying hard to dig themselves out. Mariah nodded along, clearly taken aback but listening intently as Charlotte finished.

"I'm...I don't know what to say, Mom," Mariah said, her voice quiet. "That's terrible. I can't imagine...my God. I had no idea. I should've put things together. I always took it for granted how much money Dad had. I'm so sorry..." She shook her head and stared out the window for a few long moments. Sylvie reached across the seat and gently placed a hand on Mariah's shoulder.

Charlotte felt a small burden release from somewhere between her shoulder blades. It was a start.

"I found out yesterday that the guy Ramona's been working with, Giovanni, plans to tear down the inn, despite agreeing to restore it and use it as an inn. Some tiny clause buried in the fine print. His group made some deal with a property company, and they have the power to override the agreement if they decide the inn isn't a good investment, which they will. A commercial retail center will be put up in its place. Giovanni already has shady handshake deals with people on the inside to get the zoning approved."

She heard Sylvie gasp in the backseat. Mariah put her hands to her mouth. "Oh, my God."

Charlotte sighed. "We can't have them destroy our family's home. Not to mention, if a bunch of big-box stores find their way to Marina Cove..."

Mariah nodded grimly. "Others will follow."

"That's why we need to stop her from signing. It'll be horrible chain hotels and strip malls and fast-food restaurants in no time. It'll destroy local business. Marina Cove will lose its very soul."

Charlotte pushed back a wave of nausea as she imagined someone hacking away at the walls of the home she grew up in with a sledgehammer, bulldozers and wrecking balls destroying their family legacy.

Charlotte squared her shoulders. "So my plan is simple. Since your father set me up as Alastair's equal partner, I have the ability to determine where investments are made and what's put into them. So I'm going to invest in the Seaside House." She grinned at Mariah. "We'll do it the right way this time: proper funding in place, no rushing, no cutting corners. I know it to be a solid investment. I believe in it. I can handle everything from New York, and I'll hire Ramona to manage things on the ground."

Now she was going to use her position in Alastair's company to take control of her own destiny, to create her own way. She was done letting Sebastian drive them into financial ruin, and someone needed to make a good investment for a change. He obviously hadn't intended for Charlotte to use her position like she was, but there was nothing he could do to stop her. She no longer cared what Sebastian had to say.

She looked into the mirror, catching Ella's eye. "I approached things all wrong the first time. I let my desperation get in the way...I made a lot of bad decisions. I won't make the same mistakes again. Even though I won't be in Marina Cove to see it flourish, you and Ramona deserve to finally have the inn back up and running. To stop living in fear."

Ella looked back at Charlotte for a long moment before her mouth slowly tugged up into a smile. "Well, Charlotte...I think that'll do nicely."

Mariah yipped and squeezed Charlotte's hand. "That's a solid plan, Mom. I fell in love with that house...the island, the people, everything. I know others will too."

Charlotte checked her watch and groaned. "But her meeting's at noon. At this rate, we're never going to get there in time." She felt a sudden desire to get out of her car and barrel through the stifling wall-to-wall traffic on foot. "But we have to try."

Mariah dialed Ramona's phone a few more times. "What does Dad think about the Seaside House?"

Charlotte squeezed her eyes shut and swallowed hard against the pain in her throat. "Mariah, I want to tell you why I went to Marina Cove in the first place. I want you to hear me out, and I want you to remember that this is between your father and me, and has nothing to do with you or your siblings. I want to tell you too," Charlotte said, looking behind her at Sylvie and Ella.

She exhaled all the air from her lungs. "This all started when we were dropping Allie off at Columbia."

RAMONA JUMPED in her seat when the door flung open and a tall, balding man in an immaculate black suit swept into the room, followed by four other men dressed identically. "Ms. Keller? I'm Giovanni," he said in a raspy baritone. "Nice to finally meet you in person. Welcome to MDRC Realty Group. These are my associates. Let's head to the conference room, huh?"

Ramona nodded shakily as she got to her feet and wiped the sweat from her palms. The five men guided her into an elevator, one of them punching a button for the topmost floor. Metal squealed and groaned as the doors opened, and Giovanni led them down another narrow, dark hallway.

Didn't anyone else notice the heat? It was making her nauseous, lightheaded. Lining the walls were artistic pictures of enormous hotels in black and white, all massive chains she recognized from their TV commercials, some nestled in mountain terrain overlooking forests, some high above the water on jagged cliffs. The bright fluorescent bulbs overhead flickered, revealing more frames of men cutting ribbons with giant scissors against what looked to be strip malls, the sort she'd seen scattered all over the place on her drive here, nail salons and Chinese food restaurants and pawn shops. She wondered idly why a company who dealt with such massive brands would be interested in running a tiny family inn on an island that no one had ever heard of, but her thoughts came slowly; her mind felt like it had been wrapped in hot, wet cotton.

She was led to another tiny, windowless room

with a long wooden table, pale lights flickering and buzzing overhead. Five high leather chairs on one side faced a single folding chair. Giovanni motioned for her to sit as the men filled the leather chairs. She sat down hard; she was at least two full feet lower than the men across from her. Ramona felt like a caged animal on display.

The men folded their hands on the table in unison and stared down at her as Giovanni produced a sparkling glass of champagne from somewhere, setting it down in front of Ramona and taking the seat directly across from her.

"Thank you again for the opportunity to manage your family inn, Ms. Keller. We have no doubt that once we restore it to its former glory, we'll have something that will make your family proud. This is a day to celebrate! Rest assured, you're in good hands. Now, before we get started, do you have any questions for us?"

Ramona squirmed uncomfortably in the low, hard chair. "Uh, do you think I can take a look at the contract?"

Giovanni barked a loud laugh as the other men chuckled. "Do you hear that, gents? Right down to business. I like that in a woman." Ramona averted her eyes from his hungry gaze. "Sure, sure, sweetheart. Here you are." He produced a heavy manila folder seemingly from thin air and dropped it in front of her. She was painfully aware of all five men staring down at her imperiously as she reached for the envelope with trembling hands, trying fruitlessly to steady them.

The contract looked like it was two hundred pages long. There was no way she was going to get through it all; her thoughts were coming too slowly, and the stifling heat in the room pressed down on her oppressively, making her woozy.

"Take all the time you need," said Giovanni, a wolfish grin spreading across his face.

Mariah had been staring out her window for half an hour, tears silently falling down her face, breaking Charlotte's heart in two. Sylvie was in the backseat, shaking her head. Ella hadn't said anything, but her mouth was a tight, thin line. Charlotte had first explained about Steph, and then about the six-year-long relationship with Brielle. She hadn't yet had time to process everything Brielle had told her last night, but she would never forgive Sebastian for hurting their daughter like this.

"I'm sorry I didn't tell you about Steph, and why I went to Marina Cove," Charlotte said, tucking a long strand of dark hair behind her daughter's ear. "I needed time to sort things out for myself, and I didn't want to burden you kids. I never dreamed that Brielle—" Her voice cracked, and she was rendered speechless.

Mariah brushed tears from her eyes and gently placed her hand in Charlotte's. The gesture was so sweet, so loving, that something broke within Charlotte. Sebastian had put her in a wretched position, having to explain something like this. She felt a boiling heat high in her throat threatening to pour out.

"I'm never talking to Dad again," Mariah said simply, returning her gaze to the window beside her.

Charlotte quickly swiped her eyes with the back of her hand. Despite feeling much lighter after revealing the secrets she'd been keeping, she just wasn't ready for the conversation about Christian. She didn't want Mariah to have to process too much all at once. And despite what Sebastian had done, she wasn't going to have her family torn apart any more than it had been.

"Mariah, you can't say that. I know this is all awful...but this is between your father and me. He's been good to you kids, you can't argue with that. I can't have things become any worse than they are by you or Allie or Liam cutting him off, okay?"

Mariah scoffed loudly. "But it was...despicable, Mom. Disgusting. Unforgivable."

Charlotte hesitated. She needed to be a good mother right now, and that meant putting her own feelings aside and considering what was best for her kids. "We can't change what he did; we can't control what other people do. All we can control is our own actions. I know it's hard, but I don't want him to lose you because of what he did to me. I expect you to be angry, and that's okay. I just hope you and your father can move past this, whenever you're ready. Just think about it. Please?"

Mariah sniffled and nodded once. "What are you going to do?"

Charlotte closed her eyes and focused on her breathing for a moment to steady herself. Despite watching her marriage crumble and having no sense whatsoever of the course of the rest of her life, a clarity had settled over her, steeling her nerves and eliciting a confidence that she'd never known.

Sebastian could wait. She felt none of the dizziness or inability to draw a breath or anything signaling the panic attacks that would've normally come at a time like this. One step at a time. Right now, all she had to think about was her one last hope of saving her family inn.

"I don't know," she said honestly. "And I think I'm okay with that for now."

The voice on the GPS announced their exit. They were finally here. Charlotte checked her watch, already knowing before she saw it.

It was half an hour past the start of the meeting. They hadn't made it in time.

"Maybe we can still catch them..." Ella said from the backseat, defeat edging her voice. The tires pealed as Charlotte swung hard into the first empty parking spot. The four women slammed the doors shut and sprinted toward the menacing building, shoved their way through the revolving doors, and ran up to the reception desk.

"Hi—" Charlotte spluttered, looking for a nametag.

"Brenda," said the receptionist. "Welcome to—"

"Brenda, we need to talk to Ramona Keller immediately," she gasped, trying to catch her breath. "She's meeting someone named Giovanni. It's an emergency."

Brenda nodded tersely and took them all down a tiny hallway, into an elevator, and up to the top floor of the building. Charlotte gaped as the receptionist led them down a stifling hallway lined with framed pictures of all the group's successful dealings with retail centers and hotel chains and strip malls, destroying the natural charm and beauty of the surrounding areas and putting countless local businesses out of work. She felt sick to her stomach as Brenda tapped meekly on a large wooden door.

Charlotte jumped as the door suddenly shot open an inch. She couldn't see inside, but heard a man's irritated voice. Brenda whispered, and the voice spat something back, dripping with hostility and derision. The door shut with a heavy slam that reverberated down the narrow hallway.

"I'm sorry, but we'll have to wait a moment; they're just finishing up in there—"

Charlotte shoved past the receptionist and shouldered her way through the door, a heavy wall of heat blasting her in the face. "Hey!—" Brenda cried as Charlotte burst into the room.

Ramona shot up from a tiny fold-out chair, pen in hand, a stunned expression scratched across her face. "Charlotte?" she asked, incredulous. She was seated across a long wooden table from five men in identical black suits, an open pile of paperwork scattered in front of her.

Charlotte's eyes fell on the men and she felt all the color drain from her face. She was dimly aware of her phone falling from her hand and cracking against the hard floor.

Sitting across from Ramona in one of the high leather chairs, hair slicked back and gaping at Charlotte with a deer-in-headlights look in his eyes, was Sebastian.

26

Charlotte's vision receded at the edges as all the air seemed to be pumped out of her lungs. Alarm bells were ringing somewhere in the base of her skull as she tried to make sense of what she was seeing.

Some part of her registered a voice coming from the familiar man sitting next to Sebastian. "What is *she* doing here?" spat Alastair, standing up as the leather chair he'd been sitting in skidded across the floor behind him.

Charlotte felt rather than saw Mariah come up next to her. "*Dad?*" she asked, her voice thick with confusion. The sound of her daughter's voice snapped her back into reality.

"What is this?" Charlotte managed. Sebastian

stood slowly from his chair, his expression bewildered.

"I...how did you...what are you doing here?" he spluttered. He looked around at the four women who'd entered the room. "Mariah, hi, honey," he said, smiling weakly.

"I...I came to stop Ramona from selling the inn," Charlotte stammered. Her hands shook as she looked at Sebastian. "How...what are you doing here?"

Sebastian stared at her for a moment, his eyebrows arched in puzzlement. "Why on earth would you want to stop..." He shook his head. "It doesn't matter. You were going to find out anyway. I wanted it to be a surprise, but now's as good a time as any, I suppose."

He squared his shoulders, straightened his back, and smiled widely. "Charlotte, *this* is the new investment I came to Marina Cove to tell you about. *This* is what you're going to be working on with Alastair. It's the future of Carter Enterprises."

Charlotte felt as though someone had set a fire inside her chest. Her mind spun frantically as she tried to sort out her thoughts.

"I don't understand," Charlotte said carefully. "How did you..."

"Well," he interrupted, "it's a long story, but you were the one who gave me the idea, honey. Remember when I called you a while back to tell you about the, ah, investments that hadn't panned out?" he said evasively, his eyes darting to Ramona. "You wanted to restore the inn, but you said that Ramona here had been threatening to sell it to pay off their debts? Well, that gave me an idea. I've crossed paths with Giovanni here in the past, and he's been working hard in the real estate biz for a good long while. Alastair and I pitched the idea to him, and he loved it. Still a big gamble on our part, since people don't really know about Marina Cove yet," he said, smiling at Ramona, "but when we succeeded in signing an inn on Sandridge Island, I came to visit you in Marina Cove. It works, Charlotte. Everyone wins here. Ramona here will collect a nice sum of money and the property is in Giovanni's excellent hands."

He grinned at Charlotte. "But the best part is that *you* will be handling everything for the property. Who better to run it than someone who knows it inside and out? You'll have this and the one on Sandridge Island and the others we have in the works. I'm excited, Charlotte. I'm so happy that you'll get to be a part of it." He crossed the room to stand before them. "I wanted to surprise you when everything was signed, but this is even better! You get to be here for the big day!"

Charlotte stared at him, stunned into silence. It was too much to process. In the back of her mind, images of him with Brielle were stabbing and slashing at her, but she pushed them back.

"I know about the retail center, Sebastian," Charlotte said, just above a whisper.

Alastair stirred. "How..." His eyes briefly skittered toward Ramona. "*We can talk about this another time, Charlotte,*" he said under his breath. She could feel anxiety pouring from his skin like waves of heat.

Sebastian's grin slowly faded. "The what?"

Charlotte gaped at Sebastian. "Are you kidding me? You don't know?"

Sebastian turned to Alastair, who refused to meet his eye. "I'm calling security," Alastair snarled.

"You need to know, Ramona," said Charlotte, raising her voice. "They're not going to restore the inn. They're going to tear it down—"

"Charlotte, *ENOUGH!*" Alastair yelled over her, his face turning a deep shade of red as Charlotte continued undeterred, "—and construct a huge commercial retail center in its place. They have some clause in that contract there that lets them override the agreement to restore the inn if they deem it to be an unsuitable investment."

Sebastian briefly met Charlotte's eye, his face ashen. Charlotte kneeled on the ground next to Ramona, taking her hand and squeezing it. "More importantly, I'm going to let us keep the inn. I'm an equal partner with Alastair, and I'm going to make the inn one of our investments. He can't stop me. But we're going to do it the right way this time. No rushing, no shortcuts. It'll take time, but you know as well as I do that the inn is a great investment. Now that we'll have the proper financing, we can actually make it happen."

"*Triple our original offer!*" interjected Sebastian suddenly. Everyone in the room turned to look at him. "Ramona, I'm going to give you triple what we offered you if you sign right now. What they do with the land is their business. With that much money, you'll be set for years. We won't even raze the house —okay, everyone?" He ignored Alastair interjecting hotly. "I'll find a way to call it a historic landmark or something. We'll just build next to it or around it. I don't care. This is the opportunity of a lifetime, people. Do the right thing for yourselves. For your family."

Charlotte stared open-mouthed at Sebastian.

Ramona ran her hands over her face and lifted herself from her chair, wincing slightly and reaching for her crutches. The room stilled as Ramona caught Ella's eyes. They looked at each other for a long moment, silently communicating. Charlotte just barely glimpsed a small nod from her mother. A look of resolve etched across Ramona's face.

"Charlotte, I don't care what they do with the house. It's over." She sighed. "You already tried your best, but it's going to take way too long. You can't understand...we can't wait any longer, even if we can go about it the right way. I can't take that risk, and neither can you. This is really the best thing for everyone."

"But Ramona, I'll be hiring you, you're part of the investment, we can work together...You don't have to do this—" she spluttered, before Alastair clearing his throat loudly behind her stopped her midsentence. She saw him arch an eyebrow at Sebastian and then gesture toward Charlotte.

Sebastian sighed heavily and sat back down at the table across from Ramona, rubbing his eyes with the back of his hands. "Charlotte, it isn't that simple," he said. Charlotte stood and turned around to look at him. "You're a partner, yes. But that's... more of a, uh, title."

He ran a hand through his slicked-back hair, a lock falling over his forehead. "Your role is contingent upon this deal. I can't do anything about building on the land at this point," he said, glancing at Alastair and gritting his teeth. "That deal is inked. But it doesn't matter." He was speaking to her the way someone would to calm a wild and unpredictable animal.

Charlotte thought of the six years he had been with Brielle, six long years he had made her the fool. Rage punched its way into her chest so hard she was practically seeing stars as she listened to the sickly-sweet tones meant to rein her in.

"I don't want you to get the wrong idea, sweetheart," he continued. "I consider you a partner. I love you so much, Charlotte...I want you to have something you can do with your life that you'll be proud of. But it has to be this way. The money from these deals funds the more important parts of our business...it's our way forward. Together. I think if you stop to really think about it, this is the best thing for you. For us. You need to trust me."

Brielle's words echoed in her head. *He's trying to buy you, Charlotte.* As soon as she'd heard about the job on the night he surprised her on the beach, she'd known it came with strings attached, that Sebastian was indirectly wooing her back to him. It was why she'd declined. But when she'd come back to New York after the house fire, hat in hand and out of options, his sweetness and apparent remorse had fooled her.

But now she knew what sort of man he really was. And Charlotte wasn't for sale.

Sebastian hadn't given her a job...he was using his money and influence to control her, to bind her to him. Just like he'd tried to bind Brielle to him by holding her husband's job hostage. All the years he'd spent discouraging Charlotte from working, from expanding her life beyond him...it was all to keep her under his thumb, keep her dependent. Charlotte had unknowingly allowed Sebastian to pull the strings of her life, locking her into a prison of excess and complacency, a prison of her own making.

When her father had left them for reasons truly known only to him, she'd become desperate for security, certainty of some sort...and when she'd seen that her family couldn't be there for her, she leaned on Christian. Until he left too. She fled seeking something to take away her terror of being all alone in the world with a child on the way.

She saw now that she'd unwittingly repeated the

same pattern all these years later...fleeing back to her family in Marina Cove, trying to force the family inn as a way to hang on to her sense of security... she'd kept pushing and pushing to open the inn even when she knew it wasn't the right way, all in the name of trying to get her old life back, her predictable life, no matter the personal cost.

Well, no more. She was done running, done allowing herself to be a puppet because she was afraid of the unknown. Too much of her life had been spent hiding from her past. From herself, and what she really wanted.

She looked around the room at the people before her. Sylvie, her best friend for all those years and now back in her life. Her mother and Ramona... Charlotte had finally felt the first cracks in the walls of the past hurts that had kept them apart. Mariah, her beautiful daughter, taking time away from her schooling to examine what she really wanted in her life, not afraid to stand up for herself. Charlotte thought of her father. His strong hands. Her head against his chest and the steady drumming of his heartbeat. The warmth in his eyes, the endless love he'd had for them. What he'd stood for...before he left, at any rate. How nothing in the world had mattered more to him than his family.

Her thoughts turned to Christian. The way her skin tingled against his soft touch. How her heart somersaulted when he smiled at her. She thought of the sea, and of starlight. The grief in his eyes as she'd left him to come back to New York.

She thought of all the promises they'd made to each other as teenagers, their whole life stretched out before them in infinite strands, infinite decisions and consequences, not knowing the tangled and delicate paths and detours that would tear them apart and someday bring them back to Marina Cove, the place they'd once called home. The place they had thought they were supposed to be, together.

It was time to move on from Sebastian and his attempts to control her life. Her life in the city was over. It was time to close her eyes, and take the leap into the darkness of uncertainty.

Fear of the unknown, she now understood, was the price she would pay for her freedom.

"I'm moving back to Marina Cove," said Charlotte.

Several long moments passed. Sebastian gaped at her, speechless. He looked like a baby goldfish.

"What?" said Ella, her brows furrowed. Ramona's eyes widened slightly.

Charlotte drew a long breath and let it out

slowly. She felt the tension between her shoulder blades loosen and her hands unclench. She smiled as she saw Sylvie grinning widely and practically hopping up and down in the corner.

Giovanni groaned loudly. "Can we move this along, huh? I apologize for all the nonsense, Mr. Pierce," he said to one of the men seated next to him. "Sebastian, take care of this, now," Giovanni seethed. Sebastian opened his mouth to speak before Charlotte cut him off with a sharp gesture. He immediately clamped his mouth shut.

"Ramona. Mom." Charlotte took their hands in hers. "I'm sick of letting everyone else call the shots, and I know you are too. I know this is a good offer. It's enough to take away your debt and then some. But I know you don't want them to take away our home, to destroy it. To wreck the beautiful shoreline with big-box stores and chain restaurants and God knows what else."

Charlotte closed her eyes and ignored Alastair pacing the room and huffing to himself. She looked between her mother and her sister, desperate to communicate what she was feeling in a way that would make sense. "I want to move back home to Marina Cove. I don't have all the answers, but I have some ideas. I won't promise you that it'll work or that I won't make mistakes, but I don't want to live in fear anymore. I'll come back and I'll keep working at The Windmill as long as I need to, I'll give you every penny I make so that you can get out of debt. We can do this, together."

Ella looked at Charlotte for a long moment and then shook her head. "Charlotte...I do want you to move back. I know Ramona does too. But it just isn't enough..." Her voice wavered and she paused to collect herself. "We're in trouble, honey, and as much as it kills me, I can't take that chance. Not for me, or for Ramona. Your sister has lost enough already trying to help."

"I have an idea," said Sylvie from somewhere near the door. Every person in the room turned to look at her. "Charlotte, what was the only positive thing that Felix had to say in his review?"

Charlotte furrowed her eyebrows. "He liked the pastries."

Sylvie shook her head. "No. He was *obsessed* with them. He practically composed them a love sonnet. It was overshadowed by all his renegade action hero stuff." One corner of Sylvie's mouth tugged upward. "You're incredibly talented, Charlotte. Everyone thinks so. If you're coming back to Marina Cove...I have a job for you, if you'll take it. You can be The

Windmill's new pastry chef. You'll get a share of the profits, since it'll definitely mean a bunch of new business for me. What do you say?"

A slow smile formed on Charlotte's mouth as memories of Amélie surfaced, the summer in Paris, the smells of powdered sugar and melting chocolate, hands stiff from kneading dough, records playing and lemonade and sweet sunshine. The awe in Amélie's eyes as Charlotte mastered techniques and recipes on the first try; the deep satisfaction that only comes from creating something new, something that's truly yours.

"I can help too!" added Mariah. Alastair swore loudly and threw up his hands while Sebastian ran the sleeve of his expensive suit across his forehead dripping with sweat. His eyes held an expression of pure helplessness, of panic. Mariah moved to face Charlotte. "If you're not going to be waitressing anymore, Mom, then that means there's a vacancy. I wanted to extend my leave anyway, and I can't think of a more peaceful, relaxing place to spend it than Marina Cove. But I'll earn my keep, and put my money toward the debt and the inn. Sylvie, does that work?" Sylvie nodded vigorously, flashing a thumbs-up. "What do you think, Mom?"

Charlotte felt her eyes brimming with tears. She

looked back to her mother, to Ramona. "I think Christian will still help us if we're going to do things the right way. I know we can make this work. We'll never be rich, but I know we will have enough. I can't tell you with any certainty what will happen or if anything will work out like we want it to. But it'll be our future, instead of theirs." She motioned toward the men in suits, who were growing increasingly agitated and hostile.

She took a step forward and looked between Ramona and Ella. "I'm asking you to take a leap of faith."

Charlotte held her breath. Ella squeezed her eyes shut and exhaled slowly. There were tears in her eyes as she turned to Ramona. Charlotte couldn't make out the flicker in her mother's expression; it was spoken in a language that only she and Ramona could understand after so many years together. Charlotte felt a fresh pang of grief. She'd missed so much.

Ramona appeared to understand something in her mother's face, and turned to Charlotte. They held each other's gaze. Charlotte felt a rush of emotion as their eyes locked. The long years of love and loss, of anger and of sadness filled the space between them, pushing away everything around them so it was just the two of them. At that moment, Charlotte no longer cared about her own future, her own security, the inn. She felt a hard tug from deep in her chest to wrap her younger sister in her arms, to smooth back her hair and whisper soothing words of love and protection. Charlotte's heart broke as tears sprang to Ramona's eyes.

Several long moments passed. Ramona drew a long breath, and exhaled slowly.

"Okay," she said, nodding once, firmly. "Okay."

Charlotte pulled Ramona and Ella in tightly for a hug, hot tears streaming down her face. Sylvie yipped joyfully, and she and Mariah joined the other women in a hug. Ramona reached over to the table, her eyes glistening, and dropped her pen on top of the thick papers of the unsigned contract.

Alastair yanked a cell phone from his pocket and stormed across the room and out the door, muttering obscenities. Giovanni was huddled next to Mr. Pierce, whispering and gesturing frantically while Mr. Pierce held a stony expression of pure disdain. Sebastian sat down hard in one of the leather chairs, face pale and hair sticking out on end. He looked like he was going to be sick.

Charlotte felt her chest tear open as she saw Mariah watching Sebastian, sadness etched across her face. She squeezed Mariah's hand. "We'll figure it out, okay, honey? I promise," she whispered into her daughter's ear. Mariah's eyes brimmed with tears as she nodded, hugging Charlotte fiercely.

As everyone extricated themselves from their embrace and moved toward the door to leave, Charlotte paused and turned back to face Sebastian. "Just a minute," she called to the other women. Sebastian raised his head from his hands, a weary expression in his eyes.

Charlotte stared down at him hard for a long moment. "I know about Brielle, Sebastian. We're finished. I want a divorce."

She just caught his eyes widening and the remaining color draining from his face as she turned on her heel and closed the door on him, on her old life, her heart fluttering as she took her first steps into the unknown, afraid, but filled with hope.

27

"How about some music?" Mariah asked, her hand rolling against the wind outside the car window as she and Charlotte made their way back down I-95 toward Manhattan.

Charlotte grinned at her daughter as she flipped through the radio stations before landing on oldies. She cranked up the volume and they sang loudly and off-key alongside Frankie Valli singing "Sherry," laughing so hard it brought tears to their eyes.

They were heading back to the condo to drop off the convertible and sort things out for the move, while Sylvie, Ramona, and Ella took a rideshare to catch the ferry back to Marina Cove.

Charlotte had felt lighter and freer than she

could ever remember. She was finally taking the plunge, going after what she really wanted even if she didn't know how it would turn out. The feeling was indescribable.

Despite this, something hard and heavy remained in the pit of her stomach. She looked at Mariah, who was laughing and swooping her hand up and down through the wind rushing past them, carefree as a child and as relaxed as she'd ever seen her. Mariah's workaholic tendencies often left her chronically stressed, and the last thing she needed right now was more complications in her life, but Charlotte knew that she owed it to her daughter to be honest. If Mariah was going to be living in Marina Cove for a while, she deserved to know the truth about Christian, if she wanted to.

"Mariah…" Charlotte turned down the radio. "I want to talk to you about something."

The smile left Mariah's face as she brought her hand back into the car. "What's wrong?"

Charlotte swallowed the lump forming in her throat. "Mariah, I don't want there to be any secrets between us. I don't want to keep anything from you. I love you so much…and I want the best for you. I wanted to talk to you about your father."

Mariah frowned. "I'm not ready to talk about him after what he did to you."

Charlotte sighed and shook her head. "No, honey. I mean your biological father."

Mariah stared at her for a long moment with an unreadable expression. Charlotte continued, her temples pounding. "I know I've always told you that I'd tell you about him if you ever wanted. I know you've never wanted to, and to be honest with you, Mariah, I was always relieved, because it's sort of a complicated story, and one that's still painful for me. But it's been years since I've brought it up, and so I wanted to do that now. Whenever you're ready, if you ever are, I'll tell you everything. The choice is entirely up to you."

Mariah looked down at her hands and closed her eyes for a moment. She drew a breath, and Charlotte saw her mouth curve upward ever so slightly. Mariah reached into the backseat and pulled her purse into her lap. Charlotte was puzzled as Mariah rifled through the contents before her hands emerged holding a stack of photographs. Mariah shuffled through them and handed one to Charlotte, a wry smile touching her lips.

Charlotte looked at the photograph, and her chest constricted. She recognized the Seaside House in the background, and contractors milling around as they worked; the picture looked to be right before the fire. Centered in the picture, walking with a large piece of lumber on his shoulders and looking right into the camera, was Christian. His brown eyes glittered in the sunshine, a crooked grin on his face.

Charlotte's stomach flipped over hard as she stared at him. She had no idea how she'd never noticed it before. His face was the very image of Mariah's. The same brow, high cheekbones, the same tiny dimple in his chin.

But more than anything else, it was his eyes. They were a perfect replica of Mariah's.

Tears sprang to Charlotte's eyes as she looked up at Mariah, who was now grinning widely. "I already know," she whispered, her eyes welling up. "I was taking all those photos of the inn's progress, and when I got this little beauty of a picture developed, I knew immediately. I wanted to talk to you about it, but I was worried you wouldn't want to." She blew out a shaky laugh. "Thank you, Mom. For offering to talk about it." She sniffled. "And if you ever want to tell him about me, I think you should. I think... maybe I'd like to get to know him, someday. If that's okay with you."

Charlotte gripped the picture, searching Christian's face, a flurry of emotions swelling over her. "I always wanted to tell him...I just never knew how to go about it. I was hiding, when it comes down to it. I know it needs to be done, but I'm afraid of how he's going to react. It's...it's all sort of a long story, how it all happened."

A long silence passed between them before Mariah took the picture back, holding it in her lap and tracing the edges with her fingers.

"Well, if you're game...I'd love to hear that story sometime," Mariah said without looking up, a smile spreading across her face.

Charlotte laughed through her tears. "I guess now's as good a time as any," she said as she cruised down the highway, feeling so much lighter as she released the heaviness she'd hidden away in her heart.

A WEEK LATER, Charlotte and Mariah stepped off the ferry at Hightide Port, waving cheerfully to Leo, the old ferry captain. He yelled down to them, "It's good to have you home, Charlotte!" before tipping his hat and heading back to the deck.

Charlotte raised her face against the warm

sunshine cascading down from a clear blue sky. Ollie bounded past her, leaping and rolling in the sand with pure dog delight. As they rolled their suitcases onto the street toward the inn, Charlotte glanced down at herself and laughed inwardly. A simple white T-shirt, blue capris, and the comfy tennis shoes Sylvie had lent her. A far cry from the last time she'd stepped off the ferry here, in her high heels and designer dress, unprepared for life outside the city.

As they reached Main Street, Charlotte marveled at how different everything seemed now. The people rolling past her on bicycles and motorized scooters, children playing jump rope on the sidewalk, business owners catching up with each other in front of their brightly painted shops, laughing and passing the time in good conversation. The sun shone from the great blue expanse of sky untainted by human development and shimmered through the trees, dappling the cobblestone streets below. What had first struck her as quaint and outdated now felt charming and beautifully free.

Ollie raced past them as they turned onto Seaside Lane, his tongue lolling out and nearly tripping over himself in excitement. Charlotte grinned as she saw the Seaside House down the tree-lined street, looking the worse for wear after the fire but still standing strong.

"Home sweet home," said Mariah, chuckling. "And just when I got used to sleeping in a bed again."

Charlotte laughed. "You know, you don't have to sleep on the floor with me if you don't want. I'm sure at least one of the guest rooms is in okay shape."

"Nah, that's okay," Mariah said. "What doesn't kill you, and all that. Just imagine how good it'll feel sleeping in a real bed in this house once we get things going. I want to savor that."

Charlotte felt flickers of nervous excitement as they approached the house. "I'm gonna take Mr. Ollie here for a nice walk on the beach," said Mariah.

"I'll see you later, honey," said Charlotte. Mariah chased Ollie around the house twice before she caught up with him. Charlotte watched for a long time as they headed down the beach, Ollie leaping and splashing through the crystal blue waters as the sunshine warmed the golden sand. This place was paradise.

Charlotte skipped up the steps to the porch and pushed against the heavy front door. As always, it was lodged shut. Three more times she heaved her whole weight against it, laughing to herself, before she almost fell over the threshold as it burst open. What had been so infuriating to deal with over the last weeks was now strangely delightful, an eccentricity of the beautiful inn that was her home.

"Hello, new home!" she yelled into the empty house. Charlotte could just barely detect the smell of smoke. She ran up the stairs, laughing again at the unbelievably loud creaks and pops of the old stairs.

Charlotte peeked into her parents' bedroom; her blanket was still on the ground. The room hadn't been damaged by the fire. She knew from Ramona that two of the back rooms had taken some fairly heavy damage; the sky was still visible from one of the rooms where the rain had thankfully quelled the worst of the flames. Plastic sheets cordoned the area off.

Her skin went cold as she entered the room that Felix had stayed in. He had undoubtedly created a huge obstacle for them to overcome through the damage to their reputation; the paper review and the one-star online rating would be tough to get over. But Charlotte supposed it was only fair, given how she'd handled things in her desperation.

She pulled open the shutters and then the window to let in the clean saltwater breeze. The room was flooded with brilliant, sparkling sunlight, the rays warming her face like a blanket. As she looked down into the yard, she saw someone walking toward the house. She held her hand up to block the sun. It was Christian. Charlotte squeezed her eyes shut and took a deep breath.

It was time to let go of her final secret.

She padded down the stairs, feeling like everything was moving in slow motion. As she pulled open the front door, Christian paused mid-step on his way up the porch.

"Charlotte..." he said, running a hand through his wavy hair.

Charlotte ran down the stairs toward him and wrapped her arms around him. "I'm so sorry for how I handled everything, Christian," she whispered. "I was desperate, and I handled things poorly. I thought I knew what I wanted, but I've come to realize a lot about myself lately. I hope you'll forgive me."

Christian's body relaxed, and he gently placed his arms around her, sending shivers down Charlotte's spine. Her heart started to beat faster.

"Of course, Charlotte. I'm sorry that I didn't try to better understand what you were going through."

He pulled away, staring intently into her eyes. "Is it true? Are you really moving back?"

Charlotte's mouth tugged upward. Ramona had apparently let that one slip. "Yes. I'm moving back."

His eyes were sparkling in the sunlight. "I didn't believe it when I heard it. But Ramona told me you were headed back this afternoon. I wanted to talk to you myself. So, what happened exactly?"

They strolled around the Seaside House as Charlotte explained the dramatic last-minute race to save their home, how Mariah would be staying for a while, and detailed her new job as the pastry chef at The Windmill.

"I'm really excited," Charlotte said. "Nervous, of course, but I'm excited to see what will happen. Right now, it feels like anything's possible."

Christian stopped walking suddenly. "Charlotte, if you still want me to, I'd love to start working on the house again."

Charlotte turned to face him. A moment passed. "I would love that, but you should know that money is an issue. We're all going to be working to help my mom and Ramona. I can't afford to pay all those contractors again...there's no way. Not yet, at least. I don't want you to commit to something that difficult."

He reached for her hand. "Then I'll start myself, and it will take as long as it takes. I'm not going anywhere."

Their eyes met; the intensity in his gaze made her knees tremble slightly. Charlotte felt beads of sweat breaking out on her forehead; her mouth felt dry, and her heart was now slamming full force against her chest.

"Christian..." she whispered. "Before we move forward with...the house, and everything, there's something I need to talk to you about." Charlotte felt a shudder course through her body. "Something I should have found a way to talk to you about a long time ago."

Ramona sighed as she sat down hard on her bed. Ella had gone for a walk, and Ramona was taking the time to tidy her bungalow. She ran a hand over her face and looked over at the mirror above the long dresser next to the bed.

A quiver of surprise ran through her as she gazed at the woman staring back at her. She couldn't remember the last time she'd actually looked into a mirror. For such a long time, each day had seemed like something she just had to survive, a whirlwind filled with dull panic. She had long felt that she didn't really understand who she was anymore. Maybe it was time to start thinking about that.

Since the meeting in Boston, something had shifted in her. It was as though she'd been in a dark cave for so long that it became her new normal, a life inside without sunlight, until she eventually forgot that there was anything outside the cave at all.

But now, something had changed ever so slightly. A subtle difference in the pall that had been cast over her life since the night her father had abandoned them. She felt...like she wasn't the only person in the world anymore. It was such a new feeling that she didn't trust it, expecting it to vanish between her fingertips at any moment. But it hadn't. It had been like tiptoeing toward the entrance of the cave and seeing the first glimmers of sunlight, recognition flooding her.

Ramona felt herself smile as she thought of Charlotte. They'd spent the last week texting back and forth, coming up with plans and ideas for the inn. It made her feel like they were kids again. They'd made plans tonight for an early dinner, just the two of them. Ramona felt strangely nervous.

Her fingers ran idly over the long wooden

handles of the paint brushes, over the coarse grooves of the canvas that she'd unearthed. A pain hit her squarely in the chest like a hammer. She hadn't painted since she was a teenager. After a moment, she gathered up the supplies and the easel, kneeled on the floor, and returned them to their dusty home under her bed. She couldn't. Not yet.

After showering and getting dressed, Ramona made her way toward the Seaside House. As she approached, she froze when she saw Charlotte. She was talking to Christian.

But something was wrong. She couldn't hear what they were saying, but Christian was raking his hands through his hair while Charlotte seemed to be trying to explain something. Christian had a look across his face that sent a shiver down Ramona's spine.

Not anger or hurt...It was like heartbreak. He began gesturing wildly, shaking his head before turning on his heel and walking away. Ramona started to run toward them to see what had happened. She saw Charlotte's shoulders crumple as she yelled toward Christian, taking a few steps before stopping and covering her face with her hands.

CHARLOTTE SLOWLY ROCKED BACK and forth on the white porch swing next to Mariah, lost in thought. It had been a week since she'd told Christian everything. Despite feeling a new looseness between her shoulder blades after letting go of her final secret, she'd felt wretched ever since.

"You can't blame him, really," said Mariah as she stared out across the sea. The sun was almost at the horizon; the sky was just beginning to deepen to a navy blue. A pleasant breeze whipped at them from the shore.

"No, I suppose not," said Charlotte. She couldn't stop seeing the look in his eyes when she'd told him the truth. She couldn't even imagine what he was going through, what he was thinking. If he'd ever forgive her.

"You did the right thing, Mom. I'm proud of you for talking to him." Mariah put a hand on Charlotte's shoulder.

Charlotte blinked back tears. "I'll never know if I did the right thing. I didn't want him to feel obligated to stay with me. He did what he thought was right after Elliott died. But maybe if I had tried harder to find him..."

Mariah shook her head. "Mom, you didn't know where he was...if he was even alive. Grandma and Aunt Ramona basically weren't talking to you, so you had no way of knowing he'd come back here. And besides, you were married...I totally get why you didn't think it was right to go searching for an old boyfriend. And you know what?" she said, catching Charlotte's gaze. "You can't change the past anyway, right? We're all human. All we can do is try to focus on what we can do now. "

Charlotte stared at Mariah, marveling at her maturity, her wisdom. Somewhere along the way, despite everything, she and Sebastian had managed to raise a wonderful girl, a woman. A true gem.

If she could go back to the start, she wouldn't change a thing. The twisted road she'd traveled had given her three beautiful children. It had brought her back to Marina Cove, to her mother and Ramona. To Sylvie. A second chance at building a relationship with them, a clean slate.

Despite having some solid plans in the works, things were by no means perfect. She still had to face repaying the loan shark, her mother and sister were still mired in debt, and she was sleeping on the bare hardwood of the burned-out husk of a house that might never see another guest. The father of her firstborn daughter had seemingly disappeared; she'd stopped by Christian's tiny cabin several times, and he was nowhere to be found.

But that was life, Charlotte supposed. Things weren't always tied up with a bow like they were in fairy tales.

Her mind drifted to Christian. Walking down the pier eating cotton candy with him on one of their first dates, young and nervous, heat rising to her cheeks at his easy laughter. The feel of his strong hands running through her hair as they lay in the warm sand, making shapes of the clouds in the bright blue sky above. That night on the beach, the storm raging overhead and the ring in her pocket and the look of anguish in his eyes.

She thought of the night they met. Charlotte had signed up for stage crew as an after-school activity. She'd been too afraid of performing onstage in the musical that year, and Sylvie had joined a year earlier and had the time of her life. For weeks Charlotte had been busy hammering, sanding, and painting the set pieces under the watchful eye of the stern but talented musical director. She worked hard, and did her best not to be distracted by the new boy who had joined late, the one with the wavy hair and the intense brown eyes that you could get lost in.

Charlotte instead lost herself in the magic of the rehearsals. There was a feeling being backstage in the dark in high school that was hard to describe to anyone who had never been part of it. It was a collective excitement, a collective spark; whispering and humming along to the music, brushing shoulders with potential love interests, awkward eye contact and gossip about who'd kissed whom. They were all so young, brimming with endless hope and lost in the day-to-day dramas and thrills of being teenagers.

It was opening night, and the last number was coming up. The lights blackened for the scene change. As Charlotte helped wheel a particularly heavy set piece out on stage, she somehow lost her footing and stumbled forward. She caught hold of a large piece of cloth that formed the backing of the set, and as she fell, her mind went white with static as a horrible ripping sound reverberated across the stage. Her balance shifted and she was tumbling backward, but before hitting the floor, she felt two strong arms gently catch her, easing her down softly. "I'm so sorry," she stammered as he helped her to her feet.

She could just barely make out who had caught her in the darkness. It was the boy with the wavy hair. He smiled at her. She smelled cedarwood and leather and saltwater.

"Are you okay?" he whispered. His face was etched with concern, but his eyes danced with a wry amusement. Charlotte felt the words tangle in her throat and looked to the floor nervously. She nodded.

"Good. I'm Christian, by the way," he said softly.

Charlotte met his gaze. "I'm Charlotte," she said. They looked at each other wordlessly for several long moments. Suddenly, the stage lights came back up, illuminating everything around them in harsh relief. Charlotte felt her stomach drop into the soles of her shoes as she turned to see the entire audience before her, staring at them in thick silence. At the edges of her vision she could see the director frantically motioning for them, fury in his eyes. Christian laughed, took her hand, and she giggled as they raced across the stage, her heart fluttering wildly.

As the sun inched toward the horizon and the blue sky deepened in color, Charlotte quietly rocked in the porch swing next to Mariah, deep in her thoughts. It was going to be hard to get used to the lack of certainty in her life. She no longer knew what each day would hold, the comfortable endless motions she could've gone through with her eyes closed.

But there was a certain thrill to it, a knowledge earned through pain that life wasn't meant to be lived on autopilot. It was always easier to say tomorrow, tomorrow; you just never knew how much longer you had. Time marched on relentlessly no matter how hard you tried to clutch it in your hands.

And Charlotte, for one, was done running and hiding. For better or for worse, she was at least living life on her own terms now.

"Mom..." Mariah whispered as she shot upright in her chair, looking toward the shoreline. Charlotte squinted, her stomach somersaulting as she saw a familiar figure approaching them.

Charlotte and Mariah both stood up as Christian approached the house, stopping at a careful distance. His expression held a deep, dark sorrow that broke Charlotte's heart. Several long moments passed as he shuffled on his feet. Charlotte took a tentative step forward before she realized that he was staring at Mariah.

Charlotte turned to Mariah, who stood frozen in place. Time seemed to stretch on endlessly. Christian's eyebrows knitted together, his eyes filled with grief and apprehension. He slowly started toward Mariah.

Tears sprang to Charlotte's eyes as Mariah suddenly raced down the porch steps, ran across the sand, and threw herself into Christian's arms. He picked her up in a single slow twirl and buried his face in her long hair, squeezing his eyes shut. A quiet sob escaped from Charlotte's mouth as her heart pounded. Christian held their daughter firm in his grasp and ran a hand through her hair, pulling her in tighter. Mariah's body was shaking as she wept into Christian's chest.

Christian looked up over Mariah's shoulder at Charlotte. Tears fell hard from his eyes and streamed down his face. Charlotte's stomach clenched as they held each other's gaze, all that they had lost over the long years stretching between them. After an endless moment, ever so slowly, his mouth curved slightly upward into a smile.

The sky was shimmering with streaks of brilliant violet and gold, and a warm breeze filled with tiny droplets of saltwater swept over their skin. Dolphins crested the surface of the sparkling sapphire sea.

A long time passed before Christian gently pulled away from Mariah, and together, they walked toward Charlotte. As Christian stepped up to her, he took Charlotte's hands in his own. She could feel his heat, his quiet strength, the joy and the sorrow and the glittering fear of the unknown.

Charlotte wanted to tell him so many things. The way the sunlight reflecting golden streaks in his eyes made butterflies dance around in her stomach. His strong grip, his steady presence making her feel as though she could face anything, no matter what. How he'd cradled her heart in his hands, keeping it safe until they'd lost everything, and how part of her had never let him go. But as he looked deep into her eyes and held her gaze, she couldn't find the words.

"Charlotte..." He took a long, deep breath and let it out slowly. "Would you like to have dinner with me sometime?"

Charlotte felt hot tears falling down her face as the corners of her mouth pulled up into a grin. Christian pulled her into his arms, holding her like he never wanted to let her go. Distant birds sang their heartbreaking songs to the infinite sea and sky while the sun dipped quietly below the horizon and the first glimmers of starlight fell over Marina Cove.

And for the first time in a long, long time, Charlotte felt at peace.

EPILOGUE

Ramona wiped the sweat from her brow as she submerged the rag back into the soapy water, wrung it out, and continued scrubbing one of the inn's guestroom walls. A fine layer of black soot had settled onto various surfaces in the house after the fire, and they'd been doing their best to clean up the undamaged rooms before the very long reconstruction process would begin. She was seated in a chair, her leg in its cast spread out in front of her. It would be a long time before she'd be walking without a crutch, but at least the pain had been lessening.

"Maybe we should call it for the day," said Charlotte from the other side of the room. Ramona looked out the window; she hadn't noticed the darkening sky. She didn't mind working at the house; the repetition soothed her, and it was satisfying to see the progress they made, however small.

Mariah came in from the hallway, holding a broom and dustpan. "Time to clock out already, boss?" she said with a wry smile.

"Well," Charlotte said, her cheeks flushing a bit, "Christian and I are going for a walk…"

Mariah laughed. "Well, have fun, you two." She set down the broom and lifted her patterned fabric crossbody bag over her shoulder from the floor. "I'm going to try to catch the sunset for some photos. The sky's a different color every night, it seems. I'm gonna turn it into a little collection." She waved to Charlotte and Ramona before floating out the door.

"You want to meet for lunch tomorrow? My treat," said Charlotte.

Ramona stretched, groaning as the muscles in her back seized up. "I'd like that," she said. She looked up at Charlotte. A moment passed between them, words of the complicated dynamic between them left unspoken. Like all wounds, Ramona knew, theirs would heal with time, now that Charlotte was back. Her heart didn't feel quite so heavy anymore… it had been a wretched thing, carrying the anger for so long. She felt a small smile flicker across her lips.

"Can I walk you home?" Charlotte asked, motioning toward Ramona's crutches.

"No, that's okay." Ramona settled back in her chair and reached into the bucket of water. "I think I'll go a bit longer. This is strangely relaxing." Charlotte smiled and gave her a little wave before heading out.

After a while, Ramona set the rag into the bucket, slowly stood up, and hobbled over to the window with her crutches. The first stars had come out, and a pale moonlight had illuminated the sand with a warm, white glow. Far down the coastline, Ramona could just make out two figures walking together next to the dark water lapping at the shore. She felt a familiar pang in her heart as she pulled out the silver necklace from under her blouse and gently unclasped it.

A few days ago, she'd been walking down Main Street when she heard someone shout, "Ramona! Hey, wait up!" She felt her skin go cold as she recognized his voice. Danny was making his way down the sidewalk toward her.

She felt herself pale, and her limbs were suddenly heavy. They'd barely spoken to each other since she'd ended their marriage what felt like an eternity ago.

Danny had heard about the fire at the Seaside House. He shifted from one foot to the other as they spoke, barely making eye contact with her. Which suited her fine; she knew she wouldn't be able to look him in the eye anyway.

With a tentative look on his face, he'd offered to provide everything he could manage for the restoration from his supplies store, and told Ramona that they could work out whatever payment plan they needed. He offered to give them a massive discount, which Ramona rejected outright. She'd told him that they wanted to do things the right way, and she wasn't about to put him out. He had been able to talk her into accepting a very gracious payment plan, however. It was all very sweet of him, after everything they'd been through.

Ramona closed her eyes as she let out a long, slow breath. The sound of the waves carried in from the shoreline outside. She rolled smooth metal around in her hands, fingering the golden edges thoughtfully. She blinked back tears as she slipped the silver chain in her hands back through her wedding ring. A pit of grief sat hard in her stomach, enormous and heavy, threatening to consume her.

Ramona brushed the tears from her eyes and

slowly lifted the necklace she always wore back in place, clasping it carefully.

She stared out the window for a long time, swimming in her thoughts. Suddenly, she heard someone quietly padding into the room. She whipped around in terror before she saw Ella closing the door behind them.

"Mom, you scared me," Ramona said, trying to catch her breath. "I didn't hear the front door opening downstairs."

Ella made her way across the room, standing next to Ramona. A comfortable silence stretched between them as they looked out over the shore. Ramona glanced at her mother and noticed her eyes were red and brimming with tears.

"Mom, what's wrong?" Ramona put a hand on her shoulder, her heart twisting in her chest.

Ella was watching the two distant figures strolling down the shoreline as darkness settled in the night sky. She closed her eyes and pressed her hand tenderly against her chest.

"Ramona," she said, her voice barely above a whisper. "I want to find out what happened to your father."

THE STORY CONTINUES in book two of the Marina Cove series, *The Last Letters*.

Sign up for my newsletter, and you'll also receive a free exclusive copy of *Summer Starlight*. This book isn't available anywhere else! You can join at sophiekenna.com/seaside.

Thank you so much for reading!

~Sophie

Made in the USA
Coppell, TX
09 June 2024